WHAT'S LOVE GOT TO DO WITH IT

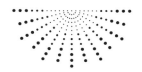

SUZETTA PERKINS

WHAT'S LOVE GOT TO DO WITH IT?

SUZETTA PERKINS

Suspense Is My Business

ACKNOWLEDGMENTS

It is with much pride that I present my new novel, *What's Love Got To Do With It*, the sequel to *Silver Bullets*. Those crazy women are back providing laughter, love, humility, and a sense of belonging. My readers…my awesome readers, are the ones who've kept these characters alive. You loved them, embraced them, talked about them as if they were real people, and compared the many similarities to yourselves. As always, thank you for being on this journey with me.

I'd like to thank my family for their continued support of what I do. My family has been amazing throughout my literary journey, and I love them to the moon and back.

The book clubs are my heart and soul. Collectively, they have provided a forum for which I could reach many, and I appreciate the warm receptions, the gifts, lunches, and a seal of approval of my literary work. I'd like to thank the **Mimosa Book Club – Richmond, VA** for the most wonderful time, camaraderie, outstanding book discussion when I visited them. Members Carol Bryant (my road dawg many years ago), Danita Hughes, Joyce Libron, Simone Thomas, Valerie Hodge, Delores (Dee) Minney-Toller, Gail Robinson, Delores Esparza, and Kathy Brown showed me sisterly love and I appreciate them from the bottom of my heart. I'm ready to come back to Richmond anytime.

I had the extreme pleasure of being invited to **Rochester, NY** by the **Successful Impressive Sisters (S.I.S.) Book Club**. My dear friend, Deborah Miller, paved the way, even flying to Rochester to be with me while on this fabulous trip. I met some wonderful women who showered me with love, a great lunch, and an awesome book club discussion. The members—Martha Richards, Shanese Richards-Sims, Joanne Mack, Gloria O'Neil, Shay Lanos, Valorie Sims, Sylvia Balkom (AKA Candy), Tynia Jenkins (Tonya), and Karen Patterson made my day. My time there was priceless; I'll be back! I must send a shout out to Luvon and Frances Sheppard, Deborah and David Miller's aunt and uncle, who provided me with the best accommodations while in the ROC. Luvon, your art is to die for.

To the wonderful ladies of **Words with Friends out of Goldsboro, NC**—Simone Knight, Montina Swift, Traci Carraway, Angela Cherry Jackson, Letetia Vann, Sonya Armstrong, and Myra Bell, I thank you for your continued support. You have proudly honored me with a book club meeting for all of my books. You deserve My Book Club of the Year Award. Thank you from the bottom of my heart. Since this acknowledgement was already written before I met with you, I had to speak to the wonderful canvas of my book cover you all presented me on September 23rd. My eyes are still wet, Simone.

Roundtable Readers Book Club—LaSheera, Hannah Lee, Kay Edmonson, Twosyn, Joyce Mayo, Sherri Shade, and Traci White, you never fail to show me love. LaSheera Lee of Read-You-Later and Event Planner of the Year, thank you for always thinking of me and for allowing me to showcase my work. The Cameras, Light, Action event was phenomenal in every way, but it was your love for readers, authors, movie producers, and the plain old written word that made it the model for all events. Thank you and the Roundtable Readers for all you do in support of authors!

While I love my book clubs, there are many readers who aren't attached to book clubs, who've supported me throughout my writing career. My sister Gloria Goward Jordan, Marsha McLean, Sharon

Evans, Keshema Jackson, Charlotte Adams-Graves, Gwendolyn McClure, Antoinette Gates, Gloria Moore-Carter, Cheryl McGhee, and Judy Jordan; I'm nothing without you. To my newest reader, Joy Johnson, thanks for taking a chance on me. I'd like to give a special shout out to my BFF for over forty years—my best friend forever, Yvonne Head, who I love dearly and has always supported my career. Love you, Bonnie. To my road dawg and BFF, Mary Farmer, thanks for always having my back.

A special and sincere thank you goes to Dr. Edward Dickerson of Cape Fear Aesthetics, who has always supported me as an author and a friend. You've always been there on my behalf and I thank you.

I've reserved this space for a woman who's always had my best interest at heart. She has always thought of ways to boost my career by promoting and putting my name out in the atmosphere for others to take notice. Mrs. Juanita Pilgrim has been the impetus and force behind my literary journey. I can't thank you enough, Juanita, for all you've been to me throughout this aspect of my career. I take pride in calling you my fan and forever friend. Thank you for being the wind beneath my wings.

DEDICATION

To my beautiful, black sisters. YOU ROCK.

WHAT READERS HAVE SAID ABOUT *SILVER BULLETS:*

I truly enjoyed this book. So glad that Suzetta included a story that represented us Silver ladies. There are so many books now about the younger adult woman. We silver ladies are still sexy and have it going on too! It made me laugh, cry, and to join in. Couldn't put it down, it is a page turner! So, looking forward to discussing with my book club sisters. – *Theresa Talley*

GREAT WRITING TRANSCENDS ALL AGES AND GENDER

Suzetta Perkins is a writer that can make a man feel right at home reading her fiction about 50-something year old women. Her story telling of women we all know in life who are living and enjoying life, might be 50 is the new 35. The women are sexy not only in looks, but also mentally confident in many ways. The demographic is sexy and classy, and any man would like to have a chance to meet the characters. In many ways, Silver Bullets allowed me a man, to see into a world beyond the surface of the demographic that Suzetta Perkins wrote about in the book. I read the breaking down of the surface and stereotypical assumptions when you don't know a female person(s) life Silver Bullets is great read, that is funny, smart, and well-written sexy conversations for a group that in these days and times is front and center and important in the world. Silver Bullets is a good book for all to read. – *Alvin L. A. Horn the author of the novels One Safe Place and Perfect Circle*

AWESOME!

Oh yes Suzetta Perkins has done it again! This book kept me on the edge of my chair (as always) wondering what was going to happen next! I even took it to work with me, as I couldn't put it down. As always, Suzetta brings these characters to life so much so that one would think that he or she is a part of the story. Even though I haven't reached my fifties yet, I definitely felt like I was a part of this group of ladies who lived their lives to the fullest! Great job Suzetta Perkins! – *Margot Pittman*

DELIGHTFUL READ!!

These 5 Silver Sistahs are a true force to deal with. They may have some internal issues among themselves, but in the end that sisterly love and bond is so strong between them, that they have each other's backs through thick and thin. They all experience everyday circumstances and issues that arise in their lives, but they all triumph over them. This book was a very good read for all, and a different read from your normal contemporary fiction. It was especially relatable for us readers in our silver years of life or approaching those years. The book lets you know that life happens, you pray about it, deal with it and kick your silver shoes to the sky and keep on moving! I also loved the book cover, which was very nice. This was the first book I read by Suzetta Perkins, and I will definitely be reading some of her other books. – *DC Avid Reader*

MATURE WOMEN WITH A LOT ON THEIR MIND

This is the first book that I've read by this author and she did a wonderful job. The characters in the book were very realistic and easy to relate to. They all had their issues, getting mad at one another, men troubles and saying what's on their mind. These women will put aside their differences and come together when one of them need that support. Anyone can relate to the bond these women share. As in any relationship, there will be some ups and downs. This book shows what each of the five friends are dealing and how they help each other. This is a must read for any woman. – *Bookworm*

CHAPTER ONE

MY NAME IS JEFFEREY SHANICE JACKSON-QUICK

*J*uly 4, 1999. It was the last time I'd been with a man. ~~Scratch that.~~ It was the last time I made love to a man. Umm.

As suggested by the date, fireworks should have been exploding for days. For sure, there should have been a celebration that lasted until we were ready to come down off the cloud—at least through the Fourth of July weekend. I was down for it, considering I was happy, life was good, and I definitely was in the mood and spirits were high.

On Saturday, July 3, my man and I had thrown a family barbecue with enough ribs, chicken, links, hotdogs, and hamburgers to feed a whole battalion at Fort Bragg Army Base and the City of Charlotte. At the end of the day and after all the picnickers had gone home with their Styrofoam trays filled to the gills with what was supposed to be my leftovers for the next week, my husband pulled me into what I claimed to be a warm embrace.

My man made love to me that night...clear into the next morning, as if this Fourth of July had been declared the last day on earth. He made me feel some kind of special—like I was his heaven here on earth and that all things revolved around no one but us. Multiple orgasms had me screaming for more and doing an all-nighter, which was right up my alley. Hell, I forget about

Prince singing about partying into the New Year like it was 1999; it was doggone July. But on July fifth, my man turned my life upside down.

Peaceful sleep was what I remembered after all of the lovemaking. My body quivered at the thought of how my man had put it on me and how he made me feel. I begged for more, but he said he was through—I had worn him OUT. But it was good like that, and I'd be a fool if I hadn't begged for more.

I pulled out of my daydream and reached over to rub my baby's back, put my arms around his waist, squeeze him a bit, and place little mock kisses along his spine, prodding him to make me over again. We'd both taken the week off from work, and I looked forward to spending quality time together. But when I turned in his direction, he wasn't there. Only the wrinkled sheet lay exposed, serving notice that he had been there.

I rose from the bed and rushed into the bathroom to start my day, eager to join my husband for a leisurely mid-morning, afternoon delight. Just as I stepped out of the shower and had wrapped my plush towel around my body, I heard a rap, rap on the door.

A smile flew across my face in anticipation of seeing my husband on the other side of the door, although at the time, I never stopped to wonder why in the hell he was knocking. It was my fifteen-year old son, HJ—short for Harrison Jr.—who'd come to tell me that his dad, my husband, my man had plucked him out of bed and said goodbye. Okay, he'd be back in an hour or two was my thought. So what was the big deal?

Today is July 4, 2014. My son and I haven't seen Harrison B. Quick since that Monday after the fourth when he vanished into thin air. He left without a trace, a word or a forwarding address. I heard through the grapevine—some old military buddies of his—that he left his place of employment and took a contracting job overseas making lots of money. My son and I haven't seen one damn penny, if there's any truth to it.

My step-sister, Queenie Jackson said she always knew Harrison was disturbed. That's what I'd expect her to say because while she always wanted a man, she couldn't ever keep one. You'd think she'd be up on her game; the heifer is going on sixty and should've learned some real life lessons by now.

My husband and I were happily married for seventeen years. We'd built what I considered to be the Quick Empire. We had good jobs, a beautiful home in the burbs, two nice cars, and were surrounded by a good group of social acquaintances. You'd say we were living the life in Charlotte, North Carolina, the Queen City, as the natives call it.

Queenie hated on Harrison some kind of bad and it's the reason I lived two hours away in Charlotte...so I'd never have to see her behind. But now I need a favor; I lost the beautiful home that Harrison and I built from the ground up. My son is grown and on his own, but me, I've been pining for Harrison for so long that I've lost the will to live along with my home. Well, I lost my home after the State of North Carolina fired me from my good paying job; they said I was non-productive. I need somewhere to kick it for a while—until I can land back on my feet.

I'm on a bus due to arrive in Raleigh any minute. I had to make this note in my journal for posterity sake, so that if something should happen to me, the reader would know my story, at least the abbreviated portion of it. My relationship with my half-sister is a large part of it.

Queenie Jackson can be some kind of evil, although she claims to be a staunch Christian. Yeah, right. She ain't foolin' nobody, especially me. When our daddy married my momma, Queenie was resentful of me. I can't help it if my parents doted on me. Her momma and our daddy had long since been an item. He married my momma and from what I later learned, Queenie's momma didn't want him anyhow—kicked my dad out into the streets. It's also true that my daddy bought my momma a cute little house in a nice neighborhood, hence some of the resentment, while Queenie and her momma were living in an old dilapidated apartment somewhere on the other side of town. You choose; you lose. That's the breaks.

Queenie is nine years older than me; that makes me fifty-one. From what I hear, though, she turned out all right. She's never been a real sister to me, but now I'm giving her the opportunity to do something about it—in her old age. LOL. Please, I'm well aware that she doesn't owe me a thing.

We've arrived at the Greyhound Station on Capitol Boulevard and it's time to get off the bus. I put my furniture in storage and packed what I could into the two suitcases that are parked in the hull of the bus underneath. Queenie has no idea that I'm coming. Yeah, it was dumb of me to put my ass on a bus and ride all the way to Raleigh without knowing if she'd let me stay. The remnants of what was once my car are sitting in a metal heap in some *junk yard after it was hit by a drunk driver who didn't have any insurance. He didn't have insurance and neither did I. And now, I'm here.*

Lord, please don't let me have to knock Queenie out in her own house should things get ugly. I'm coming humbly as I know how, with my two suitcases and a pitiful story. Help me, Jesus.

Jefferey Shanice Jackson-Quick
July 4, 2014

CHAPTER TWO

QUEENIE JACKSON

a smile of satisfaction crossed Queenie's face, as she reminisced about the romantic day she had. She was head over hills in love and Donald Griffin was the reason. He'd finally asked her to be his wife, and July 4, 2014 would never be the same. They'd been together for almost a year, and there was nothing Queenie could think of that could ever tear them apart.

Donald had become her everything and she loved the way he doted on her. He was caring and loving, always attentive to her needs. He had made her his queen and she made him her king. Queenie could already hear Donald say, *I take you, Queenie Jackson, to be my lawfully wedded wife, my constant friend, my faithful partner and my love from this day forward.* Without a doubt, that day would come—soon.

The one thorn in Queenie's side about her relationship...now impending marriage to Donald was that he was living a Christian life, according to God's word. That should've been a plus for Queenie, but she wanted more—sooner rather than later. No matter how much Queenie teased and enticed, Donald refused to peel off his clothes and enter the halls of seductive reasoning with her. Many nights, Queenie went to sleep, wondering what it was like to make love to Donald. They kissed and sometimes took their petting to the brink, but Donald always shut the hormones off before Queenie's temptation led him to sin...against God.

Queenie didn't understand it. She was a good-looking, full-figured woman who in her book was irresistible. To make matters worse, she was horny as hell and desperate for the rump in the hay. Donald had yet to fondle her breasts or peek at what the good Lord had blessed her with down stairs. Queenie's body screamed for Donald's physical affection, but when the temptation hit, he'd always stop, kiss her lightly on the lips, touch her nose with his finger, and tell her that when they were married, he would gladly give all of himself.

"Damn," Queenie said out loud to no one, allowing the thoughts of intimacy with her man to slither off of her back. Only thirty minutes had elapsed since he got in his car and headed back to Atlanta so that he could get a good night's sleep before his meeting he had to attend the next day; she could still smell the faint hint of his cologne. "But I love him, and I'm willing to wait. God sent this man to me."

Sitting in front of her vanity, preparing to take off her make-up, Queenie jumped when she heard the doorbell ring. Maybe Donald had a change of heart and decided to turn around and give her what she craved since he'd now committed to being with her forever. Without giving it another thought, Queenie rushed to the door as the doorbell rang again, slowing her gait as she approached the door, adjusting her clothes as an added measure. She fanned herself in anticipation.

Poised and ready to pounce on her man, she snatched the door open. Shock, surprise, alarm, and then anger rolled through her like an atomic bomb in only a matter of seconds. It was late, darn near nine-thirty, and the last person she expected to see was her half-sister, Jefferey, standing at her front door.

Queenie's first impulse was to slam the door in her face, but fear... maybe caution prompted her not to do it, at least not right away.

Jefferey was the split image of her father—the father Queenie had thrown away in the trashcan of her mind. She still maintained her good looks—in fact she could pass for a woman in her mid-twenties, although Queenie knew Jefferey was on the other side of fifty. Her silky, dark-brown hair draped her shoulders, and from Queenie's vantage point, the hair was all hers. Queenie took a second glance and noticed that Jefferey's eyes seemed hollow in her mocha-brown frame, and she acted very nervous, although it could've been her imagination.

"Well, look what rose from the dead. What in the hell are you doing here? And why are there suitcases sitting on my porch?"

"Hi, Queenie. I need a place to stay."

Queenie slammed the door in Jefferey's face. Her nostrils flared and she stood looking at the closed door, wondering how this nightmare began.

Two to three minutes passed. All was silent. Queenie placed her ear to the door, but heard nothing…not even the sound of a car passing by. She stepped back, contemplated what she would do, and then hurriedly pulled the door open. Jefferey was still there, her face flooded with tears.

"Come in," Queenie said in a gruff tone, moments later wishing she hadn't been so foul.

Jefferey hesitated, picked up her suitcases, walked through the door and stood in the foyer.

"How did you get here?" Queenie asked, looking beyond the door but not seeing a car.

"I took the Greyhound Bus. Look, I shouldn't have come here without asking you first, but I couldn't take rejection that far away."

"So you had the nerve to get on a bus and receive your rejection face-to-face. Why didn't you drive?"

"I was in a bad accident and my car was totaled. I lost my job, Queenie, and was evicted out of my house."

"Does Harrison know? He should have some responsibility in all of this."

"Harrison has been out of my life for fourteen years, Queenie. I haven't seen hide or hair of him. I loved that man too hard."

Queenie looked at her sister for a long time. She'd heard about

7

how Harrison had ditched her and HJ, leaving them high and dry. Even in knowing the circumstances, Queenie hadn't felt any kind of way about it. But now, looking at Jefferey, her heart softened a little.

"Come on in and make yourself comfortable. I'll put on a pot of water for tea."

Jefferey followed Queenie into her family room. "Thank you, Queenie. I owe you. All I need is a place to stay for a minute...until I can get back on my feet."

"A minute was all I was going to give you. I haven't seen you in God knows how many years. You've never called to see how I was doing. Hell, I wasn't sure if you were dead or alive. Well, I did, but you get my drift."

"The doors of communication swing both ways, but I will be the first to say that I'm sorry that it took a moment like this to find your doorstep."

"Yeah," Queenie grunted. "I don't remember ever being invited to a family reunion or any of those lavish parties you and Harrison used to throw at your fancy house."

Jefferey exhaled. She tried to remain calm. "If it's any consolation, the last fourteen years of my life have been a living hell. I don't understand how I let one man get in my system like that. We married young, but the seventeen years we were married should've counted for something."

Queenie watched Jefferey for a moment and then went into the kitchen upon hearing the whistle of the tea kettle. She came back with two cups of boiling water—the steam oozing out of the cups—and two tea bags and gave one to Jefferey. Tears continued to roll down Jefferey's face.

Jefferey wiped her face with the back of her hand and took the tea cup from Queenie. "I'm sorry; I hurt so bad inside. Insecurities have kept me from talking to my girlfriends about this."

"What about your mom... Daddy?"

Jefferey took a sip of the hot tea, put the cup down on the table and then looked at Queenie. "They're old. They're trying to hold onto what little life they have left. When was the last time you saw Daddy?"

Batting her eyes, Queenie went to her seat and sat down. "I haven't seen the old man in years. In my book, he deserted my momma and me. Even with Momma now gone to heaven, there is nothing I want from him."

"He loves you, Queenie. I believe if your mother hadn't kicked him out, he wouldn't have been with my mother, and there wouldn't have been me."

Queenie rolled her eyes. "Hold it one damn minute. I let you in here, but there's no room for you to talk about my dead momma. Momma kicked his ass out because he was a filthy, low-down womanizing bastard. I'm going to leave it at that. If I tell the story the way I believed it happened, you wouldn't like it at all."

The room was suddenly quiet. Jefferey took several sips of her tea. The sound of Queenie's cell phone seemed to be a welcome relief.

"Hey, baby," Queenie said quietly into the phone. "I love you, too." Pause. "Look, I'll call you later tonight. I've got company right now." Pause. "Love you, too."

CHAPTER THREE

EMMA WILCOX

The *Steve Harvey Morning Show* was blaring on the radio. With nothing on but her black, bikini panties and her black lacy bra still swinging from her hand, Emma stopped in her tracks when Shirley began to read from the "Strawberry Letters." She cringed, clinched her teeth, and ran to the side of her bed and sat on it, her ear tuned into what Shirley was reading.

"This is a sho'nuf crazy letter. My hand is shaking, as I try and control my laughter. It's from a Ms. I Think I Need a Man Right Now in Raleigh, North Carolina. The letter goes like this:

Emma put her hand over her mouth. Shirley Strawberry was about to read her letter to the millions of *Steve Harvey Morning Show* listeners. It didn't matter that no one knew that it was her letter; the mere fact that she did frightened her. Everyone would hear her thoughts broadcast out loud, but she waited with baited breath for Shirley's answer.

"I've been suffering alone in silence after the death of my dearly beloved. The other day, it seemed that all the organs in my body began to do flip flops, sending me a signal that had me on full alert. And then

I realized it was my heart telling me it needed a jumpstart and that I needed to pick myself up and take off the mask of loneliness. My heart said I needed companionship, although, I didn't understand, as I had been with a man...well, we hadn't done the Do. True, I didn't want any kind of commitment; in fact, the only person I kept thinking about was my deceased husband.

"He came in the middle of the night wanting to make love to me. He lied down next to me and whispered sweeting nothings in my ear. I swear I could feel his tongue tickling my inner ear. He made my body roar like when we were young and in love...the first time we discovered each other's bodies and wanted our expedition to go on for days. Our lovemaking was passionate, and I woke up after my body trembled something fierce, like I'd been in a cyclone. What made me realize that he'd actually been there was that his cum was left on the sheets."

Shirley laughed so hard, the mike kept hissing. She had a time getting back into the letter. Emma could hear laughter in the background of the radio station, too. She blinked her eyes, wanting Shirley to move on and finish the letter so she could lay down and hopefully revisit her husband, Billy.

"I've had admirers," Shirley began, "One I was partial to, but I didn't sleep with him. When I felt the wet cum, I wanted to do a Monica Lewinsky and save it...to remember the moment that my dead husband's ghost had come to me in the middle of the night and made his woman happy. I had to admit to myself that it sounded crazy and for sure no one would believe me. If I told my girlfriends, they would've had me committed to Dorothea Dix—the crazy house.

"What am I to do, Shirley? Wait for my ghost to reappear or wake up and get a real man?"

Everyone at the radio station was laughing and making crude comments about Emma on the air. Emma covered her face with her hands and began to cry, wishing she hadn't exposed herself so nakedly. But the experience was real. Billy had visited and made love to her.

She huffed, and anger consumed her as the ridicule continued.

Emma was ready to reach through the wires and strangle Shirley and Nephew Tommy. She jumped off the bed and nearly fell when the phone began to ring.

Startled, Emma stood in place not eager to answer the phone. What if it was one of her girlfriends and they'd been listening to the "Strawberry Letters" and knew that the letter was about her?

The phone wouldn't stop ringing and Emma retrieved if from her nightstand. It was Queenie, the last person she wanted to talk to. She pushed the TALK button. "Q, I'm late for an appointment."

"This won't take long, Emma."

"What is it?" Emma asked, her voice easing up a little.

"Girl, my sister is here."

"What sister? You can't be talking about Jefferey."

"That's the one."

"What is she doing here, Q?"

"She's planning on staying awhile."

"Oh, hell no."

"Oh, hell yes."

"We need to talk."

"Oh, hell yes."

"Let's meet after I go to the gym."

"What time?"

"Twisted Fork at three."

"I'm there. Oh, I forgot my most important news."

"What?"

"I'm engaged." And the line was dead.

Emma held up the phone and looked at it as if she couldn't believe what she'd heard. Surely, she didn't hear Queenie say she was engaged. Damn, she missed Shirley's advice. Hell, it didn't matter any way. She was used to doing what she wanted to do. She hit the OFF button.

Emma put on her bra, a burnt-orange blouse, and jumped into her beige pantsuit. She snatched her blonde wig off the Styrofoam head, pinned it down on her own head, and smoothed down the sides. Then she stood in the middle of the bedroom floor and began to laugh. She laughed so hard, that she had to hold her sides.

For a moment she thought about Terrance. He was a good guy, a good kisser, but he wanted to wait until marriage before he'd entertain a sexual relationship with her. He and his brother, Donald, had vowed a life of celibacy until marriage. He'd asked her to marry him, but Emma wasn't feeling it. The distance romance thing wasn't her cup of tea. If she was going to be with a man, she wanted him closer than close.

It was amazing to Emma that Queenie was still seeing Donald, but they seemed to be in love. As much as Queenie claimed she needed a man twenty-four seven to satisfy her sexual desires, it surprised Emma and her girlfriends that Donald was still an item.

In truth, Emma wasn't eager to be with anyone but her beloved Billie. Tonight, she'd have a talk with him, and if he said it was okay for her to move on, then she would. There was a new brother who'd joined Shiloh Baptist Church and was trying to catch her eye. Maybe she'd let him catch it and see what transpired.

CHAPTER FOUR

THE PRODIGAL HALF-SISTER

Queenie hated wading through the mall traffic to get to Twisted Forks. It was always crowded, partly due to Barnes and Noble and a couple of other stores that were anchored in the same area. She huffed and hurried toward the entrance to the restaurant. Maybe she needed to lose a few pounds, although Donald seemed to be pleased with what she was packing.

As soon as she entered, she saw the back of Emma's blonde wig. Queenie wished that Emma would throw it away; it had already seen its best days. Coming up behind her, Queenie placed a kiss on Emma's cheek.

"Hey, Q." Emma rose from her seat and gave her best friend a hug. "How's the engaged diva?"

Before Queenie could sit down, she waved her left hand in Emma's face. The fire from the Princess-cut diamond nearly blinded her. "How's that for an engagement ring? My man has impeccable taste."

"Indeed he does, sister. That piece of jewelry had to set him back a few thousand. I ain't mad at you. I only have one question?"

"The answer is no."

"You didn't give me a chance to ask my question."

"Emma, I know you like the back of my hand. If you were going to ask me if he gave me some, the answer is no…no, no, no, no."

"I guess that means you're going to have to move up the wedding date."

"Wedding date. That's scary, Emma."

"Q, it's what you've been waiting on for the past twenty years." The two friends laughed.

"You're right, and I finally have a man who loves me for who I am."

"What if he can't throw it down like Linden? You know…make you work hard for the climax?"

"Linden's name is no longer in my vocabulary. Let's talk about something else, Emma."

"I'm sure it's crossed your mind, you horny beast." Emma and Queenie laughed.

"Yeah, I've thought about it, but if God gave this man to me, I have to trust that God answered all of my prayers. You heard?"

Emma giggled. "I hear you. Well, tell me about your visitor. How did she look after not having seen her in God knows how long?"

"She seemed nervous and her eyes were a little hollow in that high-yellow skin of hers. Other than that she looked pretty good, even that I have to admit."

"So how did she end up on your doorstep? What was her story?"

"There's nothing to it, Emma. I thought Donald had come back to the house with a change of heart about giving his new intended some good loving. When I opened the door, there was Jefferey standing on the porch with two suitcases waiting to come in. I was pissed. The last time I'd heard from that wench was… I can't even remember. It was probably when H. J. was graduating from high school and she had the nerve to send me an announcement. Mind you, there wasn't a ticket to be a guest at the graduation ceremony, only an invitation to put some money in a card and mail it back."

"Well, what did she say?"

"She said she needed a place to stay until she got on her feet."

"That doesn't seem long, Q."

"Believe me; it won't be. I'm giving her two…maybe three months and then she's out."

"Maybe this is some kind of divine test. It's time that the two of you healed your wounds."

"Emma, I have no open wounds. Jefferey has never been a part of my life. She happens to be my daddy's other child. That's all. And who gives their girl child a boy's name?"

"There are open wounds. Your hatred for your dad is deep and you're blaming it on Jefferey. She's a product of your dad's philandering and can't be held responsible."

"Whose side are you on, Emma? Jefferey is sneaky. She's always thought that she and her mom were better than me and Momma. I always wanted to cut her nose off; it was always up in the air, sniffing at me like I smelled like dog doo doo."

"It's your imagination."

"Naw, I didn't dream that up. I'll admit I've never liked her—hated her guts. And now that Donald and I have got our lives on track, I don't want my wayward, half-sibling around."

"You're cold, Q, but I feel you. Guess what?"

"Hold on a second. Where's that waitress? I need a drink."

"I thought you were abstaining. I might have to tell Donald that you're indulging in the sauce of the world."

"I've got to drink something. He left me horny and now I've got to babysit a sister, who can't do anything for me. I know absolutely nothing about her. Here's the waitress now."

The ladies ordered drinks and salad.

"So, what were you going to tell me?" Queenie asked, taking a sip of water.

"Shirley Strawberry read my letter on the show today."

Queenie nearly choked on her water. Emma got up and patted her on the back. "Please tell me you weren't the one who wrote about the ghost coming in the middle of the night and making love to his woman, leaving nasty wet cum all over the bed."

Emma stared at Queenie. "I shouldn't have told you. I went against my better judgment."

Queenie tried to keep a straight face. "I'm sorry, Emma. But that story was too funny. You were pretending that Billie was one of those sex toys you got from the Passion Party and you were having yourself a ball." Queenie howled with laughter.

Emma got up from her seat and put the straps of her purse on her shoulders. "It was real. You can laugh if you want to, but Billie was there. We didn't need a toy to receive the joy I shared with him."

"Don't go, Emma." Queenie desperately tried to quiet the laughter inside. "Come on and sit down."

"Is it funny to you? Kiss my ass."

"That wasn't very Christian-like."

"Go to hell, Q." Emma walked away from the table.

Queenie got up from her seat and ran after Emma. She grabbed her arm and pulled Emma to her. "Girlfriend, I'm sorry. I didn't mean to upset you, but Emma that story was hard to digest. I like to have peed in my bed. Maybe you need some therapy."

"Maybe you need to sweep around your own front door first."

"Let's not argue." Queenie hugged Emma. "Let's have a drink, a salad, and a good laugh."

"As long as it's not at my expense." They walked back to their booth and sat down.

"Let me tell you a quick story about this guy I dated for two-seconds."

"When was that?"

"It's not important, Emma, 'cause I was with him all of two-seconds. I was kinda feeling him and we were on our second date. I even made him one of my special, delectable fudge-brownie cakes and took it to his house."

Emma wrinkled her nose.

"Anyway, we were in his bed..."

"You hussy. Jesus fix her."

"Let me tell the story, Emma. Anyway, he says to me that he wanted a slice of that cake. I was more than happy to oblige. Us eating cake together in his bedroom would be super foreplay for me."

"You're so nasty. All you think about is sex. Hurry up and finish your story before they bring the food. I want to be able to stomach it after this tall tale."

"Well, I went downstairs to the kitchen. Did I tell you I had on one of those short, short see-through numbers? Girl, I left very little to the imagination. Anyhow, I sliced two pieces of cake, put them on saucers and pranced my fine, fat behind back upstairs. You would've thought I was in Hollywood or on Broadway acting out a part. I tried to give him his piece of cake. Do you know what that nigga said to me?"

"I have no idea and I don't want to guess."

"That nigga said we weren't eating in his bed. I bent down lower for him to repeat what he said, titties swaying all over him, but doggone it, if that man didn't say we weren't going to eat in his bed—that's why dining rooms were invited. For sure I thought I was hearing impaired. You know me, Emma; I worked all of my facial muscles to keep from cussing him out."

Emma couldn't catch it. The shrill sound of laughter left her body until she was coughing and trying to catch her breath. "What… what did you say?"

Queenie looked at Emma, as if she didn't have any good sense. "I turned around and took the cake to the dining room."

"Did you leave?"

"Girl, that man could bake a cake in bed; he was that good. I drove a hundred miles to be with him. I had to get some for the road, and then I left his sorry-ass behind for good."

"And y'all call me dumb and stupid." Emma laughed to her heart's content. "That was a good story, Queenie. You didn't have to make me feel good though."

"Emma, that happened. You can't make up crap like that." The ladies laughed.

"At least you didn't have to see his sorry behind anymore."

"Yep," Queenie sighed. "I'm not sure how I'm going to get through the next three months with Jefferey in my house, however. What do I say to her, Emma? I almost busted her in the mouth for talking about my momma."

"That's crossing the line."

"Girlfriend threw some heavy shade, talking about... if my momma hadn't thrown my daddy out of the house..."

"What, Q? Girlfriend didn't go there."

"Yes, she did, although she tried to make it seem as if she wasn't being disrespectful."

"Jefferey needs a girlfriend intervention. I'll call all the girls tonight so we can meet for Sunday Brunch tomorrow. With this group, you'll get some answers."

"Make sure you invite First Lady. We need someone to put the fear of God in her. Thanks, Emma."

Emma picked up her glass. "To you, Q."

CHAPTER FIVE

A SILVER BULLET INQUISITION

Queenie Jackson, Jefferey Quick, Emma Wilcox, Connie Maxwell Alexander, and Yolanda Maxwell-Morris filed out of church.

"That was some good word pastor threw down on us today," Emma said. "And Q, you sang that song."

"Yes, you did," YoYo interjected. "You sang the house happy."

"Well, thank you, ladies. I'd like to introduce you all to my sister, Jefferey Jackson Quick. She'll be staying with me for a few months. Jefferey, this is Connie and baby Desi, Yolanda better known to us as YoYo, and I'm sure you remember Emma."

"Hello," Jefferey said in a sweet tone of voice.

"Hello," Emma, Connie, and Yolanda said in unison.

"How old is your daughter?"

Connie smiled. "She's two months old." Jefferey patted her on the cheek.

Emma went to Jefferey and hugged her. "It's been a long time. Good to see you."

"Thank you, Emma. It's good to see you, too."

"Hey," yelled First Lady Jackie O'Neill. Are you all going to lunch? Franklin has some church business to take care of and I'm hungry." The ladies laughed.

"Come on, First Lady," YoYo said, waving her hand. "You pick the spot." Pointing at Jefferey, "and this is Q's sister, Jefferey."

"It's been a long time, but I remember Jefferey. You must've been in your twenties the last time I saw you."

"No, I don't believe it was that long ago, First Lady. I enjoyed church today."

"I'm glad. Franklin worked on that sermon for three days. Well, let's go to Nantucket Grill. Hopefully, we won't have to wait too long."

"A good choice," Queenie said. "Let's go."

There wasn't much conversation between Queenie and Jefferey as they rode toward the restaurant. In fact, since their reintroduction two days before, the two of them barely uttered a word to each other.

"I really did enjoy Pastor O'Neill's message today, "Take Charge of Your Life," Jefferey said to break the ice.

"Yeah, Franklin, that is Pastor O'Neill, let the master speak through him. That's why I go to Shiloh Baptist; no matter what I'm going through Monday through Saturday, I'll always get a word from the pastor on Sunday.

Jefferey let Queenie's words marinate. She was in definite need of a word, some guidance, some help from somebody. In fact, she needed the Lord's divine intervention, as soon as He could deliver. There was more to the reason she'd become a residence at Queenie's house, but she wasn't at liberty to say, at least not right away. It would become evident on its own. "He was good."

Queenie took a left on Durant Road, drove a few miles and made a right on Falls River Avenue. "We're here," Queenie said, pointing to the left.

She drove into the parking lot, made a turn into a roundabout and pulled into a parking space in front of the restaurant. Yolanda pulled up behind them and when she stopped, Connie and baby, Emma, and Jackie O'Neill got out.

The Nantucket Grill was noted for its seafood ravioli, lobster rolls, and prime rib. The interior was dim with few diners inside. The restaurant was welcoming and had a rustic look to it. It made you feel like you were in the wilderness. The ladies had dined here a number of times and were always ready to sink their teeth into one of their sandwiches or slurp on the broth from their delicious lobster bisque.

After the waitress took their orders, the ladies lit in on Jefferey like reporters from the Raleigh *News and Observer.*

"You don't look like Q at all," Yolanda said, analyzing every inch of Jefferey's face, as if she was a forensic scientist. "You must've gotten your fountain of youth from your momma."

"How long are you going to be in Raleigh?" First Lady Jackie rushed to ask, not wanting anyone to ask the question before she did.

"I hear you're looking for a job," Yolanda said, easing into the conversation. "We may have some part-time jobs available at the hospital. What kind of work do you do?"

"You should've come up for prayer this morning and let Franklin hit you with some blessed oil," First Lady interjected.

Her eyes rolled around the room. Without warning, Jefferey threw both hands in the air. "Excuse me, ladies. I'm sure you all mean well, but my situation is one that I'll have to figure out on my own. I'm not ungrateful or against having olive oil splashed on my face, but while I do appreciate your concern, my situation is a private matter."

"Hmph," First Lady Jackie said out loud, secretly polling the others with her eyes.

"Okey, dokey," was Yolanda's response, as she picked up her glass of water, taking a small sip of it.

Queenie sat there with an air of indifference.

Yolanda sat her glass down and stared at Queenie. "So what say you, Q? I'm sure you have an opinion."

Queenie bunched up her lips. "My sister said she didn't want to talk about it, YoYo. I say give her that respect."

"Oh, so your sister showing up at your residence is no longer of any interest to you, although I do believe it was your idea in the first place to have this little inquisition."

"No, it was Emma's idea."

"Ain't this some crap. I couldn't have had the idea, Q, if you hadn't planted it in my head, giving me the green light to contact the others."

Jefferey abruptly rose from her seat, threw the napkin that had once sat on her lap onto her plate, and pushed back from the table. Her voice was no longer polite. "Excuse me." And she exited the dining room and headed toward the restrooms.

"Aren't you going to run after her?" Connie said, nursing her baby at the table. "This was your bright idea. We're the Silver Bullets and we don't beat around the bush. You wanted this inquisition, now be a big sister and see if Jefferey's all right."

"Who are you to be talking to me like that? I'm going to serve your rusty butt on a silver platter," Queenie clapped back. "And it's disgusting to watch a baby sucking on an old-ass Silver Bullet tittie. Speak to your sister, YoYo, about baby etiquette and decorum in public places."

"Queenie Jackson, if you don't want me to throw the rest of this water in your face, you better apologize to Connie—now. As usual, you can't handle the truth."

"No, YoYo, I've got this," Connie said, holding Desiree tight in her arm. "You're nothing but a mean ole heifer…"

First Lady rose from her seat. "Enough ladies. We haven't been out of church a good hour and you've already flipped your switches and are at each other's throats. Don't let me have to lay hands on you."

"Take a seat, Jackie," Queenie said, rolling her eyes. "I'm going to the restroom and check on Jefferey."

Everyone was silent and watched Queenie walk away. They kept quiet until she was out of earshot.

"I was about to go upside that mean ass Silver Bullet's head, talking to my sister like that. Q gets on my damn nerves. Sorry, First Lady."

"YoYo, we did hit a nerve," First Lady piped in. "There's something deep going on with Q's sister. I believe she needs some kind of help and we need to pray for her."

Desiree burped out loud, causing a minor distraction. "Desi says sorry," Connie said, chuckling and wiping Desi's mouth with a towel. "You're right, Jackie. We need to pray."

CHAPTER SIX

CRAP OR GET OFF THE POT

*B*lowing air, Queenie rushed into the restroom like an Olympic runner trying to be first at the finish line. She stopped and looked around. When she didn't see Jefferey, she strolled down the row of stalls until she came to the one at the end. It was the only stall that wasn't empty—the closed door being the giveaway. Queenie dropped her head to see if she could identify the occupant.

"What do you want?" the voice behind the door asked.

Queenie could tell Jefferey had been crying. "Crap or get off the pot. Look, Jefferey, I'm sorry about what happened out there. I didn't mean…"

"You set me up, Queenie. You humiliated me in front of your friends. We're sisters and that was the last thing I expected from you. If you had questions, why didn't you ask me rather than get your posse together and berate me in public?"

"I was at the house all day Saturday, and instead of you taking the time to have a sister-to-sister talk, you went and gathered up your girlfriends so you could discuss strategies on how to deal with me.

What do you want to know, Queenie? Wasn't my explanation good enough?"

"Lower your voice; you don't have to shout. I said I was sorry. Please come out of the stall so we can talk face-to-face. I hate talking to a door."

"We'll you're going to have to talk to it. I'm not coming out of here. I can't face your friends. I'm embarrassed as hell. I...I feel like a woman who has three heads, and everyone can't stop staring."

"So what are you hiding?"

After several minutes passed, Jefferey unlocked the stall and came out. She stared at Queenie without batting an eye or saying a word. She finally closed her eyes and took a deep breath.

Queenie stared back equally as hard. She had no clue as to what was going on inside of Jefferey's head. Something more than what she'd been told was lying beneath the core. The truth always surfaced, but for now, Queenie had to wait on it to do so. Jefferey had some wounds and they seemed to be fresh, at least that was her best analysis of the situation.

CHAPTER SEVEN

SOMETHING AIN'T RIGHT

𝓛unch was cut short once Queenie and Jefferey reappeared. You could cut the atmosphere with a knife the tension was so thick. Conversation was kept to a minimum with no reference to the earlier inquiries about Jefferey's situation.

Quiet as a mouse, Jefferey sat unable to look into the faces of the women who had mocked her earlier. She wanted to get up and run and never see these women again, only she was at the mercy of Queenie, since that was her transportation away from the place.

Jefferey picked at her sandwich and listened to First Lady Jackie O'Neill yap her lips, going on and on about nothing. She wished she'd shut up and get over herself. It was hard to comprehend how the woman she knew as her sister, Queenie, could put up with these hens. Maybe she was like them, although, as she searched her memory, Queenie wasn't a push over and didn't take any prisoners.

Queenie was noticeably quiet. Every now and then, Jefferey would glance in her direction, although Queenie didn't look back.

Reprieve.

"I'm ready to go," Queenie announced. "It's been real; time to get out of my church clothes. Are you ready, Jefferey?"

Without uttering a word, Jefferey stood up and nodded at the ladies. Emma, Jackie, Connie, and YoYo sat stiff in their seats and watched as the two sisters got up and left the restaurant.

"That was some weird mess going on," YoYo said, looking around at the others. "Something ain't right in that camp. I can't believe that Q was acting all crusty and stuffy; she couldn't be mad at us for asking the questions she wanted to ask her own sister."

"Q is conflicted," Emma said, still looking toward the door. "She and Jefferey have not had a real relationship for the better part of their lives. The wound is deep and goes way back, but I agree with you, YoYo. Something else is going on with Jefferey."

"She acts a little weird...a little crazy in the head if you ask me," Connie said, "although she sounded intelligent enough the few times she did say something."

"Be careful how you label folks," Jackie rushed to say. "We don't want to throw shade when there is none. I say the girl is down on her luck and she's got the weight of the world on her shoulders."

"You're right, First Lady. We need to pray for her instead of conjuring up ideas as to what's wrong with her." Connie brushed lightly over Desi's head. Desi was falling asleep.

"Well, ladies, it's been an interesting afternoon. Illya is supposed to be calling me around four and I need my quiet corner, by myself to talk with him."

"Do you think you and Illya will make it down the altar, YoYo?"

"Emma, marriage is a nasty word in my vocabulary. Hell to the NO! I'm not going to let a man tie me up. Illya's a nice guy, but he's on the road a lot. He is an extremely good and patient lover—makes me scream like a banshee."

"I forgot to tell you something."

"Emma, please," Jackie said standing up. "I don't want to hear about your sexual interludes. YoYo has done a good job of that already."

"I can't help it if my man takes care of me." Yolanda had to chime in.

"This is juicy, First Lady," Emma plowed on. "You'll never guess who's on their way to the altar."

"Tell us, Emma," Connie interjected. "My baby is ready for her nap and I don't have all day to be guessing. We know it isn't you; you're doing it with ghosts."

Yolanda began to laugh and couldn't control herself.

Emma's eyes were wide as saucers and she stared at Connie accusingly. The muscles in her neck were breathing in and out. "What are you talking about? And what do you mean by I'm doing it with ghosts?"

Yolanda was now choking on her spit. Water was pouring down her face.

"Girl, YoYo and I were listening to the "Strawberry Letters" yesterday, and I could've sworn Shirley was reading a letter that sounded a lot like my friend, Emma."

"Your mind is twisted, Connie. I haven't written any letter and for sure didn't send one to Steve Harvey's Strawberry Letter folks. I don't know why you want to mess with me by manufacturing some foolishness. You're getting bad as that crazy sister of yours."

"So, are you admitting you did write a letter but didn't send it to Shirley Strawberry? Tell her, YoYo. Tell Ms. Emma Wilcox that we are close to being one-hundred percent sure that the letter was hers."

Yolanda was trying to hold it in, but she couldn't stop to answer.

"I'm sick of y'all. Can't go out with folks and enjoy a decent meal."

"What did the letter say?" First Lady wanted to know. "And what made you think it was Emma's letter?"

"The person who wrote the letter said they made love to the ghost of her husband who had visited in the night and that wet spots were on her sheets—we'll that's not exactly how she put it, but I won't bore you with the nasty details," Connie said, now laughing herself.

"Well, I'm glad of that," Jackie O'Neill said, her nose turned up in the air. "That is nasty." She turned to Emma. "Did you write that stuff, Emma? Did Billy come to you in the night?"

Emma stared at First Lady Jackie O'Neill. "I can't believe your naïve brain is buying into this bull crap," Jackie. "Connie and YoYo are always conjuring up stories about other people. They need to look in their own glass houses."

"Hold up," Connie said, raising her hand. "Now what ghost do you know smells like fried chicken?"

First Lady pointed her finger. "Emma, you can't get out of this one. If you wanted to be discreet, why in the world would you divulge that bit of information? Everybody in Raleigh, North Carolina knew that Billy fried chicken every Wednesday. He's probably up in heaven fixing fried chicken plates for the angels."

Yolanda's eyes were red from crying and laughing. "You're wrong for that First Lady."

"Speak the truth, Emma," Connie said, pointing her finger in her face. "Why are you on the defensive if you didn't write the letter? Is the reason you're ill at us because we know your masturbating secret and now you're embarrassed?"

YoYo couldn't stop laughing, but she rose from her seat and went to Emma and hugged her. "Emma, it's nothing to be ashamed of. I have ghosts visiting me two or three times a night. It's those toys we bought at the bridal shower last year."

Emma wrapped her arms around her bosom. Her body began to convulse and the tears ran down like Niagara Falls.

"It's okay, E. Nobody's judging you. I've got Preston to make my sheets wet."

First Lady began to laugh.

"Why are you laughing, Jackie?" Yolanda wanted to know.

"You ladies think I'm a prude. Yeah, I'm sure you talk about me behind my back. But girls, I had a memory when you mentioned the toys, YoYo. I took my Silver Bullets and my dildos home, and hot damn, Pastor Franklin O'Neill hasn't been the same after I finally introduced him to my babies, as I call them." First Lady leaned in and tried to whisper. "The sex is wild now. Later for Samson and Delilah; we've created some new characters that aren't even in the Bible."

"Shut up, Jackie!" Yolanda howled, doubling over with laughter and holding her chest with her hands. "First Lady Jackie, we've been a bad influence on you."

"Look, I'm glad I got rid of my baby making apparatus a while ago. Franklin and I have kinky, crazy sex all the time. I thought that part of my life was going to slow down, that the well would be old and dried up after I turned a certain age, but I have to admit before you all and God…I'm a married, Christian freak that can't get enough. What goes on in my marriage bed, though, is of no consequence to no one but me and my lover, my babies' daddy, my pastor…"

"We got the picture, Jackie," Connie said, shaking her head. "The Lord is not pleased with you heathens today." Everyone at the table doubled over in laughter.

"Took my very own words and used them against me, huh, Connie?" First Lady Jackie couldn't keep a straight face and laughed some more when she saw the others working hard to contain themselves. "Oh, Emma, what was it you've been trying to tell us?"

"Jackie, my news wasn't half as good as your bit of information about your sexcapades. I needed a good laugh. But since I have everyone's attention…" Emma looked around the room and once she had everyone's attention, she blurted it out. "Q is engaged!"

No one moved or said a word for the next minute or two. It was as if everyone was processing Emma's last three words."

Everyone jerked their head in YoYo's direction when her fist hit the table. "I'll be damned."

CHAPTER EIGHT

CONNIE ALEXANDER

*C*onnie drove to her plush, four-thousand square-feet home that was located on a golf course in North Raleigh. It was a beautiful, five-bedroom, four-bath, brick dwelling that boasted the most gorgeous view of a lake and a portion of a golf course. She and her husband, Preston Alexander, were enjoying life after a drug trafficking crackdown in the city almost cost Preston his freedom and a life with his adorable wife. Now they shared a precious new addition to their family, little Miss Desiree Marie Alexander. She was the love of their lives and life couldn't be better.

"Hey, baby," Connie shouted as she entered the house with Desiree in her arms. "Where are you?"

"I'm in my office watching Derek Jeters knock another one out of the ballpark for the Yankees."

"I thought you were a football man," Connie said, stepping into Preston's office, planting a kiss on his waiting lips.

"Let me hold my baby girl." Preston took Desiree from Connie and placed kisses on her face.

"Stop kissing all over my baby."

"My baby girl…" Preston kissed Desiree again. "I am a football fan, but I've got to wait a few more months before Cam Newton and the Panthers take to the field. We've got to make our way to Charlotte this year for a Panther's game."

"Speaking of Charlotte, Q's sister is staying with her."

"I didn't know she had a sister. Did you?"

"Yes, although I'd never met her before today. She lived in one of Charlotte's upscale neighborhoods, according to Emma, had a good paying job, hob-knobbed with Charlotte's elite but is now living with Q without a job or a place of her own."

"What happened?"

"That's the big secret. Q wanted the girls to meet for lunch and maybe help her find out what's going on with Jefferey."

"Jefferey? I thought you said it was her sister."

"Everything is suspect, baby. Who'd name their girl child Jefferey? Anyway, it was a mess."

"I'm guessing that you all tore into her like a ferocious herd of lions. That crew you hang out with is merciless, and that includes my lovely sister-in-law."

"It wasn't that bad, but darn near. I'll admit the questions flew out of everyone's mouth like the girl was on trial for murder. And Q had the nerve to get all huffified when we asked for her opinion. After all, it was her bright idea to put Jefferey on the spot. YoYo was about to slap Q silly."

"All of you women are hotheads. Lord, the poor girl didn't have a chance."

"First Lady Jackie said that we need to pray for Jefferey. Something is up with her, she believes, but I'm going to stay my behind out of other people's business. I've got this little one to think about."

"The best advice I've heard from you today."

"Guess what else I heard today?"

"What could that be, baby?"

"Queenie is getting married."

Preston moved away from the computer screen he'd been staring at. "You mean the guy she's been seeing is crazy enough to want to marry her?"

Connie smirked. "I feel for him, but they seem to be in love."

"More power to him. When Linden gets a hold of the news, he's going to be jealous. Old flames die hard."

"Baby, Linden is married."

"That boy has a love Jones for Queenie Jackson. I ran into him not too long ago."

"And you didn't tell me?"

"Some secrets a man has to keep to himself."

"What did he say?"

"It's not so much what he said but how he said it. He asked how Queenie was doing and stuff like that. He may be married, but he was definitely trying to get the lowdown on your girl. I didn't tell him anything, though."

"Like you had something to tell him."

Preston pulled Connie to him, the baby now lying on her shoulder. "Look, I'm tired of this ball game. The Yankees have this one sewn up. Why…"

Connie touched Preston's lips lightly with her finger. "Why don't we go upstairs and make another baby?"

"That wasn't what I was about to suggest, woman. You better thank God for the one you have. We're getting too old to be producing a brood of little ones that we won't be able to play with when they get school age. Leave that for Kim and Kanye West."

Connie managed a fake laugh and rolled her eyes seductively. "Speak for yourself, big daddy. Let me take Desi upstairs to bed; she's fallen asleep. Momma wants some good Poppa Bear loving. I don't need another baby, only your warm arms wrapped around me. That will make me happy."

"I'll see what I can do."

CHAPTER NINE

I'M NOT MY SISTER'S KEEPER

*H*ome was the place where you relaxed, let down your hair, and did whatever you felt like doing. For Queenie Jackson, this was her haven and place of solitude when she wanted to be by herself. There were no responsibilities like children or a husband that she had to consider in her daily grind. If she didn't feel like cooking, Queenie didn't cook. If she didn't feel like making her bed, Queenie didn't do it. And if she felt like roaming through her house in her bra and panties and sometimes naked, it was Queenie's prerogative.

Jefferey's sudden appearance threw a wrench in Queenie's lifestyle. It wasn't that she didn't want to share, but the only persons Queenie had shared anything with, within the confines of her private sanctuary, were her boy toys—Linden Robinson and Donald Tillman, and she could kick them out anytime she got the urge; well Linden was no longer in her life. This new arrangement with Jefferey, though, was an inconvenience that didn't sit well, especially since she was family and there seemed to be something far deeper than Queenie had imagined motivating Jefferey to solicit her help.

When they arrived home, each sister went their separate ways. Reaching her bedroom and slamming the door shut, Queenie huffed as she took off her clothes and found something a little more comfortable to lounge in. She put on one of her colorful, floor-length caftans and sat on the edge of the bed, contemplating her next step. Jefferey had to be a little more forthcoming or Queenie was going to personally put her on a bus back to Charlotte.

Listening at the door, Queenie eased open the door to her bedroom. She moved stealthily through the hallway of her immaculate three-bedroom townhouse, finally turning the corner and entering her kitchen. It was eerily quiet, but Queenie ignored it. She picked up the tea kettle, placed water in it and put it on the stove to boil.

Without notice, Jefferey peered from around the corner. Queenie jumped and stumbled over the chair she had pulled out from the dining table.

"Why are you sneaking up on me?" Queenie asked her anger etched in her face and in her voice. "I could've hurt myself."

"Sorry." Jefferey stood and stared.

"Why are you staring at me?"

"No reason."

Queenie put her hands on her hips. She had let Jefferey in but now she was beginning to feel uncomfortable in her own home. "Why did you come here? What are you hiding? I need some answers today."

Jefferey continued to stare at Queenie. "You've never liked me, although I looked up to you."

"Tell that to someone else. I wasn't nice to you and we've never been friends."

"Dear sister, I've lived with your nasty insults and your standoffish ways, but it hasn't fazed me one bit. I've lived a good life...had a good life until Harrison decided to turn the tables on me."

"I'm not sure that it was all Harrison's fault."

Jefferey stared Queenie down. "What in the hell do you know? You've never been family to me. When I needed you, you didn't come."

"Make some sense, Jefferey. When have you ever needed me?

When was the last time you picked up a phone and dialed my number? Life has always been grand in your mind and I was always the big sister who was beneath you."

"You said it; I didn't."

They both turned when the tea kettle began to whistle. Queenie rushed to the stove to turn it off. Ignoring Jefferey's stares, she reached in the kitchen cabinet and retrieved a coffee mug and poured water into it. She got a tea bag and let it fall into the water to seep. "Would you like a cup of tea?"

"Goddammit, I don't want a cup of tea. I want to have a decent conversation with my sister."

"Hold it, Jefferey. Getting loud on me isn't the safest way of attracting my attention, if you know what I mean."

"And I wish you would throw hot water on me, you evil witch."

Queenie put the cup of tea on the table. "Bitch, that's the last time you will disrespect me in my house. I was hoping for a quiet Sunday afternoon, not some bull from the likes of you. I'm trying to be the big person, the nice person here. So you better get to talking real fast. Sister or no sister, your ass will be out on the street."

Taking a seat at the dinette, Jefferey put her elbows on the table and held up her head with her hands. "I've been through a lot. In fact, I haven't spoken to H. J. in more than a couple of years."

Queenie took a seat and watched Jefferey with different eyes. She seemed far away and not really able to concentrate. "Do you have any idea where he is?"

"No. After he finished college, he stayed in the Raleigh/Durham area. We stayed in contact for a while, and then one day his phone was no longer in service. I waited but I never heard from him."

"Did you file a missing person's report?"

"No."

"Okay, Jefferey, I've always thought you were the intellectual one. Why haven't you reported H. J. missing?"

Abruptly, Jefferey got up from the table, bursting into tears. She held her hand across her mouth and then fled the room. Queenie's eyes trailed after Jefferey, still wondering what had caused the sudden outburst. She took a sip of tea and looked out of the window.

CHAPTER TEN

YOLANDA MAXWELL MORRIS

*P*eering at her face in the bathroom mirror, Yolanda squinted and contorted her face, conjuring up a multitude of facial expressions. She took a finger and stretched the skin from her eye to her forehead and then took the fingers of both hands and dragged them along her jawline from her neck to the tip of her chin.

"Yep, Botox is the answer for these aging jowls. A nip and a tuck there, and I'll be good to go."

Dressed in a cute midi sundress and a pair of gold, Prada sandals, Yolanda took one last look in the mirror; grabbed her mini, three-compartment, strap clutch; put on her Prada sunglasses; and headed for her nip/tuck session with her favorite plastic surgeon. More black women were opting for the treatment that only white women and/or Hollywood's beauties were said to get, but if it was going to make her feel more confident about who she was, Yolanda was game. She wasn't getting any younger, and she was thinking about casting a wide net for a look at new fish in the sea.

Illya Newsome, the fine, dreadlocked, undercover FBI agent she'd met almost two years ago was slipping from her grasp. His assignments kept him from seeing Yolanda as often as she'd like. Besides, the long distance romance wasn't good for a woman who'd once vowed that she wouldn't have another permanent fixture in her life after her divorce was final, but all of a sudden craved human affection something fierce from the opposite sex. And something that Illya said during the course of their last telephone conversation hinted that he might be trying to rekindle a relationship with his ex-wife. She didn't have time for that kind of tension.

It was a beautiful, sunny Saturday in August. Summer was almost officially over. College, university and public school students were all back at school, and it was evident as she drove her Lexus on Hillsborough Street, the main thoroughfare for North Carolina State University. It was bustling with activity—even for a Saturday morning.

Arriving at her destination, Yolanda pulled into a parking space, sat a moment, took a look at her face in the rearview mirror, and then got out. Her plastic surgeon loved money so much, that his practice was open for service on weekends.

Yolanda stepped inside of the dimly lit lobby. Mood lighting was placed throughout the room and the décor made you feel warm. The walls were covered with a rust-colored wall paper that had a rippled effect. Neatly arranged glass cases were mounted on the wall and contained some of the products that were used in the practice. As you walked in, the reception desk was straight ahead and on the wall were appliques that looked like leaves forming a tree in colors of olive, yellow, and light brown. The words Beauty is our Business was embossed on the wall and looked as if it flowed through the trees.

After signing in, Yolanda took a seat and waited to be called. She pulled her sunglasses from her face and relaxed in one of the soft, buttery, leather chairs. Five minutes passed before her name was called to go back to get her Botox fix. As she rose from the seat, another patient entered the clinic, but Yolanda didn't look back until she heard her name.

"YoYo, what are you doing here?"

No one called her YoYo but her closest friends. She recognized the familiar voice without having to see her. Turning around, she took a good look at First Lady Jackie O'Neill as she pulled her sunglasses from her face. Yolanda was in a state of shock.

Yolanda drew her head back in disbelief. "First Lady, what are you doing here?"

"Evidently the same reason you came here on a Saturday morning. Girl, we're getting ready to be in the spotlight, and I didn't want the cameras showing up my crow's feet."

"What are you talking about?"

"Franklin and I are going to be on television."

"Okay. That's nice."

"I'm talking about reality T.V."

"What are you talking about, Jackie?"

"The network approached Franklin about doing a reality T.V. show called Preachers of Raleigh."

"Shut your mouth. You all aren't going to do it?"

"Why not? It will draw more members to our congregation."

"No, Jackie, people are going to talk about you and Franklin all over town, disgracing your good name. That's what happens when you get on those reality T.V. shows. The producers want you to share about your ministry, but they want the drama too. And the drama is the big part of it."

"Well, we're not going to be like those others. We have to go to New York next week to meet with some production people. Maybe we can get the rest of the girls to go…maybe see a Broadway play. I hear that *Motown the Musical* is still playing. Let's talk about it when we get finished."

"That's not a bad idea, Jackie. I've got to get my nip/tuck. I'll wait for you."

First Lady Jackie winked at Yolanda. "Okay. Get pretty."

When Jackie finally emerged from her Botox session, she was beaming from ear to ear. "How do I look, YoYo?"

"Can't tell much at the moment, Jackie. You've got to give it time to do its thing. This must be your first treatment."

"It is. Franklin has become a little more liberal about some things…if you know what I mean. He wants his wife to look good beside him, and he understands that sometimes it takes a little cosmetic change to make that happen. I feel like a new me."

Yolanda laughed at First Lady, who was so comical and animated, as she moved her arms and hips to get her point across. "Work it out, Jackie. I rather like the new you. Now, what were you saying about New York?"

"It would be great if you and the girls met me in New York and we could go see *Motown the Musical*. Franklin and I are going up on Thursday morning. I will check to see if they have tickets available for either the Thursday or Friday showing. All I need for you to do is contact the ladies to see if they're in, and I will purchase the tickets in advance. They will have to pay me back, though. I'm not rolling in the dough yet."

"Okay, I'll call Connie, Queenie, and Emma."

"I hope Queenie's sister doesn't want to go. That's a strange one."

"According to Queenie, she's been hibernating in her room. She hasn't tried to get a job and the relationship between the sisters is even more strained. I doubt seriously, if what's her name…"

"Jefferey."

"How could I forget that? What mother would name their daughter, Jefferey?"

"A mother who wanted a boy?"

"No doubt. Anyway, let me go. I've got some other errands to run. I'll get back with you tonight or tomorrow."

"Okay," First Lady said. "You're going to keep my secret right?"

"You mean that Botox secret? Girl, please, your secret is safe with me."

Both ladies laughed, strolled out of the building, and went their separate ways.

41

CHAPTER ELEVEN

A NEW YORK STATE OF MIND

The ladies were excited about their getaway to New York. Yolanda, Connie, Queenie, and Emma sat in Terminal 2, waiting to board their eight a.m. flight. They'd been giddy all morning, anxious to go to the City and get caught up in the New York state of mind.

Even Queenie seemed peaceful, considering that she was harboring an unwanted house guest. This was what she needed, although she wanted Donald more.

"I'm glad we're going up on Thursday," Emma said, rocking her one leg that dangled over the other. "I plan to do some shopping and see some sights."

"This is what I needed," Queenie interjected. "I wish Donald could've come with me. But I'm going to enjoy being around my girls since I haven't hung out with you in a while."

"Yeah, Q, we've missed you. Still babysitting that sister of yours, I see."

"YoYo, that's why this trip was so needed. Something is wrong with Jefferey, but she refuses to talk to me, although I believe she wants to, if that makes sense. There's something going on with her...maybe even mental."

"Umph," Yolanda said. "Q, I was thinking the same thing. She seems withdrawn and nervous about something. I didn't get that when I first met her."

"I'm almost afraid to leave my house for fear that she's going to steal something...ah, ah...or go through my things. It's wrong of me to indict her like that, but she's been throwing off some strange vibes that's makes me uncomfortable."

"Somehow, you're going to have to make her talk, Q. What do you do when Donald comes up to visit?"

"Connie, don't make me laugh. Donald and I haven't even done the bump and grind."

Everyone began to laugh. Queenie was the loudest of them all.

"When we're married, I'm going to tear it up." Queenie couldn't stop the tears from laughing so hard. "We go out to eat, take in a movie, or take a long ride when he comes up. I don't know what it's like to get a hotel room with him."

"Good. You need to keep that fast tail dress of yours down anyway."

"Don't start, Emma, since everyone is aware that you're having live sex with ghosts."

"Shut the hell up, Q."

Everyone fell out laughing.

"Delta Flight 6234 is ready for boarding.

The flight lasted a little over an hour. Everyone was glad when their happy feet touched the ground. Excited, the ladies got their luggage and caught a shuttle to mid-town Manhattan. First Lady Jackie was going to meet them there and do some shopping.

When the ladies reached the hotel, Jackie was waiting for them in the lobby. The spotlight was on Jackie and the girls gasped when they saw her all made up and out of her element. Jackie's hair had been done by a professional—puffed a little at the top with the sides swirling about her face. She wore a pantsuit, whose asymmetrical zip-front, tweed jacket that featured a faux-leather collar polished off the black designer, polyester-knit slacks. On her feet she wore a pair of four-inch black-leather heels that accentuated the outfit. Even Queenie smiled at Jackie's new look, giving her an elevator stare.

Queenie threw her index finger in Jackie's direction and then gave her a high-five. "Well, girlfriend, you're rocking that outfit. I can't believe that you're the same First Lady Jackie O'Neill of Shiloh Baptist Church that I know from Raleigh, North Carolina. Look at you."

Skinning and grinning, First Lady twirled around so that her Silver Bullet friends could take a good look at her. "You all like?"

"Yeah," they all said in unison.

Yolanda walked up to First Lady and whispered in her ear. "You're letting this reality T.V. stuff pump your head up."

"We all like to look our best."

Yolanda lightly tapped First Lady on the arm. "I like it, no...I love it. Divalicious. You're going to make Pastor mad."

"He got his face dusted for the audition. Three other pastors and their wives from our area are also being featured. Now hurry and put your things up so we can take New York by storm."

"I'm ready," Queenie said. "You all may have to drag me back to Raleigh."

"You said the same thing when we went on our trip to Vegas last year," Emma added. "But we know that you'll be going back, since you can't stay away from Donald for only so long."

"You know me, girl." Queenie laughed.

"Hurry up. I'll be waiting downstairs," First Lady said with a broad smile on her face. "I can't wait to go shopping again. You won't believe that Franklin allowed me to go out with one of the producers of the show and acquire this outfit. It costs some money, too. I told her that my girls were coming in today, and I want them to have the same experience. She gave me the name of a stylist they use from time to time, and guess what? She's meeting us in one hour and will take us on a shopping trip that will always have you remembering your trip to New York. After we've done the damage with our shopping, we're going to have lunch, and that will be a surprise."

"Well, shut the hell up, First Lady," Queenie said with a smirk. "It took fifty-something years for you to grow up and get with the program, and now with one reality T.V. show in the making, you're the toast of the town. I ain't mad, but damn."

"I had to catch up with you heathens. I didn't realize you were having so much fun. But so that we're clear," First Lady Jackie pointed heavenward, "my Father above is still the head of my life and Him only will I serve."

Queenie tried to look at Jackie with a straight face. "Girl, you crack me up. Come on guys; I'm ready to shop."

Connie, Emma, and Yolanda let out a chuckle, with Yolanda holding her chest. Queenie strolled to the elevator and pushed the button to go up.

"Give us thirty minutes," Yolanda said, as she and the others moved toward the elevator. "I can't wait to have some fun. Here I am New York."

The elevator doors opened and the girls were gone.

CHAPTER TWELVE

NIP/TUCK

"First Lady came to New York and lost her mind," Queenie said to the others while riding up in the elevator. "But I'm glad she's having a good time."

"Yeah, it takes some getting used to," Emma said. "We're so used to the Holy Ghost, sanctified, and filled with fire Jackie that claims she does no wrong."

The door to the elevator opened and the ladies got out.

"Ever since we went to Vegas, First Lady changed," Connie interjected.

Yolanda laughed. "And it didn't hurt that she was kissed by a handsome prince."

"A prince that she was fool enough to give her phone number to… that almost cost her marriage to Pastor," Queenie put in.

"Come on, guys, Franklin knew that First Lady wasn't capable of having an affair with anyone," Yolanda interjected. "For God's sake, First Lady was always at Franklin's beck and call. The church is her true mistress."

"Sis, let's be nice and fair. When First Lady committed herself to her man, she made a vow to love the church, too. It takes a strong First Lady to endure some of the battles these preachers go through."

"You should know, Connie. You and Preston almost didn't make it down the altar."

"But we did, Emma, and now we have our beautiful daughter, Desi."

"She is beautiful," Emma said. "Okay, let's get ready."

Queenie put the card reader in the door and pushed it open. "Ooh, la, la. Look at this suite. I guess Emma and I will take one room; Connie and YoYo, since you're sisters, you guys take the other. The rooms have double beds in them."

"Sounds good to me," Yolanda said.

Queenie began to dance.

"What's wrong with you?" Emma asked, somewhat alarmed.

"I've got to pee. My blood pressure medicine makes me have to go to the bathroom all day long. We've been moving ever since this morning, and my bladder is telling me I need to shut up and get to the bathroom. I've got to get this girdle down first. Pray for me that I don't pee on myself."

Emma laughed as she watched Queenie rush to the bathroom. "We're going to have fun this weekend. Have you guys noticed that Queenie hasn't been her usual combative self? Normally, she has to disagree about something, but she's rolling with the flow."

"You're right, Emma. Our girl has a lot on her mind. I'm sure it has something to do with her sister. That one is a mystery still to be unlocked. She seemed to be drawn to Desi, though."

"I wouldn't trust Jefferey within two feet of Desi, sis."

"I hear you, YoYo. I'm calling Preston right now and tell him that we've arrived safely in New York and to make sure he's treating my baby girl okay."

"Leave that man alone, Connie," Yolanda said. "Preston loves him some Desi, and he's not going to let no one hurt his child, including himself. I wish Momma and Daddy were alive."

"Me, too. Momma would be smiling and kissing all over Desi. Go and get ready, while I call Preston."

The ladies put on their best *Sex and the City* outfits and headed downstairs to meet First Lady.

Yolanda struck a pose at the elevator. "I feel like I'm an older version of Sara Jessica Parker, except that I'm not trying to meet Mr. Bigg. Oh, I've got some juicy gossip for you guys."

Queenie, dressed in a mustard-colored fitted dress that draped across her hips like scotch tape on a Christmas package, looked at Yolanda and shook her head. "I don't want to laugh, so whatever it is, keep it until later."

Ignoring Queenie and unable to keep a secret, Yolanda kept talking. "Guess where I ran into First Lady last week?"

"We're sure you're going to tell us," Emma said. "You better hurry up; the elevator is here."

"At the plastic surgeon's office. She got Botox."

"YoYo, you're lying," Queenie accused. "Ain't no way in hell Jackie would let some plastic surgeon touch her face."

"And how would you know?" Emma asked, getting onto the elevator but staring straight at YoYo.

"Because I got a little nip/tuck myself. I saw a few wrinkles on my face and had to arrest those jokers."

"You're exaggerating," Connie said. "Wrinkles on your behind are what you have—that cellulite is eating that butt." The ladies laughed.

"I don't have cellulite and my behind is still firm. I may entertain implants, though, to give my butt a little lift."

Everyone stared at Yolanda as if she'd lost her mind, and Emma rolled her eyes. "You need to have your brain examined."

"Don't go there, E. You don't want to get me started about the ghost in your bedroom."

Emma rolled her eyes again and waited with the others for the elevator door to open. When the door opened, First Lady Jackie was in a corner having a conversation with a much younger, black woman who had ample boobs, that spilled out of her blouse and were not hers, and long red, acrylic nails that had to measure at least three inches in length. The woman sported a beautiful, thick mane that dropped well below her shoulders.

There was nothing real in the world any more, Emma thought. If you didn't buy it or have it sewn in, you nipped and tucked it. Emma shook her head; she'd rather spread her legs and make love to her ghost.

CHAPTER THIRTEEN

DINNER AT CARMINE'S

*N*ew York was everything the ladies needed and then some. Shopping had a new meaning. Thanks to First Lady's new stylist, the ladies perused the best stores in New York and laid their plastic down on the counter every chance they got. Ignoring the cost of their purchases, First Lady Jackie, Queenie, Emma, Connie, and Yolanda shopped like there was no tomorrow, ending up with at least thirty shopping bags between them. From Chanel to Tiffany's... Michael Kors to Macy's, this excursion was the thrill of the day.

Enjoying the camaraderie, the ladies stashed their purchases back at the hotel and headed out to eat.

"I feel like Italian," Queenie suggested, raising her hand high so that the group was aware that she was first with the suggestion.

"That's fine with me," YoYo added. "A good friend of mine told me that Carmine's on 44th Avenue in mid-town Manhattan is the best in Italian cuisine."

First Lady Jackie started laughing, finally shaking her head. "Ladies, I've already taken the liberty in selecting our dining experience."

Queenie stood back on her heels and gave Jackie the craziest elevator look. "Franklin let you out on a long leash and now you think you know everything. You're the last person that I'd trust to select my 'dining experience' as you so eloquently put it."

First Lady moved forward and stopped in front of Queenie, pointing her finger in her face. "Your fat ass shopped at the best stores today because of me, and I didn't see you curb your appetite for the finest those stores had to offer."

"Did she say I had a fat ass?"

"I'm not finished, Q. I may have been bottled and tied up under my husband, but I've been doing my homework. I'm not the lost little lamb you once thought I was. Now to get us back on track, I took the liberty to make reservations at Carmine's on yesterday at the urging of my stylist, as there would be no way on God's green earth that we would've got in without one. Great suggestion, YoYo. Now do I get an Amen?"

Emma, Connie, and Yolanda gave First Lady a high-five and grinned heartily.

"I'm game," Emma said. "As long as the food is good, I'm down for it. I didn't realize that shopping could take so much out of you."

"With what I purchased, I'm going to be looking good when the camera is on me when we tape the show."

"And don't you say anything stupid, Jackie, and embarrass your friends," YoYo added.

First Lady Jackie smiled. "Did I tell you how much we're going to be making per episode of the Preachers?"

Everyone stopped, their faces fixed on Jackie's mouth. Jackie didn't say a word, but watched the expression on each of her girlfriends' faces.

"Well, what are you all going to be making?" Queenie queried, placing a hand on her hip.

First Lady laughed. "I can't tell you jealous heathens. You'd have your mouths stuck out for the rest of the trip, and I'm having too much fun."

Connie raised her hand and slapped the air. "First Lady is messing with you all. They couldn't be making that much."

"Let me say this," First Lady Jackie began. "I've acquired your tickets for the Broadway show tomorrow night and I'm going to pay for dinner. Chew on that."

Yolanda pushed a gawking Queenie out of the way and placed a kiss on First Lady's cheek. "Honey, I don't care how much you and the reverend will be earning from your T.V. show. I wanna thank you for my meal and ticket to the play."

"Picking up the tab sounds good to me," Emma hollered. "Let's go."

Queenie smiled at Jackie. "Thanks for being a real friend. Forgive me for being an ass...no, fat ass sometimes. I'm having the time of my life." The two friends hugged.

"Me too," Connie said. She went to Jackie and gave her a great big hug.

"We're going to take a cab and get this party started."

"Sounds good to me," Queenie said. "Are you splurging for the cab too?"

First Lady laughed. "Naw, the least you heathens can do is put your money together and pay the fare. We're probably not even two miles away." The ladies laughed.

Yolanda raised her hands in surrender. "We got it."

The ride to Carmine's took inside of twenty minutes due to the traffic. It was down the street from Times Square and around the corner from Rockefeller Center. Yolanda loved the hustle and bustle of the natives, the tourists, and the continuous flow of traffic as they navigated the streets of the city. The air was crisp, but it was a New York crisp. Even the sights and smells of New York were unique unto itself.

The ladies filed out of the cab, pooled their money together, paid the fare, and entered the restaurant.

The restaurant had a rustic, eclectic, romantic feel to it—a true Italian Family restaurant setting. The long leather seats and the long window that looked out onto the street made it so inviting. It was almost chaotic as there were so many people trying to get in without reservations. The ladies smiled when the greeter said to First Lady, "yes, we have the reservation for O'Neill, party of five. Is everyone here?"

The ladies followed the hostess and sat in what the restaurant described as Open Service Seating. The ladies were given a menu and were surprised that the prices were reasonable.

"Let's get a couple bottles of wine to celebrate."

Everyone stared at First Lady Jackie. It seemed that no one could believe their ears.

"What would Franklin think of you sipping on the sauce?" Connie wanted to know.

"Do you and Preston sip on the sauce occasionally?" First Lady countered.

"Occasionally? Girl, it might be three days a week, but not so much for me now since I'm nursing Desi."

"It doesn't make you a non-Christian," YoYo said. "In fact, it might make you a better one, especially in between the sheets tonight when you cozy up to Franklin." The ladies laughed. "And remember, Jesus turned water into wine. He liked the red stuff too."

First Lady shook her finger at Yolanda. "Watch it, YoYo. Blasphemy doesn't look good on you. But I do say we should have a bottle of wine and toast to our sisterhood."

"To the Silver Bullets," Emma said raising her hand.

"If I may make a suggestion," Queenie interrupted, "Pinot Grigio would be my selection. It goes perfect with an Italian meal." Everyone looked at Queenie with those *who asked you* look.

"Sounds good," First Lady stated. "We're going to have red and white."

Queenie winked at Jackie. "Proud of you," she mouthed.

The ladies ordered their food—calamari for starters, Veal Parmigiana for Queenie, Chicken Marsala for Emma, Meatballs for First Lady Jackie, Veal Saltimbocca that Connie and her sister, Yolanda shared, and plenty of Carmine salad. When the food was finally delivered to the table, the ladies' eyes jutted from their sockets. The portion sizes were way beyond their expectations.

The meal was superb and all agreed that they wanted to dine at

Carmine's right before going to see *Motown the Musical* the next day. The ladies ate and enjoyed each other's company, as if they hadn't seen each other in years.

"Don't look now, but we're receiving some friendly fire at the one o'clock position," Queenie said, staring back at the gentleman with a broad smile.

"Q, this place is full of Italians and foreigners," Yolanda said. "Ain't nobody looking at us."

"They say the darker the berry the sweeter the juice. A little chocolate won't hurt anyone."

The ladies laughed. "You're funny, Q." Connie took a look. "Damn, and he's fine. He really is looking this way."

Before anyone could utter another word, the handsome gentleman got up from his seat and strolled in their direction. Over what appeared to be a well-toned body, he wore a black linen jacket, a crisp white tee-shirt, and black gabardine slacks that were belted at the waist. His wavy, dark hair was loose and fell to his shoulders. He looked like a younger version of Robert De Niro, without the gray hair. His walk was lithe and smooth—a walk with a purpose, and it didn't hurt that the gators on his feet hugged his slim foot just so. And when he stopped in front of the ladies, he gave a slight bow and smiled.

"I hope I haven't spoiled your dinner," the gentleman said, scanning the group of gorgeous, older women.

"Not at all," Yolanda was quick to say.

"I've been admiring your beauty since you walked in. Are you all visiting New York for the first time?"

"Do we look like first timers?" First Lady Jackie asked.

The gentleman looked at First Lady for a moment, smiled and then formed his words. "Yeah, but that's okay. As long as you're having a great time, that's all that matters."

"The food is excellent," Connie said, wanting to put in her two cents, dabbing her face with a napkin.

"We're planning on coming here tomorrow evening," Emma added. "The food and wine are that good."

"Wonderful."

Yolanda stared the newcomer down. "Does the gentleman have a name?"

"I do. My name is Stefan Morsilli. I'm a musician in town and I love this restaurant. And your name?"

Yolanda blushed and laid her hand on her chest before looking around at the others. "Are you talking to me?"

"Yes, you. What is your name pretty lady?"

"Ahh, ahh, Yolanda...Yolanda Morris." Yolanda saw the stares coming from her girlfriends.

Stefan picked up Yolanda's right hand and placed a kiss on it. "You're beautiful. In fact, all of you women are beautiful. African-American women always look so young, no matter how old they are."

Queenie began to laugh. "This is too funny. He's calling you old, YoYo."

"YoYo?" Stefan looked perplexed.

"That's my pet name. Yolanda is my given name."

"Oh, I see. But I didn't call you old. I'd say you're probably in your late thirties."

Yolanda stuck out her chest and grinned like a clown at the circus. "Did you hear that ladies? Stefan said that I look like I'm in my thirties, silver hair and all. This girl is on fire." Yolanda danced around in her seat.

Stefan's eyes roamed over Yolanda's body. "Did I say something wrong? You're probably in your twenties and I made a grave mistake by..."

"Let me stop you right there, cutie pie," Queenie said, holding her hand out for him to shut up. Pointing in YoYo's direction, "that woman right there is probably old enough to be your mother...maybe grandmother." Yolanda shot Queenie a nasty look.

"She doesn't look it. I'm forty-nine. The only difference in me and others my age who are in my game is that I didn't let drugs eat my insides out. I've taken good care of myself. Truth be told, my mother is black and my father is Italian."

Shocked looks crossed the ladies' faces for a second time tonight.

"Well, you've got good genes and you do look good, honey," Yolanda said. "A girl doesn't tell her age, but I will say that I've got a few years on you. I'm sure my silver hair gave it away."

"No, that couldn't be true. You're beautiful."

"Well, thank you, Stefan. I accept the compliment."

"Ladies, why don't I pick up the tab for you tonight?"

"Say what?" Queenie's face softened and nodded her approval of Stefan.

"Thank you, Stefan. My name is Jackie O'Neill." Jackie extended her hand out to Stefan, who took it and placed a kiss on the back of it. "I was going to pay, but…"

"Put your money away, Ms. O'Neill. I've got this. What do you ladies have planned for the rest of the evening?"

"Well, I've got to get back to my husband. We're in town meeting with T.V. execs about a reality show that we're doing."

"Good for you," Stefan said. "The best of luck."

"Thank you, Stefan. Ladies, I'll take a cab back to my hotel, as it looks like you all might be staying a little while longer. I'll meet you here tomorrow at four."

"See you tomorrow," Yolanda said, winking.

The group watched as Jackie disappeared into the crowd.

"I'm playing at a club in SoHo later tonight. Be my guests, if you like."

Yolanda spoke up for the group. "Stefan, we'd like that."

"Where is SoHo?" Queenie asked. "You're not going to kidnap us and take us to some island that we can't get off of?"

The girls laughed. "Q, you are a mess. SoHo is right here in New York City. It's the real artsy part, and yes, Stefan we are game. Is the group in agreement?"

Connie took a sip of her drink. "We came to New York to have fun. I'm in."

Stefan turned toward Yolanda. "Your energy is bouncing all over me. There's something about you that makes me want to know more."

Yolanda smiled. "The night is young. Maybe you'll discover what it is before we have to bid farewell."

CHAPTER FOURTEEN

THIS GIRL IS ON FIRE

*Y*olanda Maxwell-Morris had not anticipated meeting the Italian stallion. Stefan was a great host and tour guide as she, Connie, Queenie, and Emma hung close to him the rest of the evening, navigating their way through the city in his Bentley that he'd stashed in a parking garage near Times Square. Stefan showed them a good time, eventually ending up at a quaint little night club in the center of SoHo—with Yolanda hanging on his arm.

Jazz music flowed from its center and the girls loved every minute of it. Stefan led them to a table up front, and then he was off, probably backstage to get ready for his set. He was in a band, although he preferred to play solo.

"Trying to put your hooks in that one I see."

"Q, you are observant, however, I wouldn't say that I was trying to hook the dude. I'm having a good time like the rest of you. But did you get a whiff of that cologne? My goodness, he smells good."

"Don't forget, sis, that you're still seeing Illya."

"Connie, I believe that relationship is dead in the water. I told you all he was acting strange and I can't do these long distance things for any length of time."

"So, YoYo," Queenie began, "if your Italian knight in shining armor wants to take whatever this is a step further, what are you going to do? He lives in New York and you're in North Carolina. Sounds like long distance to me."

"Dang, guys, I just met the guy. I'm not trying to get married or have his babies. I'm having a good time, and you should be, too. I can't believe you've turned this into something serious. Let's enjoy the music."

"Umm hmmm," Emma said under her breath, scanning the faces of the other detractors.

A bottle of wine was sent to the table, the ladies sat back and relaxed. After a few sips of wine, an announcer peered on stage and engaged the audience.

The lights were dimmed and the curtains rolled back. On stage was Stefan holding an acoustic guitar, along with three other guys—one with a base guitar, one with a flute posted at the tip of his mouth, and the other on the drums.

The guys began to play. Then Stefan stepped to the microphone and began singing a sultry number that was full of base, soul, and dripped with sensuality. It was a love ballad, and Yolanda surprised herself, as she fell hard like a bear caught in a trap at the words and the rhythm of the beat.

"You captured my soul in your hands, you made me feel like a wanted man...your beauty arrested me, and now I only want to be...in love with you."

Yolanda wasn't sure she heard the rest of what Stefan sang, but she did know that the song hit deep within. Her eyes were closed for longer than she'd imagined and opened them only at the snap of Queenie's fingers.

"What's come over you, girl?"

"Q, I'm not sure."

"Surely, you're not letting those man's lyrics pull you under. Snap out of it."

"Why are you so worried? You have Donald. I'm not in a competition for anyone. I'm only having fun this one night in New York. Leave me alone."

"Okay, but Emma and your sister are sitting here watching you, too. Don't be a fool for lust."

"I'm not going there with you, Q. We've had a good day. Listen to me; leave it alone."

"Okay." Queenie didn't say another word.

Stefan and his band played for the next couple of hours. He smiled as he approached the table. "What did you ladies think? Did you enjoy the music?"

"It was beautiful," Yolanda said with baited breath, while the others looked on.

"What did you think, Q?"

"Stefan, I loved it. You're a good blues singer. Must've come from your mother's side of the family." Stefan and Queenie shared a laugh.

"You're a good singer," Connie said. "I'm ready to download it on my MP3."

"I do have songs available for download," Stefan advised. "It's more of what you heard tonight."

"It was great," Emma added, shaking her head in agreement. "Enjoyed it so much."

"Well, are you ladies ready to return to the hotel?"

There was a unanimous yes.

Yolanda sat in the front, while the others hopped in the back seat of the car, admiring its beauty. The group chatted all the way to the hotel, recounting their evening. Pulling up in front of the hotel, Stefan jumped from the car, opened the back door, and helped Queenie, Emma, and Connie out. Stefan scurried back around to the passenger front side and got back into the car. He touched Yolanda's arm, and she melted in front of him, not sure of what had transpired. It was as if Stefan had cast a spell and she had fallen under it.

Moving closer to where Yolanda sat, Stefan kissed her. All was not lost on the others, who stood on the sidewalk waiting for Yolanda to emerge. Yolanda felt Stefan's lips on hers, and in one swift motion wrapped her arms around his neck and kissed him back. And when their lips parted, Stefan ran his arm down the length of hers.

"I want to see you again," he said.

"I'd like to see you, too. We'll still be here in the city tomorrow, and maybe we can…"

"Great. I'll meet you all at the restaurant at four. Better yet, I'll pick you all up, and maybe go to the play with you, if that's okay. But I'm talking about more than that, beautiful Yolanda."

Surprise was written in Yolanda's eyes. A sudden jolt…an electrical current ripped through her body. It was almost sinful the way she felt at that moment, but she liked the way it made her feel. And then the words that Stefan sang rushed back to her. "I want to see you again, too," she heard herself say.

Yolanda kissed Stefan again, their fingers entwined. And then she exited the car, shut the door and watched as he pulled away from the curb.

"This girl is on fire!" Yolanda said out loud. She dismissed the stares of her girlfriends who couldn't in the least bit comprehend how she felt.

CHAPTER FIFTEEN

ANOTHER NIGHT ON THE TOWN

he next morning, the women rose and began preparations for the day's events. They were excited about going to see *Motown the Musical*, as well as returning to Carmine's for dinner. Connie, Queenie, and Emma couldn't wait to call First Lady and tell her about the rest of the evening the night before. They were all sure that it was a New York City infatuation, and that as soon as they got on the plane, Stefan Morsilli would be another fling in Yolanda's daily diary.

The day was perfect for breakfast and a little sightseeing. They ladies ventured to Ground Zero, where once stood the Twin Towers and then ventured to the Statue of Liberty for photo opportunities. Not wanting to be late, they headed back to the hotel to freshen up and wait for Stefan to pick them up.

Yolanda wore a red, long-sleeve bandage dress by Herve Leger that she picked up at Macy's. The dress stopped right above her knees and boasted a scoop neck. The dress looked as if it was wrapped tight around Yolanda without any room to breathe. But she looked good, capping it off with a silver, sling-back shoe and matching clutch.

The others looked equally as put together—Queenie in a rich blue-green, shimmery cocktail dress; Connie in a black cocktail dress that was draped with beads that resembled icicles; Emma dressed in a black and white polka-dot cocktail dress with black panels running on either side; and First Lady Jackie in a simple but elegant sky-blue, long-sleeved dress, that fell below the knees.

"You're wearing that dress, YoYo," First Lady Jackie said as she entered the ladies' room. "Don't let Franklin see you; you know what they say about a woman in a red dress."

"That they're hot; this diva sure is."

"Okay, YoYo, have it your way."

"I'm here to have fun, First Lady. Don't let me have to whack you with my purse. Now, we better go down so Stefan won't have to wait on us."

"I'd better call to check on Jefferey," Queenie said, pulling her cell phone from her bag. "She's been acting so strange, and I feel obligated…at least a little bit since I am her sister."

"Go on and be the big girl, Q," Emma said.

"I'll be the big girl all right." She winked at Emma and pressed speed dial for home.

Queenie let the phone ring and ring, but Jefferey never picked up. To relieve her mind, Queenie dialed again, but still no answer. Maybe Jefferey was in the bathroom and couldn't get to the phone. She'd call again before going to the play.

"Q, are you ready?" Yolanda called out to her.

"Yep, let's get this party started.

The ladies wined and dined at the expense of Stefan Morsilli, who somehow had matriculated his way into their women's group. Queenie, Emma, and Connie had summed it up in a few words—the man had eyes for their friend and sister, YoYo. While the moment lasted, for sure anything beyond that evening was a rap, the ladies took the gracious liberties that Stefan offered without batting an eye.

After dinner, Stefan drove the ladies to the Lunt-Fontanne Theatre on 46th Street for the seven-thirty show. Unable to get tickets for the sold-out musical, Stefan dropped the ladies off with promise to pick them up when the show was over. Yolanda seemed disappointed, but as soon as she and her girls were inside the theatre, her mind switched to seeing the actors perform rendition after rendition of her favorite songs popularized by Motown greats like Diana Ross, Smokey Robinson, Marvin Gaye, Stevie Wonder, The Temptations, the Jackson Five to name a few.

"First Lady, you got us some of the best seats in the house," Emma quipped, delighted at how close to the stage they were.

"Thank you, Emma. I wanted to show my friends that I could have a good time."

First Lady Jackie and Queenie slapped hands. The ladies sat in their seats and waited for the show to begin.

"You and Rev go on and do your reality T.V. show. If that's what brought you out of that pent up shell you were in, I'm glad to see it."

"Well, Q, it's about time, don't you think?"

Queenie smiled at First Lady and nodded her head.

First Lady Jackie tapped Queenie on the leg. "So how are things at home…between you and Jefferey?"

"I'm not sure, Jackie. She barely talks to me, although I'm the one giving her shelter. But there is something going on with her and I aim to find out." Queenie sighed. "Let's not spoil the mood talking about my long, lost sister."

"Okay."

At seven twenty-five, there was an announcement that the show would begin promptly in five minutes. People scurried to their seats and settled down until the curtain opened.

The cast was comprised of actors who had graced Broadway in other performances. The singing was superb, and the ladies rocked their heads and snapped their fingers to "I Heard It Through the Grapevine," "What's Going On," "My Girl," "Dancing in the Street," and so many others. It was a first-class act, and the ladies would remember this night forever.

At the show's end, Yolanda took out her cell and called Stefan. "Hi, Stefan, the show is over."

"How was it?"

"Fabulous. The girls and I enjoyed it so much."

"Wonderful. I'll be there in approximately fifteen minutes. Stay inside. I'll call when I'm curbside."

"Sounds great. We'll be waiting."

The ladies followed the crowd out of the theatre, reminiscing and reenacting some of the scenes in the play.

"I had a good time tonight," Emma said, taking a breath. "I needed this. I feel like I've come alive, singing all those old songs that took me back to a time in my life when I was happy."

"Girl, you better start living again," Yolanda stated emphatically. "Yes, Billy is gone but never from your heart. It's time for you to do YOU."

"Yeah, you're right, YoYo. Speaking of moving on, did you call that new boyfriend of yours to come and pick us up?"

"He is not my boyfriend. He's my boy toy while I'm here in New York."

Queenie stared Yolanda straight on. "Girl, who are you trying to fool? That man has your nose wide open. You can say what you want, but we see another."

"That's right," First Lady Jackie interjected. "It was all over your face when your new friend couldn't get a ticket to the musical. Since he was connected and all, I thought he'd have no problem. But it was your sour face that told the story."

"She's right, sis," Connie said, now laughing along with Queenie, Emma, and Jackie. "Fess up; you're smitten."

Yolanda smiled. "He's a nice, handsome, charismatic guy, but I don't do the swirl thing. I love my men black and sometimes as black as the ace of spades. That Italian brother ain't it, and I doubt that he could satisfy this girl, if you know what I mean."

"Save that bull crap for someone else, YoYo," Queenie stated. "We've all been witnesses to how you acted when Illya walked into that restaurant. You were the first person up from the table to introduce yourself like some little hoe. And how is he anyway?"

"Q, take that back." The others ladies giggled and Yolanda looked away as her cell phone began to ring.

Yolanda held the phone to her ear without saying a word. And then she noticed everyone staring in her direction. She regained her composure before saying, "We're on our way out."

CHAPTER SIXTEEN

WHAT'S LOVE GOT TO DO WITH IT?

The ladies jumped into Stefan's car and continued chatting about the musical, all except Yolanda. She looked straight ahead and thought about what the others had said about her and Stefan. This was their last night in New York, and while she enjoyed Stefan chauffeuring them around and paying for their meals, she was going home alone. She had a New York fling that she and the girls would talk about from here to eternity, and love had nothing to do with it. And a long-distance relationship to a man much younger than she, who was only smitten by her obvious beauty, was out of the question. And she was no one's whore. In fact, she was selective in choosing her men.

"A penny for your thoughts," Stefan said offhandedly, taking a hand off the wheel and placing it on top of hers.

Yolanda flinched, temporarily distracted from her daydream. She turned toward Stefan's smiling face. The words she formed in her brain wouldn't come through her mouth. Easy does it, she told herself. Let him down lightly; you don't want him to feel like he was being used. And yet, that's exactly how it seemed to her, although something else in the back of her brain that radiated to her heart was saying something totally different.

"Thinking… I was thinking about the great time I've had these past two days," Yolanda said in a soft voice.

And the car became eerily quiet. Not a word was said for more than three minutes.

"Would you ladies like to have a nightcap?" Stefan offered. "This is Friday night and by New York standards, the night is way too young for you to hibernate."

"Stefan, you've been a doll and we thank you for showing us a good time," First Lady said. "If you'd drop me off at the Sir Francis Drake, I'd appreciate it. I've got to spend some time with Pastor."

"Yeah, right," Queenie said, giving First Lady a high-five.

"We might as well go back to our hotel, too," Connie said. "Don't you agree, YoYo? Although we aren't leaving until tomorrow evening, I need some down time after running around the city all day, and I've got to check up on my family."

"You heifers can turn in if you want to," Emma began, "but I'm ready to party."

Queenie gave Emma a hard stare. "Emma, you're going with us."

"What are you going to do, YoYo?" Emma pushed. "If you're hanging out, I'm partnering up with you."

Stefan glanced in Yolanda's direction while keeping an eye on the traffic.

"I guess I can hang out a while longer. How often do I get to New York?"

Stefan smiled.

Pulling in front of the Sir Francis Drake, everyone said their good-byes to First Lady Jackie. She and Pastor O'Neill would be returning to Raleigh on a different flight. And they were off again.

Arriving at their hotel, Connie and Queenie immediately jumped out of the car after thanking Stefan for showing them a good time. Emma didn't move until Queenie pulled on the back of her dress and gave her the eye. Reluctantly, Emma got up and got out, her mouth bunched up in a pout.

"I guess this is it," Yolanda said to Stefan, unable to look him straight in the eye. "Since Emma isn't going to hang out with me, it's probably best that I go with the ladies."

"Take a ride with me; I promise to bring you back in one piece."

"I've had so much fun these past two days. I can't impose on you anymore."

"You're not imposing on me at all." Stefan reached into the console of the car and pulled out a small blue box. He gently placed it in her lap. "For you."

Yolanda gasped and drew her hands to her face in disbelief. "I..I..I can't accept this."

"Open it...please?"

The ladies were still standing on the sidewalk, waiting for some kind of confirmation that Yolanda was either coming with them or staying with Stefan. They didn't move from their spot.

Nervous fingers opened the box. Yolanda threw her hand over her mouth when her eyes studied the contents. "Why me? I didn't do anything to deserve such an elegant and expensive gift. I can't accept this, Stefan."

"You're worth your weight in diamonds and pearls. After being with you the last day and a half, I want to find out all there is to know about you. You have captured my heart in ways I couldn't imagine."

"But how can that be? My friends have been with us the entire time we've been together. Yes, we stole a kiss here and there, but a beautiful ring from Tiffany's was the last thing I expected."

"You're magical, you're funny, and you make me want to dance all night. This may sound strange to you, but the moment you stepped into that restaurant, I knew. It was in the way you moved across the room, the way you smiled, and it was the way you were wearing that dress tonight. But it's more than that, YoYo. You made my heart flutter. Sitting next to you has been the hard part; I want to touch you, kiss you, and tell you how much being in your presence has meant. I'd like to show you the world; I can afford it."

"What are you trying to say, Stefan?"

"You've already asked me that, YoYo, but if I must say it again without sounding redundant...I want you. I want all of you, and I want to fall in love with you if I haven't already."

"You don't know a thing about me."

"I want a chance to get to know the real Yolanda Morris. Now put that ring on and tell your friends that you'll be out for a while and that I'll take good care of you."

Yolanda looked back down in the box, picked up the ring, and slid it on her finger. "It's beautiful and it fits. How did you know the size?"

"Remember me asking you about your shoe size?"

Yolanda smiled. "Yeah, I remember; you got me there." She blushed. After a moment, she rolled down the window and looked back at her girlfriends who were stuck like statues to the concrete. "I'll be back in a little while. Don't wait up for me."

Queenie shook her head and the trio turned and marched inside the hotel. Stefan pulled away from the curb.

"Where are we going?" Yolanda wanted to know.

"My penthouse overlooking the Park."

"As in Central Park?"

"One in the same."

CHAPTER SEVENTEEN

A WOMAN'S WORTH

*A*s much as Yolanda hated to admit it, she rather enjoyed the attention Stefan was giving her. Love had nothing to do with it. At least that's what she kept telling herself. She sat back and enjoyed the ride, which was shorter than she'd imagined.

Pulling up to the curb, a doorman walked to the passenger side and opened the door for Yolanda. She looked in Stefan's direction, smiled, turned, and gave the gentleman her hand. In the next minute, another gentleman appeared from somewhere inside of the building and took the wheel for Stefan. That's when Yolanda knew for sure that Stefan had means, and there seemed to be limitless amounts of it.

Stefan held out his elbow, beckoning Yolanda to put her arm through it. And through the door they went as the doorman held it wide enough for them to get through. They walked to the elevator and rode it to the twenty-fifth floor.

Silence covered them. Jitters erupted in Yolanda's stomach, as she tried to anticipate what was coming next and why she was there in the first place. Rocking on her heels, she looked down at the gorgeous Tiffany ring and quickly looked away, not wanting Stefan to ask what she was thinking. And then the sound of the elevator that announced their floor startled her back to reality.

"We're here," Stefan said, smiling as he looked down at Yolanda. They exited the elevator, turned left and stood in front of large wooden door.

Butterflies replaced the jitters, or they could've been one in the same. Yolanda took a deep breath and moved forward after Stefan opened the door. Her eyes became an enormous camera lens as she snapped picture after picture. Yolanda thought the Bellagio was magnificent, but this apartment, condo, or whatever they called it was drop, dead gorgeous and more beautiful than any residence she'd ever seen or been in. The apartment boasted a grand view of Central Park that was so breathtaking that she couldn't stop gawking. It was as if she was on top of the clouds; and she didn't want to come down.

When she came up for air, Yolanda caught Stefan staring at her.

He smiled. "Admiring your beauty; you're an attractive woman."

"Stop it, Stefan. I'm way too old for you. I've had a fabulous time..."

Before Yolanda could get the next word out of her mouth, Stefan's mouth was on hers. He held her tight and ran his hands down the length of her body, stopping at the base of her buttocks and easing his hands down slowly. Squeezing the round mounds of flesh through the fabric of her dress, Stefan moaned...Yolanda moaned. There was passion in every twist of their heads, as fire and desire exploded to the surface.

Releasing his embrace for only a second, Stefan scooped Yolanda up into his arms and carried her to his massive bedroom. Although the room was dressed up in masculine attire, Yolanda loved the black and white contrasts of the décor, the motifs, and the bed that was draped in all-white bedding that she found and loved in the large hotels.

The softness of the comforter engulfed her body. She felt like a baby in the television commercial where the mother places the baby in a soft blanket that had been washed in Downey. And then he was lying next to her, his breathing heavy, nose nestled in her hair, and his finger outlining the contours of her face.

And he kissed her again, holding her chin in his hand. Before another minute had gone by, Stefan lifted her body slightly, unzipped her dress, and began to peel it from Yolanda's shoulders. He placed kisses all about her neck, across her shoulder blades, and down to the cleavage that exposed natural, tender breasts. It was erotic and sensual. Stefan nibbled for a minute before reaching up and pulling the dress off the shoulders to her waist.

With eyes closed, Yolanda loved every minute of it. It could've been a fairy tale, but it felt so real. She loved the way Stefan took his time with the little things, not too anxious to get to the good stuff. That made it more exciting, intoxicating, and she lay there and let him take charge at will.

When her dress was fully off, Yolanda felt a cold chill run across her body. Her lacy, red undies clung to her like icing on a wedding cake. Stefan toyed with her, tickled her with his tongue, but the real show was about to begin when he abruptly stopped, stepped out of his clothes, and looked down on her.

The man was hung like a stallion. That had to be the black side of the family. His muscles rippled like waves on the ocean, and the hardness of them made Yolanda weak. She couldn't wait to feel him.

He took his time seducing her body. With one swift move of his hand, her breasts were released from bondage, free to fall into his waiting hands. He took them, squeezed them, and gingerly sucked the now extended and swollen nodules like they were a tropical fruit. And then he found the real fruit of her passion and without permission, delicately parted her legs and entered, but not before covering his massive hardness with a golden sheath.

Yolanda had died and gone to heaven. This man, this creation of Italian and black, rode her like a thoroughbred horse. His knees dug into her sides as his pelvis met hers, riding and grinding to the finish line. Moans of pleasure and joy were ushered from Yolanda's mouth, begging him not to stop. This girl was on fire, and she couldn't get enough of what the young buck, Stefan, had to offer.

His back arched and her body began to tremble. Simultaneously, they gave up the ghost and fell together, their breathing the only thing that could be heard.

Wiping sweat from his brow, Stefan kissed Yolanda. "I want you. I want to take care of you. I'll do whatever it is that'll make you happy. It's been a long time since I've felt this way, Yolanda, but my desire for you is strong. I'll protect you with everything I've got. Whatever you need, it's yours." He kissed her again.

"Right now, I want you to make love to me again."

"So, you enjoyed it." He picked up her hand with the glistening diamond and kissed it.

"It was everything I needed and then some. You're a wonderful lover, Stefan. It's been a long time since I've been made love to like that."

"Just know that you're more than the sex; it was damn good for sure. But you, my lady, are a queen. I can't explain it, YoYo, but my search is over."

"You're only infatuated with me; yes, the sex was good, but I may have been an easy acquisition."

Stefan raised his head, holding it up with his arm. He laid a finger on her lips. "Please, don't ever say that again. Don't play with my affections. What I feel for you is real. Don't make me bare my soul when I've already delivered it to you on a silver platter."

Yolanda stared him straight in the eyes. She could tell he spoke the truth of how he was feeling...that this wasn't a quote, unquote booty call. It was more than sex; he made love to her...he made music like a violinist strumming the strings of his Stradivarius violin. It was a work of art. Yolanda felt the pain, pleasure and the ecstasy, as the warmth of his passion flowed through her.

"I want you, too."

CHAPTER EIGHTEEN

DON'T THROW SHADE

*T*he ladies landed in Raleigh without fanfare. Although the trip was fun and everyone had a good time, no one said much on the flight home. Yolanda hadn't arrived back to the hotel until eight that morning, all bright and cheerful and still in the same party dress she wore the night before. Connie seemed to be holding back some repressed anger that had built up from worrying about her whereabouts. But no one had any idea that the feeling that had flown through Yolanda's loins from being with Stefan were still strumming softly.

Back on North Carolina soil, the ladies hugged one another and prepared to go their separate ways. "Ladies, I had a wonderful weekend. Don't forget about the yard sale at the church this Saturday," Connie said. "Q, bring Jefferey; it might do her some good to get out."

"We'll see."

"Ladies," Yolanda said, taking in a deep breath before continuing, "I want to apologize for my selfishness last night. I could've called; I should've called, but the moment didn't present itself."

Everyone stood stone silent. When no one said anything, Yolanda tried again, not sure of what she wanted to tell the ladies or what she wanted them to say. "Stefan was so easy to talk to. He showed me New York from a fascinating point-of-view."

"I bet he did."

"Q, don't go there."

"You made me go there, YoYo. When we were in Vegas last year, you all were brutal when I stayed out with..." Queenie snapped her fingers. "I forget his name now..."

Emma started laughing. "You are too much, Q."

"But on the real, and I'm not trying to throw shade, YoYo, you didn't know if that white man was a serial killer or not."

"Hold it. Hold it, Q; he's only half white..."

"No, let me finish. That he's half white doesn't change a damn thing. You went out by yourself to God knows where, in a big freaking city with a man you didn't even know."

"Let me take it from here," Connie said, interrupting Queenie's flow. "You're taking too long to get to the point." Redirecting her attention, "You're my sister, YoYo, but damn if you didn't act like some damn tramp, running after that slick Italian gangster."

"Isn't that what I just said?" Queenie rolled her eyes at Connie.

"Whatever, but YoYo is the only sister I have and damn it, she pissed me the hell off. What if you'd been strangled and left for dead in some dark alley? If that man had put your brain into a squirrel, you'd climb up a tree backwards. That's how stupid you were. The least you could've done was had the decency to call and let us know that you were all right."

"Did you sleep with him?" Emma asked, getting her three cents in.

Yolanda rocked back on her heels and looked at the three of them. She wanted to tell the whole world how she felt, but instead told them the opposite. "I've listened enough. Why is it that every woman who goes off with a man has to have slept with him? Stefan showed me New York City by night and then we talked and talked until I fell asleep."

"Sounds like a contrived story to me," Connie said, with no expression on her face. "I'm your sister; I know you and your hot tail."

"Vulgarity doesn't become you, Connie. I can't believe that you won't accept the truth of the matter—that goes for all of you. My God, I had a wonderful evening, without sex, with a man who adored me," she lied.

"You're a liar."

Yolanda's face became contorted and if looks could kill, someone would be dead. "Take it back, Q. Take it back or I'll kick your fat ass right in front of this terminal. Don't you ever open your mouth and disrespect me…call me out of my name again."

"Damn, I'm not trying to get into a tongue-wrestling match with you. I didn't mean to…"

Yolanda threw her hand in Queenie's face. "Be careful how you throw shade. Your glass house has smudges all over it."

"Cool it, sis," Connie said. "Queenie isn't by herself in how she feels. We panicked. We had not heard from you; that was disrespect-ful. It was a beautiful weekend until you ruined it by running behind some young thing that was preying on your vulnerability." Connie threw her hands up in the air. "I'm done; you're safe now. Let's go."

Emma said nothing but followed Queenie to her car and got in. "We were hard on her, Q. We probably shouldn't have said anything. After all, YoYo is a grown woman and can take care of herself."

"You make sense. As hard as it was to believe, she was probably telling the truth."

CHAPTER NINETEEN

BACK TO REALITY

*A*fter dropping Emma off, Queenie headed toward home. The outburst with YoYo bothered her. She hadn't witness Yolanda's fury in a long time. If anyone had come to her like that, she would've hit back hard, and why should Yolanda be any different. The truth was all of them cared about Yolanda...each other, and until Yolanda returned to the hotel, they were afraid.

Life moved on. Yolanda would get over this small dent in their relationship, and they would be a happy sisterhood once again. Queenie had real worries and they were at home.

All looked calm, as she pulled up into her driveway. She pulled her jag into the driveway and into the garage, turned off the motor, and exhaled. Taking a minute to relax, she closed her eyes and prayed that she'd find things in decent order when she entered the house.

Queenie dragged her suitcase behind, as she peeked into the house. All was quiet, almost too quiet. "Hello." No answer.

Before retreating to her bedroom, Queenie looked around the house, going from living room to the kitchen, the guest bathroom and finally her master bedroom. Everything was in order, with no sign of Jefferey.

"Jefferey, are you here?" There still was no response.

Queenie climbed the stairs two at a time. The door to Jefferey's room was closed. She knocked, but there wasn't an answer. She stood outside for two minutes, praying that there was nothing wrong inside.

Getting up enough nerve, Queenie turned the knob and pushed the door open. Jefferey was wrapped tight in a blanket and sound asleep in the bed. As Queenie drew near, Jefferey nearly jumped up off the bed, startled by her sister's appearance.

"Were you trying to scare me?" Jefferey's eyes were bucking wild, as if she were trying to get her bearings.

"No, I kept calling you and I didn't get an answer. I've only been home a few minutes and was just checking on you."

"Oh." Jefferey brought her legs around and sat them on the floor. "I was tired."

Queenie frowned as she looked at her disheveled sister. "What have you been doing while I was gone?"

"Uhh...uhh, still trying to get a job. It's hard without a car. But, I'm going to get one," Jefferey rushed to say.

Queenie sighed. Their relationship was already unhealthy and she wasn't sure that she could communicate with Jefferey. Their conversation was so limited that it frustrated the hell out of her. "Okay, I'm home now. I'll fix us something to eat."

"Are you going to church tomorrow? I'd like to go."

Queenie had planned to skip Sunday service, but if her sister had an interest in going, she'd make that sacrifice. Anything she could do to get Jefferey up and running and possibly back to Charlotte was a step in the right direction. "Yes, I'm going. Also, Connie invited us to a little gathering next Saturday at her house. You've been invited."

Jefferey hesitated. Then she spoke. "She's the one with the baby."

"Yep, that's Connie."

"She was nicer to me than the rest of your friends."

"They're silly women. Don't take stock in what they said. Every one of them has their own issues."

Jefferey seemed to ponder what Queenie said. "Okay, I get that."

Queenie started for the door and abruptly turned around. "Are you okay? You don't seem to be yourself."

"I'll be fine as soon as I get back on my feet. There's nothing for you to worry about, Q." Jefferey looked after Queenie as she turned to exit the room.

"Okay. I'm going to fix something easy since it's already late but I'm famished. Come down when you feel like it."

"I will."

CHAPTER TWENTY

SOMETHING AIN'T RIGHT IN THE CAMP

*a*fter changing her clothes, Queenie moseyed into the kitchen to find something quick to fix. Since everything was frozen, she went to the pantry and pulled out two cans of tuna. Queenie loved tuna, and a tuna salad would settle nicely on her stomach.

Onions, eggs, scallops, pickle relish and mayo, along with the right seasonings were the ingredients that Queenie liked to put in her tuna salad. She put the eggs on to boil and chopped up the other ingredients in her dicer. As she commenced preparation, Queenie's thoughts went back to her weekend—the fabulous time she had with her girls and Yolanda's frivolous antics with the pretty, Italian man. Maybe she was jealous and she wanted some of the attention Yolanda had received.

She'd talked with Donald once while in New York and he respected her space to have fun with her friends. But now she needed him…wanted to talk and share ideas with him.

Donald was calm and unassuming. His faith in God and the principles for which he stood on provided a firm foundation for their love to grow. Only if Queenie's desire to have a sexual, physical relationship with her man wasn't always so strong each time they were together, maybe she'd appreciate him more. But who could blame her? Donald was Richard Roundtree *fine*.

She thought about all the losers—Linden Robinson, the six-foot, nut-brown, bald-headed brother who used to rock her world and set her ooh-la-la on fire; Joe Harris, aka the pimp that stole Christmas, who tried to stay in her sheets and between her breasts; and Anthony Rutherford from Vegas who she'd never had the pleasure of trying him on for size, although she wished she had. When she added it all up, Donald was the person she was supposed to be with. He was God sent and Queenie didn't want to blow it.

Throwing all the ingredients together, Queenie waited for the eggs to finish boiling. The quiet in the kitchen was interrupted by her cell phone ringing. She lunged and snatched it off the countertop where she'd placed it. As if a bell had gone off in her head, she realized that it wasn't Donald's ringtone.

Queenie glanced down at the number without a name in the cell's window. It was a Charlotte number, but the only person she would've communicated with from that area was upstairs in one of her bedrooms.

Quickly and before the caller hung up, Queenie hit the TALK button. "Hello?"

"Hello, is this Queenie Jackson?"

"That was the number you dialed."

"Queenie, this is Harrison… Harrison Quick, Jefferey's husband."

Puzzled, Queenie pulled the phone away from her ear and looked at it. Squinting her eyes, she put the phone up to her ear when she heard the caller asking *are you still there*. "Harrison Quick?"

"Yes, it's me. I'm sorry to have bothered you, but you were the last place I considered looking for Jefferey."

"What do you mean looking for Jefferey? Aren't you two divorced?"

"Queenie, it's a long story. Jefferey is in trouble."

"What kind of trouble?"

"I'm not sure. She reached out to me over a couple of weeks ago through some friends, and I came rushing home to see about her. I've been in Charlotte a week, and as yet, haven't been able to locate her."

"Why would she call you if you aren't together?"

"Besides the fact that we have a son, Jefferey and I aren't divorced."

Queenie gasped and almost dropped the phone. "She told everyone…"

"That's a conversation for another time. My wife is in trouble; I'm not sure what the real story is at the moment. She up and left the house, her car, and her cell phone is dead. I've been unable to reach her. My last hope was that she tried to contact you. I know it was a stretch considering your history, but it was worth a try."

Queenie sighed. "I'd like to help but I haven't seen her," she lied. "If she contacts me, you'll be the first person I'll call. Is the number that's showing in my caller-ID a good number to reach you?"

It was time for Harrison to sigh. He called out his number to Queenie and she verified that it was the same. "For the record, it wasn't me that didn't want to come around or invite you to our place. I loved Jefferey, but she pushed me away. Her behavior had become extreme, almost as if she had a mental breakdown."

"She fought me time and time again, acted out so bad that she'd become hard to live with. I tried to get her some help but she refused. And then she would act like nothing had happened. Our world was all right again. But when she did the flip flops, it was a nightmare. Truth be told, H. J. was afraid of her. And on that beautiful July 4th day after all of the festivities, the family had gone their separate ways, and we had retired for the night, the bitch tried to kill me."

"What? Kill you?" Queenie grabbed for her heart and looked up toward the ceiling.

"We had mad sex that evening… late into the next morning. After two or three hours of mind-blowing, raw, unadulterated…"

"I get it."

"Anyway, I was through for the night. But my wife wanted more, and when I didn't give her what she wanted, the bitch took a pair of scissors off of her nightstand and punctured my arm. I began to bleed, but I caught her arm when she tried to come down with another blow.

She became violent, cussing and struggling to free herself from my grip. I was finally able to snatch the scissors from her hand, but I had to get out of there."

"It was then that I recognized that something was seriously wrong with her, Queenie, but she wouldn't let me help her. She wouldn't let me near the house, but I went in and got my things when she went back to work. I've paid the mortgage and car notes all of this time and left her to deal with the cell phone and utilities. She had a good paying job. She was once an intelligent woman."

"Where have I been all of this time? I got a contract overseas so that I could get away. Just so that you're aware, this spiral downfall of Jefferey's didn't begin the night it all came unglued. It had been festering for some time, and I believe it's a demon she's been battling. She didn't want me around, so I took care of my wife from a distance."

"You know, Harrison, it's a hard story to believe, considering what I've heard in the streets and from Jefferey."

"It depends on your source."

"That's true. To hear Jefferey tell it, it was all on you. Where is H. J.?"

"He's in D. C. working at the Pentagon. My boy is doing things. I don't know a lot about what he does, but it has to do with Intelligence." There was a long pause. "He doesn't want to have anything to do with his mother."

Queenie stroked her neck with her hand. "Wow, I don't know what to say. My relationship with my sister hasn't been ideal. On the low, I'm probably a large part of the problem. I was jealous that she got to live with my daddy, while my momma and I had to suffer. Even after all of the years that have passed, I still carry a grudge."

"Don't sweat the small stuff. Maybe one day you can salvage your relationship. Divorce should've been imminent for me, but I loved that woman—still do. During the good times, she was a jewel. I'm going to let you go, but please contact me if you should hear from Jefferey."

"Well…" and Queenie stopped when she saw Jefferey standing in the doorway. "I will, and thanks for calling."

"Thank you. You can call me at any time, at any hour."

"All right. Take care." Queenie hit the OFF button.

"Who were you talking to?" Jefferey asked with a frown on her face as she entered the kitchen in bare feet. She looked to where the eggs were in a rapid boil on the stove. "You better take them off the stove before they're scorched."

Queenie stared at Jefferey. "We're going to have a conversation, and you're going to tell me the truth."

CHAPTER TWENTY-ONE

ZERO TO FIFTY

efferey went to the table and took a seat, her eyes steady on Queenie. Her face was somewhat composed, trying to give the appearance that all was serene in her world. She crossed her legs and bounced the one on top slowly, irritating Queenie to no end.

"So, Q, who were you talking to?"

It was Queenie's turn to stare, her eyes narrowing as she pierced through Jefferey's wall. "It was a personal call, which means it's my business who I was talking to."

"Well, sister dear, it became my business when my name dropped from your lips."

"When was the last time you spoke with Harrison?"

Jefferey flinched, uncrossed her legs, and stared at Queenie. "We haven't been together in fourteen years."

"That's not what I asked you. Are you running from him? Is that why you left Charlotte and came running to Raleigh?"

Jefferey stood up and threw her hands out, pointing a finger at Queenie. "Who made you judge and jury? I told you why I was here and I didn't say anything about Harrison. I've lost everything and I didn't have anywhere to go. It was a mistake coming here, but I had no choice at the time."

"The whole scenario as to why you're here is not making sense to me. As a matter of fact, I don't believe you. Do you want to know who called me? Of course you do. That's what this conversation is all about. Your supposed to be ex-husband, Harrison, called my number looking for you. He shared some things with me that have my bottom lip pinned to the floor."

Jefferey began to stutter. "Who... who... who you going to be... be... believe? Your sister or... or... my ex?"

"This is no stage production, so don't pretend with me. You can stutter all night, but you are a liar. Harrison told me that he's been paying your mortgage and car note, so you losing your house and possibly the bit about the car being in an accident are all lies. Funny thing is, Harrison said that you two are still married."

Tears formed in Jefferey's eyes. "Everybody is trying to ruin my goddamn life. Everyone wants to control me, tell me how I should do this and that, but no one wants to hear what I have to say." Jefferey stepped on top of the chair she was previously sitting in and lashed out at Queenie. "You're a selfish, mean monster who can't stand that I'm much prettier than you. You point your ugly finger in my face and talk about me behind my back. Harrison, Momma, and Daddy are all takers. They take, take, take but no one gives a damn about me."

"Get down from that chair, Jefferey, before you fall. I don't know what you're talking about; you're not making any sense. You need help."

Jefferey jumped down from the chair and screamed. "You're an ugly bitch that thinks you're better than me."

Slap, slap.

Stunned, Jefferey shook her head, regained her composure and headed for Queenie. With her fists, Queenie hit Jefferey in the shoulder finally throwing up her hands to ward off the onslaught of blows Jefferey delivered to her face and body. And when she was able to seize the moment, Queenie knocked Jefferey to the floor and jumped on top of her.

"Bitch, I've got a bloody lip and you've got to leave here...now. You can't stay here tonight; one of us might end up dead and it's not going to be me. You need help. You need psychiatric help. So help me God, I'll kill you if you lay another hand on me."

"Get off of me, Q. I hate your guts."

"The feeling is mutual; I hate yours, too." After a moment, Queenie eased up a little. "I'm going to get up now and get my phone, and if you so much as look like you're going to hit me, I will call the police."

Jefferey lay on the floor, her breathing labored. She continued to lay there even after Queenie got up and retrieved her phone. Keeping an eye on her sister, Queenie dialed Harrison's number.

"Wow, that was fast," Harrison said, excitedly into the phone.

"Harrison, I wasn't honest with you. Jefferey is here. She heard me talking to you, and she lost it. Can you come and get her? If not, I'm calling the police. She assaulted me, and now I don't feel safe in my own home."

"I'll be there as soon as I can get there. Please don't call the police. It won't do her any good to be locked up."

"Get here quick. She's gone from zero to fifty in two-seconds flat. I can't be held responsible for what I may do next if she gets beside herself again."

"Okay. I'm on my way. Oh, I need your address."

Queenie gave Harrison her address. "Thanks. Hurry."

CHAPTER TWENTY-TWO

WHO'S GIVING ADVICE?

*W*asting no time, Queenie called Emma and asked her to come over right away. She gave her the low down on what happened between her and Jefferey, her nerves now in disarray.

Jefferey peeled herself from the floor and turned and looked at Queenie with downcast eyes. "Hey, sis, I'm sorry," she said, as if nothing had happened.

Queenie took a good look at Jefferey without saying a word. So many things were running through her mind that she wasn't able to decipher. She was trained to be observant, but she had no idea who the person standing in front of her was.

"Sit down and I'll make you a cup of tea," Queenie said to Jefferey. "It'll be calming."

Jefferey sat down and let out a sigh. "I'm sorry, Q. My brain went on lock for a minute. I behaved badly, but I didn't mean to."

"Why? Where is all of this coming from? Are you still married to Harrison?"

Jefferey put one foot up in the chair and leaned her head against her leg, grabbing the back of her upper thigh with her arms. "I still love him."

Queenie waited for more, but that was all Jefferey would say. She said it over and over again, as if she was trying to convince herself that she still loved Harrison. Queenie fixed two tuna salads and brought them to the table. As soon as she sat down, the doorbell rang, startling Jefferey.

"Who's that at the door, Q? Are they coming to get me?"

"Is who coming to get you?"

"The men in white?"

The countenance on Queenie's face changed to sadness. Had her sister been locked up before? She had to get to the bottom of this. Queenie raised her hands to calm Jefferey down. "No, sis, it's Emma."

"I like Emma. She wasn't nasty toward me."

Queenie said nothing but went to the door to let Emma in. Before Emma was completely inside, Queenie grabbed her and hugged her. "I've bit off more than I can chew," she whispered in Emma's ear. "Jefferey needs help. She's fabricated all of these lies about her marriage and her living conditions."

"It's going to be all right."

"It will be. Harrison is on the way. Let's go into the kitchen before she accuses us of talking about her, which is exactly what we're doing."

Emma smiled and followed Queenie into the kitchen.

"Hi, Jefferey," Emma said as she entered the room. She walked to where Jefferey sat at the table daydreaming and gave her a hug.

"Hi, Emma. You smell good."

Queenie watched the little reunion from a safe distance. She felt her lip that was now swollen and was glad that Emma was there. Should she need a witness, in the event of another showdown at the O.K. Corral, Emma would be it.

"Can I have one of those salads, Q? You know I love your tuna salad."

"One coming up." Queenie fixed Emma's salad, brought it to the table and sat it down.

89

"Did you have a good time in New York?" Jefferey asked Emma, as if all was normal in her world.

Queenie was surprised, as Jefferey hadn't bothered to ask her about the trip.

"We had a good time, right, Q?"

"Yep. The food was good and *Motown the Musical* spoke to me."

"Yeah, we grew up on Motown," Emma said, reminiscing a little. "But what about YoYo and that Italian stallion?"

Queenie kicked Emma under the table, while Jefferey seemed intrigued.

"What about YoYo?"

Emma took her time trying to explain. She caught Queenie giving her the side eye. "It was nothing. We were at a restaurant, and this guy kept looking at her. We teased YoYo something terrible about that guy's infatuation with her, whether it was real or not."

"Oh," Jefferey said. "I was thinking she went out on a date or something."

Emma kept her composure. "Naw, she probably wished she had. Are you dating now?"

The question caught both Queenie and Jefferey by surprise. Jefferey looked at Queenie and turned away. "No, I've been too wrapped up in self-preservation. Anyway, it's hard to let another man into your life when your husband was once your whole world."

"I can empathize. Billy was my world. We were married almost as soon as we got out of high school. He made a career out of the military, and I was with him on every part of that journey. Thank God, the Vietnam War had ended by the time he entered the Army, and there were very few military conflicts that needed his service. We had three children, who went on to be successful, and Billy and I were content in enjoying our lives together. Nothing prepared me…"

Emma stopped and closed her eyes.

"You don't have to talk about it." Queenie got up and massaged Emma's back. "We all loved us some Billy."

Emma wiped her face. "I've been trying to move on since his death, but it's been hard. When your whole life revolved around that one person and they're no longer there, it's like losing a part of yourself."

Jefferey watched Emma closely with guarded eyes. She seemed to hang on to every word Emma said.

Emma shook her head. "I've been trying to purge myself of the dread I have for meeting other men. Sometimes I feel like Billy is standing over me, watching everything I do. I'm sure it's my active imagination, but I can't help it. Terrance is a nice guy, but I was used to having Billy with me all the time, even when we were upset with each other."

"Pray and ask God about it," Queenie finally said. She sat back down in her seat and ate some of her salad. "Donald is coming up the weekend we have our rummage sale at the church. I hear that Terrance is coming with him."

Emma froze and sighed. She took a bite of her salad and remained quiet.

Jefferey reached over and placed her hand on top of Emma's. "It's going to be all right, Emma. Change is good sometimes. I wished I'd been a better wife and mother."

"Oh, don't go blaming yourself for your failed marriage. Life happens. You have to pick yourself up and go on."

"Thanks, Emma. You have to do the same. Maybe Terrance is the man for you."

Queenie couldn't believe that her bitch of a sister was offering advice, when she was the one who needed it in the worst way. It made her want to puke, as she watched Jefferey pretend that she was consoling Emma when all the while her life was a bold-faced lie and the truth wasn't in her. She prayed that Harrison would come soon and she'd be rid of the pain in her ass.

CHAPTER TWENTY-THREE

SUGAR COOKIE INTERVENTION

*B*iting her nails, Queenie got up and paced the floor, looking at the clock ever so often. Emma stayed about as long as she could; she had to get up early for church and be in place as the choir's director.

Just as Emma was heading for the door, the doorbell rang.

"Hold on a moment," Queen whispered. "I want you to meet someone."

As Queenie opened the door, Jefferey came bouncing through the foyer; on the front porch stood Harrison Quick.

It had been years since Queenie last saw Harrison, more like fifteen and maybe then some. She believed that he was a year older than Jeffrey, which made him around fifty-two. His body was a mass of steel. His chocolate-mocha body was covered by a pair of crease-pressed denim jeans and a red Polo shirt that was unbuttoned at the top that exposed a few gray hairs. The massive muscles in his arms rippled like thunder. She now understood why Jefferey was always thirsty for his touch. Queenie loved a man who was rough, tough, and built like Paul Bunyan. Mmm... mmm... mmm. The only thing that gave away his age was the streaks of gray that ran blindly through his hair. The man was drop-dead, gorgeous.

Queenie smiled. "Come in."

Harrison smiled back, wiped his feet on the mat outside of the door and entered. Although Queenie and Emma stood in front of him, his eyes immediately went to Jefferey.

"Sugar Cookie."

Queenie and Emma passed each other a puzzled look.

"Hey, Baby," Jefferey said in return, the smile on her face radiating like the sun. "How are you?"

"I'm fine. Excuse my manners, ladies," Harrison said. "How are you both doing?"

Both Queenie and Emma nodded. Although Emma had been on her way out, she turned around and followed the crew into the living room.

Harrison looked around the room and acknowledged how beautifully decorated Queenie's condo was and that her taste in furniture was exquisite. This man was totally the opposite of the man Jefferey had painted. He was refined and articulated well. Queenie had been impressed with his sincere concern for her sister. Sure, he was nice the few times Queenie was in his presence. But no one really knew what went on behind closed doors. And it's behind those doors and Jefferey's ridicule of him that caused Queenie's rush to judgment.

"How are you, Jefferey?" Harrison asked with concern in his voice. He took a seat on the Queen-Anne sofa, while Jefferey sat in a high-back chair across the room. Queenie and Emma sat on the Queen-Anne love seat that was positioned next to the sofa.

Jefferey didn't respond. She stared at Harrison for a minute then let her eyes fall away. She seemed oblivious of Queenie's and Emma's presence.

"Sugar Cookie?"

Jefferey smiled and looked back up at Harrison. "I always loved it when you called me Sugar Cookie. It made me feel special...like I was your one and only sweetheart and soulmate."

"You've been my one and only for a long time."

93

Jefferey dropped her head and seemed to be in deep contemplation. Slowly, her head rose, and she stared again at Harrison. "Why are you here? Why have you come here?" Then she looked around the room and then accusingly at Queenie.

"I've come to take you back to Charlotte...to take care of you."

"I can't go back there. No, I won't go back there. I'm staying here with my sister."

There was silence in the room. No one moved or said a word. Everyone in the room seemed to ruminate on Jefferey's words. Then Harrison asked the question again.

"How are you, Jefferey?"

"Can't you see that I'm fine? There was no need for you to come here; no need at all."

Harrison's eyes dropped and then he sighed. "Do you recall asking my good friend Derrick to get in touch with me, even though you had all of my contact information?"

Jefferey began to rock back and forth. "I don't know what you're talking about."

There was a chill in the air. This was going to be harder than Queenie thought. She figured that as soon as Jefferey saw Harrison that she'd run to him, but this didn't seem to be the case.

And then Emma got up from her seat and went to Jefferey and rubbed her back. "Remember when you said that you knew what it was like to lose someone? Well, if you want, maybe you can put it back together again. Your ex-husband is here and wants to help you."

"We're still married," Harrison corrected. "I'm trying to bring my wife home."

Emma squinted. It was evident that Queenie had forgotten to give her that piece of information or had she forgotten she told her. "Okay, your husband wants to help you. He's the answer to your prayers."

"He's going to take me to the crazy house, and I'm not crazy. Those people are disgusting and despicable and I will not be subjected to that form of harassment."

"When did you go to such a place?" Harrison wanted to know. "I've not once caused you any harm. True, I've attempted to get you help, but you wouldn't allow me to do so. I'm sorry that I stayed away so long, but I couldn't help you the way things were."

"You didn't try hard enough. The easy road out is what you took, Harrison. You left me...me and H. J. all alone to fight our battles."

"Listen to yourself. I've always been a loving husband to you, Sugar Cookie. I did the best I could, considering all that our marriage has endured. Sure, I could've divorced you. That certainly would've been the easy way out. But I didn't because I loved the sane part of you. I still love you."

Jefferey threw her hands to her face and began to cry. Without giving it another thought, Harrison was by her side, consoling her. Pulling up her chin with his hand, he first wiped the tears from her eyes and kissed her on the lips. She pulled back, sighed, and grabbed Harrison around the neck and hugged him for dear life.

Joy was written on Queenie's face.

CHAPTER TWENTY-FOUR

NEARER MY GOD TO THEE

Q ueenie ran to the church house. Harrison had gathered up Jefferey's belongings and headed back to Charlotte earlier that morning. There was a lot to thank God for and Queenie couldn't wait to get under the influence of the Holy Spirit and express her gratitude.

The young adult choir sang; they sounded like song birds. Emma did a good job in getting the most out of them.

When Reverend Franklin O'Neill got up to speak, it was the first time that Queenie noticed the camera crew. Maybe her mind was on Jeffery and their fight the night before, but now that she was fully aware of what was going on, she straightened up in her seat and patted her red natural hair in place with her hand.

Reverend O'Neill was skinning and grinning. On the piano was his wife, the First Lady of the church, dressed in her finest. After he prayed and read the scripture, he took as his subject, "Yield Not to Temptation."

Queenie thought it rather funny that he was preaching on a topic that implicated himself. Yielding to the world's view of seeing preachers and first ladies scrap it out on television for the sake of reaching "the world" was a little like talking with a forked tongue. But what did she care? She'd look her best when the camera lens panned in her direction, and since Reverend O'Neill said that *The Preachers of Raleigh* would portray ministers in a different light, who was she to judge, although she knew, like everyone else, that it was all about the ratings. All of it was inconsequential though; Queenie's burden had been lifted, and she could get on with her life.

She listened intently as Reverend O'Neill spoke about temptation as he read Romans, chapter six and verse three from the New International Version of the bible.

"Do not offer any part of yourself to sin as an instrument of wickedness, but rather offer yourselves to God as those who have been brought from death to life; and offer every part of yourself to him as an instrument of righteousness." Franklin wiped his brow. "Some of you may think that the First Lady Jackie and I participating in this reality show is an instrument of wickedness." I've already heard the rumors and the rumblings, and I understand that may be your view due to other shows you may have seen, but I'm using this medium… this social media outlet to draw others to Christ. Yes, I may pocket some change, but the Lord's tithes will be paid.

"Sometimes we're tested to see if we're about God's business. It's all about your good intentions… or your bad intentions. There may be someone who needs your attention, or there may be a sister or brother in need of a place to stay, food to eat, or clothing to keep them warm. We turn our backs on them because we feel that it isn't our burden to bear. Everything you have belongs to God. Are you doing what the Lord has asked of you or are you allowing the devil to temp you into believing that it's not your responsibility?

"Don't be guilty of judging me for what you perceive as iniquity when your heart isn't right and you've yielded to the temptation of disbelief. I've prayed about these cameras coming into my home… the church house. I'm not playing with Him. I want to be nearer to my God, and He's told me to preach the gospel to all who will hear."

Queenie sat back and let the Reverend's words marinate. She

thought about Jefferey and the events that led up to having her deported from her home. Jefferey needed help, help she was unable to give. While she wanted to close the door in her face, she opened it up and let her stay. Maybe this was the wrong time to feel guilty about all that had gone down between them, but she had lent a temporary hand to help her sister. And then Jefferey had to go and mess things up, causing Queenie to show her other side—the side she preferred to keep locked in a cage. She'd done her best.

Cameras present or not, Queenie was ready to go. She barely listened to the rest of Franklin's sermon—his droning on and on about not yielding to temptation and half of it not making any sense to her. He must've felt some guilt if he had to talk about it for the next forty-five minutes. Queenie needed a word, and Franklin wasn't delivering.

Finally, the congregation was asked to stand and sing Nearer My God to Thee. Even the song didn't move her, although her goal was to go to heaven when her life on earth was over.

She breathed a sigh of relief, satisfied when service was over. She was ready for some company and a good meal.

Connie, Preston, and baby Desi waved to her and headed out of the sanctuary. First Lady Jackie was all up under the Reverend, acting as if she was a real actress. She saw Emma's finger go up, signaling for her to wait up. YoYo moved in her direction with a big smile on her face. Queenie was happy to have these women, these Silver Bullets, in her life, but her mind kept going back to Jefferey.

"Hey, Q," Yolanda said. "I'm famished. I've got to get out of here after that tired message. I haven't a clue who Pastor was trying to get a word to."

"It sounded as if he was trying to convince himself that what he was doing was God's work. He said he prayed about it, but I think the brother is a little convicted."

"Girl, I think you're right. Here comes Emma. Let's get out of here before Jackie decides she wants to tag along."

"Hi, ladies," Emma said, joining the two. "Where are we going for lunch? Jackie won't be able to join us. She and Pastor have to meet with the other pastors and their wives who are shooting the reality show with them."

"Good," Yolanda said. "Let's go to Braza Brazilian Steakhouse at Brier Creek."

"Good choice, YoYo. Champaign Sunday Brunch at the Braza; here I come. I've got so much to tell you. Emma already knows most of it."

Yolanda looked between Queenie and Emma. "It's about Jefferey isn't it?"

Both Queenie and Emma shook their heads in the affirmative.

CHAPTER TWENTY-FIVE

LAST CHANCE FOR LOVE?

*T*he Braza Brazilian Steakhouse was crowded with afternoon diners. The ambience was inviting—its low lights providing calm and comfort. The ladies loved this place, as it made you feel like you were dining in an exotic place in the midst of a rain forest.

Although the restaurant was a tad bit pricier than others in the area, it was the cuisine—the unlimited skewers of fire-roasted meat and vast appetizer and salad bars, that made this a popular place to eat. And having the meat served table side was the icing on the cake.

The ladies were seated and choices made. The atmosphere was ripe for Queenie to share her ordeal with the ladies. She had both Yolanda and Emma's undivided attention, and she needed to get how she felt off of her chest.

After getting their appetizers and salad, the ladies sat back, ate, and listened to Queenie rant on and on about the phone call from Harrison, Jefferey's melt down and her smack down, her calling Emma to be with her, and Harrison finally arriving to save her from hell.

"My sister should be locked in a mental institution. If Harrison hadn't been available to rescue Jefferey, she'd be in a straitjacket at this precise moment."

"Isn't that's a little harsh, Q? I'm with you on her needing help, but there has to be some underlying something that's caused her outbursts. She seemed sane when she was at the restaurant a few weeks ago."

"You weren't there, YoYo. Emma can vouch for what I'm saying. Anyway, she lied about losing her home and car. Harrison's been taking care of her mortgage all this time, and I'm sure the car was paid off. But this is the kicker. They're still married; Jefferey nor Harrison ever filed for divorce."

"Jefferey was out of control, YoYo. I witnessed it firsthand. The girl was pitiful. I agree she needs help, although, I'm not sure she needs to be in a straitjacket." Emma caught Queenie staring. "I'm just saying."

"Well, I've got something to tell you," Yolanda began. "New York is following me to the Triangle."

Queenie looked at Yolanda with disapproving eyes. It was apparent that Yolanda had no interest in talking about her situation with Jefferey. There was no way that what Yolanda had to say even compared with what she'd already put on the table. Queenie shut down and listened with one ear.

"My Italian stallion is arriving in the Triangle tomorrow. I'll be picking him up from the airport tomorrow evening."

The waiter came by with a skewer of pork. Queenie and Emma had a few slices placed on their plates.

"Why?" Emma asked. "Why is he coming here?"

"That's a dumb question, Emma. He's coming to see me."

"But... but you just met him and he's much younger than you. I don't understand how a man who supped with you a couple of times is all of a sudden jumping on a plane to visit, unless..."

"Unless what?"

"Unless you did the nasty with him and he's coming back for nasty seconds. You must've put an older woman hurting on him."

Queenie began to laugh. "Emma, you are too funny. I told y'all that Miss Prissy over here gave that man some of her banana pudding."

"Now that's nasty, Q," Yolanda said shaking her head. "You heifers are so insecure. You wouldn't know what love was if it hit you in the face."

"Love? How in the hell did you come up with that four-letter word?" Queenie asked. "You were in New York for a hot chili second, and no one in their right mind is going to spend money to hop on a plane to come see your old-ass rusty butt unless he's panting after something that turnt him up, as the young hip-hoppers say. And you, of all people, should know better. You're too old for these young playas."

"Leave it to you to spoil an afternoon." Yolanda snapped her fingers. Then she raised her hand. "No, you aren't going to spoil my afternoon. While you're still waiting on Donald to tickle your... your whatever, I'll be enjoying a romantic moment with my new boy toy."

"You're a nasty hussy, YoYo. Staying out all night, worrying us to death, doesn't mean anything to you. Was it that good? Did it make you feel like a new woman?"

"It wasn't the first time I've come out of a hotel room early in the morning. But let me share this with you, it was mind-blowing, Q. He had a tongue like a lizard. Hmm... hmm... hmm."

"Oh my God," Emma said shaking her head. "There was no need to share that disgusting information with us."

"You old bats act like you're living in the stone-age. And, Q, I know better. I see you sitting over there with you face twisted into a pretzel, but we all know about your nasty habits. Does the Pimp that Stole Christmas ring a bell?" Yolanda began to laugh and so did Emma.

"YoYo's got a point, Q. You are the queen of turning *them* out."

Queenie began to smile. "I am aren't I? I'm going to break Donald one of these days."

"After they play the wedding march." Emma grabbed her side and gave Yolanda a high-five.

"It's okay. At the end of the year, you all will wish you were in my place. I'll have a husband I can come home to every night..."

"Guys, hold up for a minute," Emma said, holding a hand in the air. "Why are we talking about sex like it's the only reason we want a man? I want someone who I can share my thoughts with, cuddle up to, take care of, go to the movies with…"

"We get it, Emma," Yolanda said. "I hear you. For me, it isn't all about the sex either; Stefan is my last chance for love. Yes, his bio isn't as full as I like, but that man really cares about me. He wants to give me the world. I want someone who'll treat me like I'm worth more than a stopover for some banana pudding. But, girls, that man is a true stallion in every sense of the word and I rode him like I was in the Kentucky Derby trying to get the big prize. Talk about satisfied. He's only five or six years younger than me."

"What about Illya Newsome?" Emma asked, taking a bite of food.

"Yeah, what about him?" Queenie asked, pushing for a response.

"What about him? He's history. I've already called him and broke off our relationship. How often did I see him anyway? His work was dangerous and most times it kept us apart. Anyway, he didn't take it personal. I mean, he didn't put up a fuss. I have my suspicions; I think he's seeing his ex."

"You didn't waste any time; I liked him," Emma said thoughtfully, twirling her fork. "He was a real gentleman and a scholar. This young thing is going to break your heart."

CHAPTER TWENTY-SIX

LOVE DON'T LIVE HERE ANYMORE

a blank stare zig-zagged across Jefferey's face as Harrison barreled down the highway on his way to Charlotte. Hardly a word was spoken between the two, although Harrison tried without success to engage his estranged wife in conversation. She was estranged in that they'd been separated almost as long as they'd been together physically, and Harrison feared that this was the end of the road.

He sighed as the miles flew by on this lonely stretch of Interstate eighty-five. What could he say to Jefferey to let her know that he was there for her?

"What are you going to do to me when we arrive in Charlotte?" Jeffery finally asked, her head now turned in Harrison's direction. "Are you going to have me committed like my son did…the son I gave my all to when you up and left me?"

"No, Jefferey, I have no plans to put you away. I'd like to be there for you if you'd let me."

"Our time is over. I'm no good for you. I'm on all kinds of meds…"

"That you apparently haven't been taking."

"Don't judge me, Harrison. You have no idea what I've been through. Raising a child on my own, scared half the time and believing that I wasn't a good enough mother and that I was going to fail H. J. like I failed you has been difficult for me. I had the best... you were my best friend. I loved you with all my heart and soul, but you couldn't help me fight my demons."

"Do you understand why I left, Jefferey? Do you really understand? Sugar Cookie, I didn't want to leave you, but you made it impossible for me to stay...to live with you. Even your momma and daddy said they understood. They begged me to take H. J. with me, and I probably should've done so. However, I realized that in doing so, you wouldn't have fared well. H. J. was probably the only sane part of you that kept you from... from...."

"Going crazy? I didn't understand then. My head was in turmoil. I'm not sure where or when all of it started."

"What happened to you that may have caused this side of you to go haywire?"

"Don't you think I've wondered about that, Harrison?"

"A lot of psychologists say that repressed feelings due to something that may have happened early in a person's life, manifests itself later. Are you hiding any secrets that you haven't been able to talk about?"

"Don't try to psychoanalyze me. Who in the hell do you think you are—God? You, Momma, and Daddy always tried to control me."

"That's not true, Jefferey. Don't tell that lie on me. All I've ever tried to do is love you. You were my soulmate. I've loved you unconditionally. Why do you think I haven't divorced your ass all of these years? Everyone has told me how stupid I was not to go on with my life...that you weren't right in the head and that you weren't going to get better. Yet, I wanted to believe that things would get better, that I could come home to my wife and start where we left off."

"But you left anyway. We'd made mad love to each other that night..."

"And you tried to kill me... for what reason, I don't have a clue."

"I saw you and my best friend, Keisha, hemmed up in the kitchen on the fourth when everyone else was outside. I've always suspected that you all were having an affair."

"That's a lie, Jefferey. Why are you fabricating these stories?"

"Oh, she denied it to, and I would've hurt her too, if I had something to hit her with. I saw the two of you hemmed up in a corner…"

"We were making plans for a surprise party for you. Keisha knows you better than anyone, and she came to me with the idea and I was excited about having this elaborate event to celebrate my wife's birthday."

"Tell me anything, Harrison. I can't prove it anyway."

"You need help, Jefferey."

"I'm not going back to that place. They made me crazy and angry and I'm not either one. I'm of sound mind. I'm of sound mind. I'm of sound mind." Jefferey sat back in her seat.

"Why did you go to Queenie's? Why did you seek her out when the two of you don't even have a relationship?"

Jefferey said nothing and remained quiet.

"We're almost home. We… I have to make some decisions."

Jefferey said nothing.

Harrison exited the freeway and stopped at a STOP sign. All of a sudden, the passenger door of the vehicle flew open and Jefferey jumped out, leaving the door open. She ran down the street toward an abandoned building.

Exasperated, Harrison reached over and closed the door and turned right. He was unable to pull over and stop due to the cars that were right behind him. When he was able to do so, he made a right turn and tried to circle back. The series of one way streets made it difficult to end up where he wanted.

Harrison parked the car on a side street and began his manhunt. He ran up and down several streets in hopes of catching a glimpse of Jefferey. He wiped sweat from his brow as his attempt to find his wife left him anxious and exhausted. He huffed and puffed, as he continued to patrol the streets, but still no sign of her.

Heading back to the car, Harrison threw his hands up in the air. For the first time in years, tears streamed down his face. He couldn't do it anymore. Love was slowly fading from his heart. He'd get help for her, but he was through.

Finished.

Done.

Getting into his car, he drove around some more until he had exhausted all of his energy. Sighing, he touched a keypad in his card and the phone began to dial. The phone rang and rang until it finally went to voicemail.

"Queenie, this is Harrison. Your sister jumped out of my car and I've yet to locate her. I'm calling the police; I'll call you with an update." Harrison ended the call and drove aimlessly through the streets of Charlotte.

CHAPTER TWENTY-SEVEN

REALITY CHECK

*P*astor Franklin O'Neill and his lovely First Lady, Jackie O'Neill, pulled up to the palatial home of the Reverend LeLand James and his wife, First Lady Oneida James. Two other pastors and their wives were to join them at a luncheon given by the host.

"This is a nice place," Jackie said to Franklin as they strolled on the concrete walkway that cut through a manicured lawn that was so green that it looked as if it was freshly dyed that morning. This estate in Chapel Hill, North Carolina boasted an acre and a half of land. It wasn't a lot, but it kept the neighbors at bay.

A pair of circular steps, met the couple at the massive all-brick, tri-level house surrounded by magnolia trees whose flowers were now gone, but the leaves still welcomed visitors. Upon reaching the beautiful, hand-etched glass door, Franklin rang the doorbell. A young, African-American woman, dressed in a tailored-two piece, navy-blue suit answered the door.

"Good afternoon and welcome to the home of Pastor James and

First Lady James. Smiling, the young woman invited the O'Neill's in, her hand pointing the way."

"Thank you," Franklin said, passing a 'what do you make of this' look in Jackie's direction.

The couple followed the young woman down a vast hallway with beautiful oriental rugs covering portions of the hardwood floor. The hallway opened up into an open-ceiling living room that was at least twenty-five feet high with four skylights welcoming the afternoon sun. Large potted plants were strategically located throughout the room, and the furniture was made of fine brocade fabric. Off in a small alcove was a white, baby grand piano. *Their congregation must be paying the reverend a handsome salary,* Jackie thought.

There was laughter coming from one of the rooms. Pastor James and his wife, followed by Pastor Richard and First Lady Gloria Griffin entered the room.

"Here they are," First Lady James said as she walked up to the O'Neills and gave them a Holy Ghost kiss on either cheek. The Griffins followed suit. "Would you like ice tea, Coke, or water?"

"Yes, thank you," Franklin said. "Coke is fine for me. How about you, sweetheart?"

"I'll have sweet tea," Jackie said.

"Franklin, we're going to discuss the three-day revival we talked about last week once the cameras get to rolling," Reverend James said. "Any questions you may have, jot them down so we can have cue cards made in the event you forget. We're waiting on Pastor Martinez and his wife to arrive. I believe we're scheduled to begin shooting in an hour. The first part of this episode will be the luncheon that will include the wives."

"Sounds good," Franklin said. "I'll move over to the side and get my questions written down."

"I hear you're slaying them in the spirit over there at Shiloh," Pastor Richard Griffin said. "I've got to come over and visit one Sunday...maybe you'll let me preach. How many are in your congregation?"

Franklin looked up from the piece of paper he was writing on.

"The Lord is slaying the folks in the spirit. I'm only His vessel." Franklin looked thoughtfully at Pastor Griffin. "Will check with my staff to see when it would be a good time for you to speak. This revival will probably take care of that though."

Pastor Griffin began to laugh. "You don't want me to come over to Shiloh and cut up. Don't worry; I'm not trying to take your members."

"I hadn't given that a thought," Franklin said, and turned away and began to write on his paper.

Jackie caught the exchange. She knew Franklin better than anyone, and she'd bet he was over in that corner fuming. But she also knew that Franklin wasn't going to let anyone cause him to fall from grace, especially some bootleg pastor that had only a year ago set up camp in North Carolina. That's why he stayed prayed up. Franklin told her that he'd read an online article about Griffin being booted from his congregation in Denver. It was amazing what you could find on the World Wide Web with the Google search engine.

The doorbell rang interrupting Jackie's thoughts. Pastor George and Victoria Martinez had arrived. It was time to get the party started.

Lunch went off without a hitch. With the cameras rolling, each of the four pastors spoke about their ministry, while the first ladies spoke about supporting their husbands. It was a lively discussion.

When lunch was finished, the men retired to a large library that Pastor James had custom made. The textured, brownish-purple wallpaper with its egg-shell colored ceiling trays held up a five-tier walnut bookcase that covered three sides of the room. The bookcases held hardbound theological literature, every bible commentary there was no doubt, and oodles and oodles of reference materials. The other pastors were in awe.

The women remained at the dining table that was cleared of their luncheon dishes and replaced with a dessert plate filled with sweet potato pie and a cup and saucer for those who wanted coffee. With the cameras still rolling, the ladies kept it real, venturing into a little gossip about news at other congregations. When coffee cups were filled, First Lady Gloria Griffin turned in Jackie's direction.

"Jackie," Gloria began, "I understand that you went to Vegas and met someone who called your house, upsetting your husband."

"There's no harm in meeting people, Gloria. I'm always an ambassador for the Lord."

"But in a two-piece bikini after getting a Brazilian wax?"

The other two First Ladies stared—first at Jackie, then at Gloria.

"It was a one-piece bathing suit for your information. Now, I didn't come here to discuss what I did in Vegas a year ago. That was a personal vacation and has nothing to do with why we're here today."

"It is relevant in my book, Jackie. We preach and teach abstinence, living a holy and acceptable life unto God, yet, the rumor mill is gushing with tales of you giving your phone number to some man that kissed you while you were lying out at the pool. What kind of example are you?"

"I am a child of the most-high King. That's all you need to know. And for your information, I'm not going to sit here and let some former stripper, who bought her way to First Ladyship, ruin my good name. Now sit back and shut-up. Jackie O'Neill don't play that."

First Lady Gloria Griffin, in lady like fashion pushed back her chair from the table and stood up. And as if an electrical current had gone through her body, she stuck her finger in Jackie's face. "Maybe you weren't aware that you're on a reality television show and we've got to give the viewers what they want—fire and brimstone. I can't help it if I've done my homework."

First Ladies James and Martinez looked alarmed.

Jackie politely left her seat and grabbed Gloria's finger and pushed it back. "Reality check." Then she turned toward the cameramen and held out her hand. "Turn the cameras off. This is for the eyes in this room only."

The cameramen moved away from their equipment, but the ladies didn't know that the cameras were still running.

"You're nothing but a heathen going straight to Satan's fire. And the next time you put your finger in my face, I'm going to break it and ask God for forgiveness later."

"Come on, Jackie," First Lady Oneida James said, finally cutting into the war of words. "Gloria brought this on herself but let's try to maintain some kind of decorum. We don't want our show to be representative of what people are accusing us of doing—making profit while exploiting the sanctity of God's holy establishment."

First Lady Martinez was mortified as she sat in her seat gauging the events going on in front of her. Her pupils seemed dilated and her body stiff.

Jackie sat down. Her sigh was almost audible in the next room. "Please accept my apologies for my outburst, ladies. God is not pleased at how I acted, and in no way shape or form was this representative of how Jackie O'Neill carries herself or reacts when pushed to the brink." Jackie sighed again and closed her eyes, whispering a small prayer under her breath.

Gloria also sat down but stared darts in Jackie's direction. "I want to apologize also for my outburst, but I don't apologize for stating the truth."

Jackie refused to look in Gloria's direction. She allowed the insult to go in one ear, although it was stuck in trying to get out of the other. Jackie banked it in the back of her mind. She'd have to pray hard to release the anger that was building inside. Maybe she and Franklin should bow out of the show, although she knew her husband's passion of winning souls for Christ was the only reason they were doing it. She ignored Gloria for the moment, but if she thought that she was going to make a public spectacle out of her, First Lady Gloria Griffin needed to think again.

CHAPTER TWENTY-EIGHT

72-HOUR HOLD

Queenie enjoyed lunch with her girls and now headed home. She laughed out loud, as she thought about freaky Yolanda and her new boy toy. More power to her. If the young stallion floated her boat, she wasn't mad.

There was a sense of relief as Queenie pulled into her garage. She looked forward to the peace and quiet. Her house would be empty and she'd be free to live her life without walking on eggshells or wondering what bag Jefferey was going to come out of today. Having Jefferey in her home in no way brought them closer together or even remotely touched the surface of why their lives were torn at the seams. Her hands were washed of the matter.

Emotional scars from being separated from her father at a young age were at the crux of Queenie's hatred for her sister, although it wasn't Jefferey's fault. But Queenie harbored those ill feelings when she saw how much better Jefferey and her mother were living than she and her mother. They struggled, while Jefferey seemed to have everything, everything that included her father.

Queenie grabbed her purse off the front seat of the car and went into the house. She deactivated the alarm and went to her bedroom where she plopped down on the edge of the bed, took off her shoes, and finally her stockings. Next she took her cell phone out of her purse so that she could call Donald.

Without taking off her clothes, she laid across the bed and swiped her finger across her phone that gave access to all the applications. She had a message; maybe it was from Donald, but upon viewing the list, it was from Harrison. He and Jefferey must've arrived in Charlotte. She'd call Harrison later.

Relaxed, Queenie scrolled down her recent calls and found Donald's name. Just as she was about to tap on the telephone icon, the phone rang. It was Harrison calling. Reluctantly, she answered it.

"Hey, Harrison, I saw that you called. I trust you made it to Charlotte in one piece."

"Well, Queenie, we did make it to Charlotte, but as soon as we were off the freeway, Jefferey jumped out of the car and ran away."

"She did what? Are you kidding me?"

"No, I'm not kidding. I drove around, walked around for at least an hour, but I couldn't find her. I went to the Police Department to file a missing person's report, but they said she hadn't been missing long enough. Even after I gave them the circumstances and Jefferey's condition, they said I had to wait. I'm at home, but she hasn't been seen."

"Damn it." Queenie sighed. "Something is wrong with that girl, and we've…you've gotta put your foot down and do something. When she first arrived, she seemed normal…sane. She recited her pitiful story about losing everything and how you had done nothing for her since the day you walked out on her and H. J. I want to be there for her, but for the love of God, Harrison, I can't. She disrespected me in my home…"

"She's sick, Queenie. I only wanted you to let know what was going on. If I haven't heard from her in the next few hours, I'm going to call the police again. "Don't worry about it."

"Harrison, I'm…I'm sorry. I didn't mean to be so insensitive."

"It's cool. Don't worry about it; I'll handle it. After all, I'm her husband and she's my responsibility. Good night."

The phone was dead. If Queenie needed to say anything else, the opportunity was gone. She detected a little animosity in Harrison's voice, but he'd be all right after a while. If he knew that her sister was sick, why did he go so long without trying to get her help? It wasn't her problem, and like Harrison said, she wasn't going to worry about it.

She touched the telephone icon with her finger and waited for the phone to ring at the other end. On the second ring, she heard his voice.

"Hey, baby. How's my wife-to-be doing?"

"Hi, sweetie. I'm doing great. Emma, Yolanda, and I went out to lunch today after church, and we had a good time as always. We recapped our trip to New York."

"I can't wait to hear all about it. I'll be up this weekend. I hope I won't be in the way with you all having your church yard sell."

"Of course not. You're going to be helping me."

"Q, I was thinking. I want to take you out on a romantic date after the yard sale."

"Okay, I...I would love to."

"I'll have a few surprises too."

"Can you give a girl a hint?"

"Noooo, that would spoil the surprise."

"I can't wait."

"How's your sister? Have you two broken the ice and forgiven each other?"

"Are you serious? My sister lashed out at me last night and I had to get her out of my house. Lucky for me, Jefferey's husband called looking for her; he saved me in the nick of time. He took her home to Charlotte."

"But I thought you said that Jefferey and her husband were divorced."

"So I thought, but according to Harrison, my sister made all of that up to get sympathy. Truth is, they haven't been together in years. So her version wasn't too far from the truth. She didn't lose the house, although I believe she did lose her job. I pray that she gets well."

"You should've sat down with her and tried to get to the bottom of the friction in your relationship. You both need to heal."

"While I know you mean well, Donald, this is a discussion that I'm not ready to have with you at the moment. I need to talk to a friendly voice, one who has my best interest at heart."

"I do, Q. I love you, but I'd also like to see you and your sister mend your relationship. I've been praying."

Queenie's phone began to buzz. It was Harrison on the line. "Hold on, Donald. Harrison is on the line. I need to get this."

"Okay."

Queenie clicked over to Harrison. "What's up, Harrison? Did you find Jefferey?"

"Yeah, she's locked up in a temporary mental facility for seventy-two hours. That's as long as they can hold her. Someone called the police after they saw her walking around aimlessly in the street. Thank God she wasn't hurt."

Queenie placed her hand over her heart. There was a sense of relief. "Thank God she's all right; thank you for sharing the information with me."

"No problem." And the line was dead.

Queenie switched back to her call with Donald. "Look, baby, I've got to go. I'm still talking to Harrison about Jefferey," she lied.

"Okay. I'll call you tomorrow."

Queenie clicked the OFF button and dropped the phone on the bed. She turned on her side and cried.

CHAPTER TWENTY-NINE

YOLANDA MAXWELL MORRIS

*I*t was a brisk, zesty morning. The air smelled clean when Yolanda stepped outside. She embraced the elements as if she'd been peeled from a cocoon, experiencing nature for the first time.

There were plenty good reasons why she was in such a good mood, and it was going to be difficult waiting for the five o-clock hour to arrive. Her new man was arriving at Raleigh/Durham Airport on a flight from New York at eight-thirteen in the evening, and she couldn't wait to see him again. Although she'd been home only a good day, they had talked incessantly off and on for the past twenty-four hours. The only break she had from him was when she went to church on Sunday and had lunch with Queenie and Emma afterwards.

As a hospital administrator, she made sure the hospital was staffed appropriately and that the nurses were prepared to carry out their duties for the day. For the majority of the day, Yolanda completed paperwork, made and revised schedules accordingly. She met briefly with the new hospital chief, and when the clock hit four forty-five, she gathered her belongings together. Today, she planned to be the first person out of the double doors.

Yolanda rushed to her car, got in and made a mad dash to the house. It was already clean, but she took one last look around to make sure everything was in order. Then she stripped and jumped into the shower and scrubbed with her favorite Bath and Body shower gel. Hurriedly, she got out, toweled off, and prepared to get dress.

The night before, she'd laid out a short, black-fitted dress that accentuated her beautiful curves. After putting them on, she adorned her feet with a pair of red, four-inch stilettos. She refreshed her make-up, following it up with a deep-red lipstick.

Looking in the mirror, she smiled back at the woman who stared at her. She brushed the sides of her hair down with her hand, moved her head at different angles to make sure everything was in place, and smiled again. There was nothing in the reflection that gave away her age other than her silver hair that was said to be her crowning asset.

Quickly, she brushed her teeth and sprayed on her favorite perfume by Givenchy, 'Angeou Demon – LeSecret.' She sniffed. Stefan had told her how sensuous her body smelled and how her perfume had driven him wild. Tonight, she planned on driving him wild with pleasure and hoped he'd come with a ferocious appetite. She was the menu.

She had plenty of time to get to the airport, but she wanted to get there early so she wouldn't feel rushed. It was seven-fifteen, which gave her plenty of time to get to the airport, stop at Starbucks and get her favorite Chai tea.

Feeling refreshed, Yolanda drove her Lexus to the airport, parked, and went inside. Instead of getting her tea, she went inside one of the lounges and opted for a Long Island Ice Tea instead. Sitting at the bar, she leisurely sipped her drink, looking from time to time at her watch to check the time. Stefan said he would call as soon as the plane landed.

Before she had finished her drink, the bartender sat a fresh one down.

"I didn't order another drink," Yolanda said, looking at the bartender quizzically.

"No, but the guy straight across from you did," the bartender responded, pointing his finger in the direction straight across.

Yolanda looked up and followed the length of the bartender's hand. She froze at the sight of him. His dreads were pulled back into a ponytail and his white teeth glistened against his golden-brown skin. Never in her wildest dreams had she expected to see Illya Newsome again. Her mouth dropped to the floor and suddenly she wanted to flee.

Before she could get up from her seat, he was next to her. She could feel his breath on her neck as well as the slight smell of Scotch. He sniffed.

"You smell good, almost intoxicating."

"How are you, Illya? Are you back in Raleigh?"

"I'm fine, and yes, I'm here for a short piece. How was your trip to New York?"

"It was great. The ladies and I had a good time."

"So, may I ask why you're at the airport? I thought you arrived home on yesterday?"

Yolanda didn't want to answer the question. She didn't want to give Illya any reason to suddenly come crawling to her. He'd been absent from her in a strange kind of way, and now that he was here, he didn't excite her like he had over a year ago when she first met him. He was still fine as wine—dreads and all, but she had a new taste in her mouth—a fresh, new flavor.

Ignoring the question, Yolanda sipped her drink and put it down. "So, where have you been the past two months? I understand that you weren't at liberty to tell me while you were on assignment, but now that you're here in Raleigh..."

"This conversation is going nowhere. I realize that our being together was tough. Long-distance relationships usually are." Illya cupped Yolanda's chin in his hand. "You're beautiful, and I love you. It broke my heart that you wanted to end what I thought would be forever. There must be somebody else that caused you to call me out of nowhere and deliver the hurtful news."

Yolanda looked into Illya's eyes. They were so tender and warm. She remembered the first time she kissed him—his lips were soft and cuddled hers like a pillow. "I'm sorry."

Illya dropped his hand from her chin. "Are you sorry because you don't love me anymore or sorry that you ran into me and now you have some explaining to do?"

"My God, Illya, be blunt about it."

"I say you have something to hide. Who are you waiting for?"

"A good friend of mine."

"Do you mind if I wait with you?"

"Yes, I do mind." Yolanda looked at her watch and then scooted down from the chair. "I've got to go. It's was good seeing you again."

"Don't do this, YoYo. Remember I'm the FBI, and I'll always be able to find you and know what's going on."

"Illya, it's over. It's been over. Your mind, as well as your body, has been elsewhere."

"Where has my mind been besides on my work?"

"How about your ex-wife for starters?"

Illya looked perplexed. He arched his back and stared at Yolanda. "Are you for real? I can't believe you hit me below the belt. What an awful thing to accuse me of."

"Well, haven't you re-associated yourself with your ex? Every time we've spoken to each other, you kept mentioning things you had to do in conjunction with her."

"We have children together."

"Children who are both grown and on their own. I didn't ask you to make a choice between me and them, but I somehow got the distinct feeling that you and your babies' momma were rekindling your relationship."

"Did you ever ask me if that was so? You have another agenda, and you're using what you perceive to be a "rekindling" of a marriage that was broken and never to be put back together again as an out for you. Well, lady, you have my permission to move on."

"I didn't need your permission, Illya."

"So, it is another man."

"I didn't say that."

And then he noticed the ring...the large diamond ring that could've served as a lighthouse. His eyes went back and forth from the ring to Yolanda's eyes... eyes that he probably felt had lied to him. He didn't hear anything else she said.

"Have a nice life." And Illya was gone.

Yolanda looked at the closed door that Illya had walked out of. Her mind wandered to the places they'd been as a couple, a place that had a lot of gaps, supposedly due to his job. The memories of their time together were vivid but wonderful, and she would always encapsulate them in her heart.

She looked at her watch again. It was five minutes past eight. In ten minutes, Stefan Morsilli would be here, and all thoughts of seeing Illya were dismissed. She finished the drink that Illya sent over and left a tip for the bartender. As she was about to leave, her cell phone rang.

"Hi, YoYo. I'm on the ground in Raleigh, North Carolina. I can't wait to see you."

"I'm here at the airport and will wait for you in baggage claim. I can't wait to see you either."

"I'll be there as soon as I get off the plane. Kiss, kiss."

"Back at you."

Yolanda ended the call, smiled and headed for the American Airlines baggage claim area.

CHAPTER THIRTY

WHAT BECOMES OF THE BROKENHEARTED?

She watched as Stefan Morisilli came into view as he rode the escalator down to baggage claim. That African-American, Italian-American combo was pulling on her heart strings. He had a swagger that said he was rich and refined, and that he was fifty-percent hood. The blue-iridescent suit covered his body like a thin shell on a M&M candy—umm, umm, and his jet-black, wavy hair hung at the shoulders and swung slightly when his head turned.

He spotted her and acknowledged the recognition with a big smile. Yolanda smiled back, waving her hand. As soon as Stefan rolled off of the escalator, he moved toward her, put both arms around her waist and kissed her full throttle on the lips.

"Hey, YoYo," Stefan said, after pulling away to look at her. "You smell good."

Yolanda smiled. "Hey, yourself; I'm so glad you're here."

"I see you're wearing your ring."

"It's beautiful and makes my hand look like a million dollars."

"And it looks beautiful on you. Since I only have a day, let's not waste it standing in the middle of the airport. I don't have any checked-in luggage, only the bag I'm carrying. We're free to go. Let's do dinner and then…you know what I want."

"I hope it's me."

"Only you."

The couple held hands and exited the airport. Illya Newsome stood off to one side in the shadows and observed them as they walked past. A slight hint of jealousy coursed through his veins. His woman was with another man. Yolanda had been right about him spending more time with his ex-wife. He'd found out that she had breast cancer, and he was trying to be a good ex, because that's who he was as a person—a person who was always giving to others with no one returning the favor.

His heart hardened, Illya resolved within his soul to get Yolanda back by any means necessary.

CHAPTER THIRTY-ONE

SAY MY NAME

$\mathcal{A}$rm in arm, Yolanda and Stefan strolled to her car, laughing at various intervals, recalling moments they'd recently shared. Stefan was so accommodating and so loving that Yolanda had to wonder if he was real. She wasn't an heiress to a large fortune, so that certainly wasn't his attraction to her, and she wanted to believe that it was much more than the sex. Yes, the sex... the loving was uhm, uhm, good.

"Although I ate there yesterday with Queenie and Emma, I want to take you to the Braza Brazilian Steakhouse. You will definitely appreciate the ambience and menu."

"Anything but Italian. I eat that stuff twenty-four hours a day. You'd think with my mother being black that she would have a steady stream of greens, cornbread, and fried chicken, but no, she caters to my father's every whim."

"How do you get along with your mother?"

"My mom is a jewel. I love her more than life itself. She reminds me a little of you. She's a little taller and slightly wider than you, and that's from eating all that pasta. Her boobs are much bigger to my dad's delight. There's something about African-American blood that keeps us looking young much longer than a Caucasian. My mother doesn't look a day over forty-five, although she doesn't look like her age, which is sixty-nine. And I'm her only child. That means I'm her baby."

Yolanda laughed. "I understand. Boys always tend to gravitate toward their mothers."

"I do a lot for my mom. She's a recording artist, also. In fact, she comes from a whole line of musicians."

"Get out of here. What's her name?"

"She uses her stage name, Tracey Porter."

"Are you for real? I've heard of her, in fact I may have some old albums of hers."

"Yeah, she actually cut two albums back in the day. At one time, she used to sing with her sister, my Aunt Marjorie. My mother is a bluesy jazz singer. When hip hop hit the scene, her kind of jazz almost became extinct, but she still sings at small clubs in the City. She's where I get my creative genius."

"I've got to meet her."

"You will."

The couple let their hair down and enjoyed each other's company. Stefan enjoyed the meal and dubbed the restaurant "their place."

There was a full moon in the sky when they walked outside. Stefan put his arm around Yolanda's neck and drew her closer to him.

He bathed her in kisses—on the cheek, forehead, neck and lips. Yolanda was in wonderland, high above the clouds. The coolness of the night air engulfed them, but they seemed content as they walked toward the car.

"Let's get some coffee before we turn in; I won't be doing a lot of talking later. I want to look at you and drink in your beauty. I can't explain it, YoYo, but you've turned my heart upside down. I've been with a lot of Italian women, but there's something about my mom's heritage…my heritage that makes me appreciate a sister like you."

"How so?"

"You're smart, intelligent, and have…" Stefan snapped his finger, "the word escapes me, but this aura about you that is no-nonsense. Women tend to try and cling to me. I believe they think I'm going to skyrocket to fame and they want a piece of the pie whenever I get there. But not you; you're comfortable in your skin and in the woman that I'm becoming to know. Unassuming is the word I was trying to come up with, but I mean it in a way that says, I'm Yolanda Morris, and I know who I am. I'm repeating myself, but I can't help it."

Yolanda tucked her head under Stefan's arm. His praises of her were so refreshing and unpretentious. She had to wonder if she resembled the woman he'd described. It felt so right. "Caribou Coffee is close by. Let's go there."

They spent less than a half hour at Caribou's and headed for Yolanda's. Silence engulfed the car as Yolanda drove toward home, but the silence was golden as Stefan gently massaged her free hand while gazing at her profile. Yolanda had so many questions she wanted to ask, like how could he afford the things he did on a musician's salary and what industry was his father in. It was believed that most Italians, especially in the New York/New Jersey area were mobsters. But that wasn't important at that moment.

Upon reaching her house, Yolanda ushered Stefan in. Holding hands, Stefan sized up her place and shook his head ever so often.

"Gorgeous house; you must have a maid to keep it clean."

"I have someone who comes in here twice a month, but that's it. This is the house that my ex and I lived in before we divorced. I got the house and Lexus and a sizeable sum of money, and he got a summer house we had together and the woman that came between us. It was a good deal. I'm happy."

Stefan laughed. "It's great that you can look at a bad situation and still come out on the happy end of things."

"It's his loss. I loved my husband and gave him some of the best years of my life. We were married for thirty-two years, had two children, and are now free to live our lives as older grown folks."

"I'd like to fit into your life...somewhere between happy and ever after."

YoYo smiled and then hit Stefan on the arm. "You're crazy. Come on and make yourself comfortable."

Stefan took Yolanda's arms and pulled her to him. He dropped his head a little, and pushing hers back, pressed his lips against hers. He nearly swallowed her tongue whole, lavishing her with sensual kisses. He went from her mouth to her neck and back again. Yolanda kissed him as forcibly as she'd been kissed, all tuned into the moment.

Their hunger for each other was apparent, neither wanting to stop the passion that consumed them in order to take off their clothes. Taking a breath, Stefan backed away, stepped out of his suit in less than a minute, and the rest of his articles of clothing with it. He stood in front of Yolanda stark naked, salivating at what stood before her.

Her clothes were next to go, as Stefan assisted her in peeling off the black-fitted dress from her body. He had fun doing so. He kissed her from head to toe, sinking his nose deep into her flesh to absorb the aroma of her perfume. Lacey panties and bra were next, as he quietly slid the bra straps from her arms and unsnapped the back in one fell swoop as if he'd done it with a switch blade. And then with magical fingers, Stefan slid her panties off.

STEFAN WAS MESMERIZED by her beauty and the shape her body was in for her age. He'd seen her before, but then it was more lust and a sudden need to control and pleasure the woman who had tugged at his male psyche. But she was beautiful and he was completely captivated.

Not letting another moment go to waste, Stefan made love to Yolanda, completely absorbed in gratifying her in such a way that would leave her filled and begging for more. He caressed her breasts, feasting upon them like a hungry lion. But it was the art of seduction —the skillful way in which he bathed her body sensually that set the tone for the rest of the night. He knew she'd forever be a slave to his and her desire.

Stroking her with his tongue, he continued to assault her body, causing her to moan out loud. Tender kisses were planted along the way until he came to the fork in the road. The tunnel of love stood in the middle and beckoned him to travel the straight road.

Stefan was hungry and served up pleasure as if there were no end. Yolanda responded to his tender strokes of love and enjoyed her body's response to his touch. Her body rose and fell until she could no longer suffer the affectionate and salacious assault of his tongue. And out of the deepest part of her, she roared in ecstasy.

Giving her momentary relief, Stefan kissed her thighs and watched as her breathing slowly returned to normal. She wrapped her legs around his body for the finale, and he entered her. The intensity of his strokes was so high that Yolanda dug her fingers into his back.

"Say my name. Say my name," Stefan begged.

"Stefannnnnnnn.Stefannnnnnnnn."

"Say my name, girl. Saaaay my nammmme."

"Stefannnnnnnnnnnnn."

CHAPTER THIRTY-TWO

OH, NO HE DIDN'T

They lay spent on satin sheets, their bodies satiated to the tenth degree. The warmth of the hot water as they showered together was like drinking of cup of chamomile tea. It was soothing to the body and relaxed their inner and outer souls.

Their lovemaking was a wonderful sexual experience that Yolanda didn't want to wake up from. This man had made love to her like no other, and that included her ex. It was as if Stefan had gone to school and had some kind of formal training in the art of sensual, sexual seduction. It was mind blowing, and the desire for more that throbbed between her legs was a true testament of how exciting, articulate, and skillful her lover was. But she also liked and was slowly falling in love with the person behind the persona.

His arm was gently wrapped around her waist. Every now and then, his hand would reach for a breast that he caressed like he was examining a flawless diamond. She kissed his hand, squeezed her eyes shut, and thanked her lucky stars that she'd found real romance, possibly real love. Could this work out? She wasn't sure but she was willing to give it a try.

Sleep overtook them, darkness crawling all around. They slept peacefully as time ticked on. Birds were chirping, adding a new dimension to their day. Darkness had become light as night turned into day.

Somewhere in Yolanda's brain she heard a noise. She tried to ignore it, but its persistent ringing caused her to raise her head. The familiar tune of a now ex-flame made her snatch her cell phone off the nightstand.

"Hello," she said in a soft, sleepy voice.

"So, you're still in bed with God knows who."

"It's five damn o'clock in the morning. What do you want?"

"YoYo, it's me, the one who has mad love for you. You've never spoken to me like that."

"There's always a first time, and this is it. Now, I'm going to hang up and go back to sleep."

"I'm not giving up on you. We were meant to be. You are my woman."

Yolanda sighed. "Let's talk about this later."

"How about tonight?"

"That won't work. I'll get back with you." And Yolanda clicked off the phone.

"Was that your boyfriend," Stefan asked, now lying on his side with his head leaning on his arm and his mouth twisted in a sly smile.

"He was my boyfriend. Distance and some other things kept us separated most of the time."

"Distance is a funny word. Will that work against us?"

Yolanda realized what she'd said, now that the fog in her brain had disappeared. It was too early in the morning to try and have an intellectual conversation. "I hope not."

Stefan smiled, pulled her chin close to him and kissed her lips. "If distance was going to be a problem, I'd have to do something about it."

"Like what?"

"Move to Raleigh."

"What about your music?"

"I can gigs here, otherwise, I'd commute back and forth, and I'd take you with me."

Yolanda smiled too. "You'd do that for me?"

"Hell yeah, baby." Stefan held Yolanda's face in his hands and kissed her full on. "I'll go to the ends of the earth for you. You're a hell of a woman, inside and out."

Yolanda kissed Stefan with all she had. "Stefan," she stammered, "I don't know what this is, but I think I've caught the bug. Whoa. I've tried telling myself that this has all been a dream. I met this single, younger man this past weekend and he made my heart throb, along with some other things. All jokes aside, I'm feeling you like nobody's business. I can't explain it…"

"Say no more, love. I know what I feel, and the damn thing is real. It doesn't seem possible, and to those looking from the outside they'd say it was ludicrous. But my heart doesn't lie to me; I'm in love with you."

Stefan held Yolanda and kissed her passionately, squeezing her tight.

"I want to be your knight in shining armor; I want to be your yen to your yack. I love you, Yolanda Morris. I've been debating if I should go home tonight or stay. My mother has a gig tonight and I promised to be there, otherwise, there wouldn't be anything to ponder. Having said that, I want to be there for you and make you happy."

"Stefan, you're scaring me. I've waited for a man like you to come along…a man who was passionate about life and about me. Don't get me wrong, I'm a very intelligent, self-sufficient woman, who has no problem taking care of self. But to have a partner with the same ambitions as myself, would make my world even more special."

"Enough said. I may be younger, but our age difference is only a number. I am the one for you, YoYo; I'll prove it over and over again. I love you."

They kissed like star-crossed lovers. "How about breakfast, my African-American Italian stallion?"

"Damn. Breakfast sounds good, if you're on the menu. Can you accommodate?"

"The eggs, bacon, toast, and coffee rolled into one."

"Will your boyfriend be a problem?" Stefan asked off the cuff.

"You're the only man in my life, Stefan. I'm one-hundred percent in the corner of your ring. But so that we start off right, my ex-boyfriend saw me at the airport last night. It's funny how I was not important to him until he saw me. I told him I was waiting for someone without details, and he got a little snippy. I don't doubt that he hung around to see who I was meeting. He's FBI, and being nosey is his business.

"Aww, FBI. For Bro's Information (FBI), I'm your man now. He might as well get over it. Enough of that kind of talk; I'm ready for breakfast."

"One platter of Yolanda coming up!"

CHAPTER THIRTY-THREE

WEDNESDAY NIGHT MEETING

Wednesday nights were choir rehearsal night. Queenie, Emma, Connie, Yolanda, and First Lady Jackie were all there. They sang, but they couldn't wait for choir rehearsal to be over. And when Emma, who was the choir directress, dismissed the evening's gathering, the five friends couldn't wait to get their chitter-chatter on.

"I've got something to tell y'all," Yolanda said, throwing a teasing smile at the others.

"So do, I," First Lady Jackie said, throwing up a finger. "This reality show business is going to make me lose my religion."

Queenie held up her hand to get in a word. "Let's get away from the church. Why don't we go to Waffle House off the Beltline?"

Emma frowned. "It's a weekday, Q. I've got to go to work in the morning."

"Like the rest of us don't have to."

"Sounds like a good idea to me, even though I hate the way my clothes smell after I leave the place," First Lady said. "But I'm game."

Connie looked dejected. "Preston is watching Desi; so I better get home."

"He'll be all right, sis. My brother-in-law can handle his daughter. As long as there's baby milk in the fridge, Desi will be all right."

"You're right, YoYo. I'm so attached to Desi, I hate to let her out of my sight, except for going to work. It took me fifty years to have this baby, and I'm going to be present in every aspect of my child's life."

"We hear you, Connie, but you need to take a moment for yourself," Emma added. "A grumpy wife and mother don't make Preston a happy man."

Queenie shook her head. "Please, Emma. Preston doesn't seem to be lacking for nothing. Can I get a witness, Connie?"

"You're right, Q. My man is completely satisfied. Now let's get away from the church talking about our extra-curricular activities. I'm game."

The ladies left in their separate cars and arrived at the restaurant almost at the same time. They got a table by a window and began to talk over each other. Even the waitress couldn't get a word in edgewise.

"Okay," Queenie began, "we're going to let the waitress take our orders and then we're going to pick a number from one to five. The number you pick will determine the order in which you speak. Since I'm orchestrating this, I'm going to be number one. The only numbers I will write on this piece of paper will be two through five."

"That is so wrong on all accounts, Q," Yolanda said, rolling her eyes. "Play fair."

The waitress sighed as she stood with her pencil and pad. "May I interrupt you all for one minute? You do want to eat, I'm guessing."

Everyone laughed.

"Please take our orders and forgive us," First Lady Jackie said. "These old sisters are afraid they're not going to get a chance to talk—some of us hoard the conversation." First Lady looked in Queenie's direction. "I want scrambled eggs, bacon cooked crisp, pancakes, and coffee."

"Darn, Jackie," Emma said. "You're going to eat all of that and then go to bed?"

"When I finish telling you all what happened at the taping of our show, I will have used up all the calories."

Queenie looked at First Lady with a puzzled look on her face. "Damn, I mean darn, Jackie. What happened?"

"I'll tell you when it's my turn."

The ladies ate and reminisced about their time in New York. It was the consensus of all that everyone had a great time.

Sipping on her sweet tea, Queenie raised her hand. "Yours truly has number one. That means I will go first in telling my story."

"Whatever," Yolanda said under her breath.

Queenie threw her hand at her. "Whatever. Anyway, my sister is no longer with me. After we left you all on Sunday, I went home to what I had hoped would be peace and quiet. Little did I know that Jefferey was going to act out. But first, her ex-husband, who is really her husband, I'll explain later, called looking for her. Jefferey had reached out to him before she left Charlotte. My brother-in-law told me that they weren't divorced, that he's been paying the mortgage all along, and that my sister may be a little mental. When I tried to talk to that fool about it, she went off on me. She tried to hurt me. You can still see the bruise on my lip."

"The girl needs help," Emma said. "I was there, and something isn't quite right upstairs, if you know what I mean."

"So, where is she?" Connie wanted to know. "I don't want that crazy woman around Desi."

"I want to know why Jefferey's husband didn't get her any help if he knew she was crazy," First Lady Jackie added.

Queenie rolled her eyes and smirked. "Jefferey tried to kill Harrison; at least that's his story." Everyone gasped. "Harrison drove to Raleigh, at my request, to pick her up. God knows I was a happy soul. However, Harrison called several hours afterwards to say that Jefferey jumped from his car once they arrived in Charlotte, but she was later found roaming the streets. She's being held at a psychiatric facility for seventy-two hours. I'm not sure what will happen after that."

Yolanda stretched her neck. "You've got to save her, Q. She's the only sister you have, and this is the time you need to put on your big, girl panties and step up to the plate."

"You would say some foolishness like that because you don't have a sister like mine. My story is so different from yours."

"Well, my number is five, so you'll have to wait to get my juicy tidbits."

"I pulled number two," Emma said. "I had a great time in New York; I needed it. Otherwise, my life is still empty. I heard that Terrance may be coming up this weekend with Donald. Maybe I'll get a chance to talk to him, if he should stop by the church yard sale. I'm not throwing myself at anybody, though."

"He's such a nice guy," First Lady Jackie said. "I could see you with him, Emma—a good Christian man."

"Yeah, but I miss my Billy. He was the man for me."

Everyone was quiet for a moment, almost as if they were giving reverence to Billy's memory.

"Well, I pulled the number three," Connie said, holding up the piece of paper. "Preston and I couldn't be better. God has been a blessing to our lives. He gave us a beautiful daughter in our old age."

"Fifty isn't that old," First Lady Jackie said.

"By whose definition?" Queenie wanted to know. "All of your asses are old. Yeah, I'm old too, but remember, we are Silver Bullets and we're fierce, fabulous, and sexy."

Yolanda slapped Queenie's hand. "I heard that, Q. Fierce, fabulous, sexy, and in love."

Everyone at the table stared at Yolanda. She held up the piece of paper that had the number five on it. She looked into the faces of her dear friends and began to laugh. Number four, go ahead."

First Lady Jackie O'Neill plowed head on into her story about the altercation she had with First Lady Gloria Griffin. "I don't know how that woman knew I'd been to Vegas and that some man had kissed me and called my house."

"Say what?" the ladies said in unison.

"Yeah, and she tried to belittle me in front of the other two wives, calling me out on my Christianity. I wanted to knock her to the floor, and I was heated enough to do so. The day had gone so well, but then it had to turn ugly. That heifer is not there for the right reason. She kept saying 'this is a reality T.V. show and we've got to give the people what they want. I told her she was going straight to hell…"

"Oooh, sistergirl, you were some kind of mad." Queenie slapped Jackie's hand.

"I was mad, but I had to pull myself back to reality and remember why we were doing the show. I didn't want to embarrass Franklin any more than I had, although I found out later that he had his own run-in with the First Lady's husband. I'm not going to lose my place in the Master's Book of Life. I'll quit before I let my guard down like that again."

"When does it air?" Yolanda asked. "I'm going to have a front row seat."

"It's not funny, YoYo. I can't believe church folks…First Ladies can be so mean."

"What did the other ladies do?" Emma asked. "Enjoy the show?"

The ladies laughed out loud. Queenie, Connie, and Yolanda were doubled over in laugher.

"That's about the size of it, Emma. After everything was in calm down mode, First Lady James had the nerve to try and put an end to our bickering with her proper self." Jackie's lips were bunched like a prune, and the ladies laughed some more.

Holding up her number, Yolanda began. "I have the number five. They say you save the best for last."

"Whatever."

"There you go again, Q. Don't be mad because my story is better than yours. But to cut to the chase, Stefan, my African/Italian-American stallion came to visit me on Monday. Oh, my, my, what a wonderful visit it was. He wined and dined me, and then we went to a café and drank coffee before retiring to my house. And then it was on like popcorn. Everything sizzled and popped.

"Stefan and I are in love."

137

"Please," Q said, throwing her hand in the air. "You just met the boy. He must want something from you."

Yolanda wiggled her finger. "What can I offer him that he doesn't already possess? He's no boy by any stretch of the imagination. We not only made passionate, intoxicating provocative, titillating love, but we talked about our future. He's even willing to relocate should that be necessary."

"Yeah, yeah, yeah." Queenie sighed out loud and threw her hands up in the air.

"Don't hate, Q. I haven't told you the other part of the story; it's the part that messed me up. I went to the airport a little early so that I could be calm when I saw him. Since I had time, I stopped at one of the lounges and ordered a Long Island Ice Tea. You won't believe who sent me a drink. I never once saw him until that moment."

It was Connie's turn to harass her sister. "Don't tell me it was Illya, the man you kicked to the dirty curb to be with some youngster."

"You're right, sister dear. There was Illya Newsome in the flesh. I haven't seen him in a good month, and on the night of all nights, there he was sitting across from me. He came over and wanted to know why I was there. I told him I was waiting for someone and didn't offer any more. He buzzed off, but you won't guess who called me at five o'clock in the a.m. the next morning wanting to talk?"

Yolanda looked at her friends who were staring at her like a freak, like she was some loose cannon getting ready to go off. Quietly she said what everyone already knew. "Yes, Illya called to say that he wasn't giving up on me and that we were meant to be."

Yolanda sighed. "Am I conflicted? Yes, but my heart, and if I was a betting woman, my chips are on Stefan. He brings a new kind of freshness to the word love."

"What's love got to do with it?" First Lady Jackie asked. "You got a good screw…"

"Jackie, I can't believe that came out of your mouth." Yolanda took a last sip of her cold coffee on that one.

"Waitress," Queenie shouted. "We need another round of coffee. We might be here all night."

The waitress complied and came running with a pot of fresh coffee.

Yolanda composed herself. "Jackie, I'm going to let you slide, but three strikes you're fair game. Love has everything to do with it. Stefan is the real deal regardless of his age, and he's willing to go above and beyond to prove it. In fact, I'll be meeting his mother soon."

Connie shook her head. "You've lost your mind, YoYo. I can't believe my big sister is falling for some bull crap like this. I'm with First Lady; the boy blew your brains out as well as the other part of your anatomy. How much did he give you? Two, three, four hundred dollars or was it a complementary piece of jewelry to match your ring?"

Yolanda stood up and hit the table. Everyone jumped. "I can't believe my own sister would stoop so low as to call me a whore."

"She did," Queenie said under her breath, casting her eyes downward.

First Lady Jackie couldn't repress her thoughts on the matter any longer. "You need to keep those legs of yours together and ask for God's forgiveness before you burn in Satan's fire. All this intoxicating love stuff with a man you're not married to is an abomination before God."

Yolanda rose from her seat with tears in her eyes. "For everyone's information, I'm no one's whore. Whatever your opinion of me happens to be is just that, your opinion. I'm falling in love with Stefan, and Illya lost out. That's the end of this conversation." Yolanda tore up the piece of paper with the number five on it, threw it in the middle of the table, sat down, and sipped her coffee. She glared at Connie, but didn't say a word. Then she rose from the table with her purse in her hand. "I'll see you at the yard sale on Saturday." And she was gone.

CHAPTER THIRTY-FOUR

ILLYA NEWSOME

*A*ngry was how he felt when he laid his cell phone on the nightstand. Sure, it had been a minute since he'd last seen Yolanda. His life was complicated, but he always resolved to be the best man that he could be. When his daughters called him about his ex-wife's condition and her needing assistance, he was there. In truth, he felt sorry for her, and she even seemed to be a different person—more mellow and forgiving.

Illya ran the video tape in his head of Yolanda embracing the younger man at the airport. He hadn't taken her for granted, but he never thought that she'd dump him the way she did, all for the sake of being with someone who was a stranger. After all, they had spoken right after Yolanda arrived in New York. The relationship seemed to be in check, although Yolanda was a little short on words. When had this new man in her life materialized? Was she having an affair in the midst of what he considered their time together?

He got up, dressed, and called his contact. Another FBI case had come up that drew him back to Raleigh. It concerned a kidnapping of a prominent news anchor from Virginia, whose captor was believed to be hiding out somewhere in the surrounding area.

But he had another investigation of a personal nature he needed to handle. He was going to find out who this new interest was that Yolanda had suddenly abandoned him for. If there was any information, hopefully incriminating information, he would serve it to her on a silver platter.

Illya didn't like being served notice that his time had expired, especially when he felt more for Yolanda than he'd acknowledged. True, he wanted to take it slow; he'd been burned badly by his ex-wife. Trust issues were at the forefront, but he hadn't realized that dragging his feet meant losing his girl.

He was going to become Yolanda's superhero—win her at all costs by any means necessary. She was his destiny.

CHAPTER THIRTY-FIVE

HARRISON B. QUICK

*H*e walked from room to room, recalling old memories when he lived in the house with Jefferey and his son, H. J. It was a proud moment when he and Jefferey purchased their home in what was then a new neighborhood of up-and-coming black socialites. They'd arrived and were accepted into the community as if they'd always belonged. And they thrived as a couple, their social status intact.

He pushed open the door to the master bedroom and stood in the doorway, scanning the contents. Everything was the same as he'd remembered. However, the memory of that night when he was attacked by the woman he loved after having just made love to her caused him to retreat. In fact, there were too many memories of fond times that had been overshadowed by that fateful night.

The house seemed smaller. He walked to the spacious kitchen and looked out of the large bay window that looked out into the yard. The cluster of pine trees that served as shade at their family picnics stood tall but lonely. A tear streaked Harrison's face.

As much as he tried to deny it, the love was gone. He couldn't stomach any more. It was time to leave. Jeffery was being released.

A stoic Harrison arrived at the treatment facility where Jefferey was being held. He looked at his watch; it was two-thirty in the afternoon. Jefferey could only be held for seventy-two hours, and now it was time to pick her up. Harrison wasn't sure what he was going to do about his wife, but he realized that what he should've done all those years ago was now eminent.

Divorcing Jefferey consumed his every thought. He truly had loved this woman once, even after all that she'd done to him and their son. H. J. had begged his father not to leave his mother, although Harrison had never shared with him the real reason he decided to leave...had to leave. It was for his survival. Harrison had promised within himself that those he left behind wouldn't have to suffer, although H. J. would go through more than he ever knew.

He rang the bell for the attendant and stood waiting to be given access. In the next minute, a red-haired, rather stout white woman unlocked the steel door and let him in. Harrison looked around the lobby area that was devoid of a human presence, and just as he choose to lean against a wall, Jefferey, led by an attendant dressed in white, came around the corner.

Jefferey looked haggard but soft, if it was possible to be both at the same time. She smiled when she saw Harrison and seemed grateful for his presence.

Harrison signed some papers and spoke briefly with the attendant before leading Jefferey out of the facility. On the Sunday they had rode into town, he was willing vessel to do what it took to make her well. At this moment, his soul wasn't so willing, as the woman before him needed more than he could give.

"How do you feel?"

"Like I've been released from prison. I don't have any idea what got into me, Harrison. I've tried so hard to work through my issues, but I can't seem to control my emotions and actions when this thing I can't explain comes over me. I'm so sorry for getting out of the car. I felt like you were going to abandon me, and I got scared."

Harrison was silent for longer than he'd planned. In his mind, he had come to the end of the line with Jefferey. She needed more than he could give, and he wasn't willing to deprive himself of a decent life with someone who didn't care about him any longer. Abandonment was a hurtful word, and the last thing he wanted to do was hurt her. But he couldn't live with the person who walked beside him.

"We'll work through it," he finally said. "Let's go home and get you comfortable. Are you hungry?"

"Yes, I'm famished."

Guiding her with his arm around her shoulder, Harrison led Jefferey to the car. "How about eating at TGIF? It shouldn't be too crowded at this time of day."

"That's fine. I'm hungry; all I want is a burger and fries."

Harrison smiled. He drove on in silence for the duration of the trip. "We're here."

Before Harrison could come around and get the door for her, Jefferey got out of the car. It worried him a little, as it seemed to be a replay of only a few days ago, but all indications were that she seemed to be normal—at least at the moment. The true gentleman that he was, Harrison walked to where she stood and closed the car door. They walked into the restaurant, putting their lives on hold for a few hours.

CHAPTER THIRTY-SIX

I AM THE FBI

*I*llya divided his time between his paid gig as an FBI agent and his personal endeavor in finding the name of the mysterious man that snatched Yolanda right from under his nose. He'd watched Yolanda the night he ran into her at the airport, hoping to get a glimpse of the person she was meeting. Shock was the emotion that came over him, when he saw his lady smiling at the younger gentleman with the wavy hair, whose arm she melted into upon his arrival. Illya checked and wrote down the name of the airline and flight number at the baggage claim turnstile, assuming that it was the flight the gentleman Yolanda met was on, although he hadn't retrieved any luggage.

His badge and a special favor from an inside contact paid off. He was able to obtain the manifest for the flight he targeted, which narrowed his search to one hundred and seventy-six passengers. Once he eliminated all of the women, using deductive reasoning based on their names, the list had dwindled to one hundred and ten names.

Sitting in a coffee shop not far from the airport, Illya browsed the list again and again. He recalled that the gentleman accompanying

Yolanda appeared to be of Latin decent, although he could be wrong. The man's shoulder-length, wavy hair said he was in the ballpark, although as he browsed the list again, the two Hispanic/Latin male names listed were paired with a mate.

Illya's eyes floated down the page as he continued to cross through name after name. And then he stopped.

"Stefan Morsilli," Illya said out loud, taking a sip of his black coffee.

He tapped the piece of paper with his pen, rubbed his chin, and circled the name. He'd run the name through the FBI database to see what he could find. He tapped the paper once again. This was the right name; he felt it in his gut.

Reaching into his pocket, he pulled out a couple of dollar bills and left them on the table. He was anxious to discover who the man was behind the mask and what specifically he wanted with Yolanda.

CHAPTER THIRTY-SEVEN

CALM BEFORE THE STORM

The next few days flew by. Harrison was grateful for the calm. Jefferey seemed her old self and at ease with her surroundings.

Harrison wasn't sure what to do with himself. He'd taken a month's leave of absence from his contract job overseas, and now he was itching to get back to it. He had to make up his mind soon, as to what he was going to do. His reporting date was the last Monday in September.

Conversation was strained. It was hard to find the right words without upsetting Jefferey. He was happy to be in the moment of no turmoil, but the quiet was sometimes intimidating; there was no telling what Jefferey was thinking.

He'd made some minor repairs around the house, stopped, and came in to get a cold drink of water. It was a beautiful fall morning, and although the weather was cool, the sun was shining.

He marched into the kitchen and went to the fridge. Before the door closed good, he uncapped the bottle and was pouring the water down his throat. With his head held back, he allowed the refreshing liquid to cool him down, and when he dropped his head back down, he nearly jumped off the floor.

The sun's ray cast a light on the silhouette that sat in the shaded area of the kitchen. There sat Jefferey at the end of the table quiet as a mouse. She watched Harrison as he soothed himself with the cool water.

"Hi," he said. "How long have you been sitting there?"

"Long enough to watch you get water out of the fridge."

"Oh. Why didn't you say something?"

"I was admiring you. You still have a good work ethic. It's so good to see you floating around the house, taking care of this and that."

"Well, it had to be done," Harrison said with resignation. "I was up early this morning; I cut the grass and trimmed the hedges. I placed some straw in the areas that needed it." Harrison took another swig of water.

"You're a good man, Harrison. That's why I married you. You were a good man."

Harrison managed a smile. "I've always tried to be the best that I could be…for you and H. J."

"And you always were. I'm the failure in our marriage. I may be on meds, but I'm smart enough to realize that it was my doing…my illness that has brought me to the place I'm in. I hope you can forgive me for all I've done to you, our family, and my parents."

"I've forgiven you a long time ago, Jefferey."

"God knows I wish we could recapture our life that's been on hold for fourteen years."

Harrison winced and folded his arms in front of him. He couldn't look at her. This certainly wasn't the right moment to tell her that their lives would never be the same and that he wanted a divorce. She seemed fragile, and he danced around her statement. "We've changed. Life will never be the same as it was, Jefferey. We're too old and set in our ways for one thing."

Jefferey laughed. "You're right about that. All the body parts aren't functioning like they once did."

Harrison smiled and shook his head. "You said it."

"Harrison?" There was a long pause.

Harrison waited, not sure what to expect next. His breathing was audible and he was a little on edge. There was no way in the world that he wanted Jefferey to have hope.

"Harrison, would you make love to me?" Jefferey turned away and closed her eyes.

Harrison couldn't believe his ears. The last time he made love to her came flooding back like a raging river. They had passionate, mad sex like they always did, but then she went crazy—a psycho—when he refused to go another round. She tried to stab him…kill him, and the memory froze like a stalactite in a deep, dark cavern.

He weighed his answer. They hadn't even slept together in the same bed since he'd brought her home. Harrison searched his heart, his soul for an ounce of love or something to make him feel something for his wife, but there was nothing—nothing but an empty wasteland that didn't call her name.

"I'm sorry; I shouldn't have asked." Jefferey got up from her seat. She seemed frustrated. She began to pace and started to leave the room.

Harrison went to her, grabbed and held Jefferey, hoping to quiet the storm he may have caused to rise within her. His face was contorted with confusion and strife. He moved back and lifted her chin with his hand and kissed her on the forehead. Jefferey reached up and placed her arms around his shoulders, so tight that Harrison fidgeted.

He pulled her face up again and looked into her eyes. "It's not that I don't want to make love to you," Harrison lied, "it's that I still have vivid memories of that night… the night that you tried…"

"It's okay, there's no need to bring it up. I remember it too." She let her arms fall by her side and blew out hot air. "I'm sorry," she said again and stormed out of the room.

Harrison looked in the direction that Jefferey took her exit. He exhaled and was now frustrated at this turn of events. "I've got to get the hell out of here. Soon."

Jefferey retreated to her room, closed the door, and fell on top of the bed. Tears formed in her eyes, and she cried, closing her eyes to shut herself off from the world. After a few moments, she wiped her face with her hand, sat up, and looked around the room. She got up and retrieved her journal. She turned to the last entry in her book. It had been a while. In fact, she hadn't written anything in it since the day she arrived in Raleigh.

Turning to a blank page, Jefferey touched the paper with her pen. Nothing was forthcoming. She looked at the blank page for a minute, but still no words flowed through her pen. After fifteen minutes, she had a renewed sense of things, and Harrison was the first word she wrote in her journal.

Harrison, my dear husband, Harrison. I was so happy to see Harrison when he showed up at Queenie's. I wanted to leap into his arms and hold him. I wanted to tell him how sorry I was for trying to inflict harm on him and to make him understand it was the illness. God it wasn't my fault that I was having a mental breakdown. I learned that my Grandad Harold on my mother's side was also afflicted with a mental disease, but everyone kept it a secret for far too long.

I love Harrison and I've got to let him know before it's too late. I want him and H. J. to be a part of my life again.

I haven't seen H. J. in a long time. He hates me, too. I nearly destroyed his life, interfering by setting up roadblocks to keep him all to myself and away from the other people in his life he loved. I didn't want him to play sports in high school. I didn't want him to go away to college. I didn't want him to have a girlfriend or a guy friend for that matter. And when he was able to get away...when he went to college, he didn't come back.

I especially hate that I told Queenie all those lies about Harrison walking out on me and the bit about losing the house and the car. I've become a pathological liar when it's convenient, but it was necessary at the moment. My man came back to me. Maybe H. J. will too.

Jefferey stopped writing and got up and put her ear to the door. There wasn't much she could hear from the master bedroom that was on the second floor. She put her ear to the door, listened to see if she could hear any movement at all. Hearing nothing, she went back and sat on the bed, picking up her journal once again.

I'm happy that Harrison rescued me so we can resume our life together. I will never let him go; he'll never leave me again. I love him; he loves me; I'm still his Sugar Cookie. Harrison will make love to me. I won't accept no as an answer.

Jefferey Shanice Jackson-Quick
September 14, 2014

CHAPTER THIRTY-EIGHT

DISCOVERY

*I*llya was on a mission. He now had competition for the lovely Ms. Yolanda Morris, and at the moment, his competitor had the edge on him. It wasn't that he'd taken for granted that Yolanda would always be waiting for him when he returned from his sometimes laborious and long undercover missions, but he hadn't seen it coming—a new man in her life after she'd told him that he was all that she needed. Evidently, that was a lie.

Googling Stefan Morsilli's name didn't bring up a lot of information. He was a jazz musician in New York and played from time to time with some greats. But as his eyes wandered further into his Stefan's Wikipedia, a name caught his attention.

He hadn't seen the name Tracey Porter in ages. The Tracey Porter he knew had a sister named Marjorie, and the two of them were singers. He and Marjorie were an item during his college years at NYU, that is until he met his former wife and married her. Marjorie never accepted his apologies for breaking off their relationship, but in less than a year, she was only a name.

Illya read on and his mouth flew open. Tracey was Stefan's mother. But the boy's last name was Morsilli. Maybe she had adopted him.

Excitement rose within Illya. He had to find Marjorie and reintroduce himself into her life. Maybe she had forgiven him as nearly two decades had passed since they last communicated with each other. If he was serious about reclaiming Yolanda, the woman he had grown to love and was very fond of, he had to arm himself with as much ammunition as he could in order to stage a coup. If that meant re-establishing a relationship with an old flame to keep the fire burning under the present flame, he'd have to risk it. Was Yolanda worth it? A resounding *yes* rung in his ears.

CHAPTER THIRTY-NINE

WAITING FOR MY BOO

Walking around in circles, Queenie went into the bathroom and looked at herself in the mirror. She patted her red Afro in place and blinked several times to make sure her false eyelashes were secured properly. Licking her teeth with her tongue, Queenie picked up a tube of tangerine-colored lipstick and painted her lips. She winked at herself and smoothed down her cashmere sweater and slacks that were the same color as her lipstick. A gold, twenty-inch rope necklace and twenty-four carat hoop gold earrings were the only contrasts. Pleased with what she saw, she walked back into her bedroom, retrieved her purse from on top of her bed, and headed out. She looked around the house and was happy that all was in order.

Queenie's excitement was boiling over. Today, her fiancé, Donald, was arriving in town and she couldn't wait to see him again. She hated that she had to participate at the church yard sale, but she was going to put in her fair share so that she could take her leave as soon as Donald arrived.

Swinging her purse over her shoulders, she set the alarm and exited the house through the garage and got in her car. As she backed out, she thought about Jefferey and how they'd left their relationship. It was not good, but Queenie was happy that Jefferey was out of her house, even out of her life, and that Harrison was now taking the reins. Maybe she would give Harrison a call sometime next week. Right now her focus was on seeing her baby again.

Queenie pulled up to the church and was surprised to see that her girls were already there and that people had already begun to arrive, although the posted time of the yard sale was eight o'clock. There was an array of things for people to purchase from clothes, shoes, electronics, and, of course, desserts and other baked goods.

"Hey, Q," Emma said, as Queenie sauntered over in her direction. "What's the good word?"

"My baby is coming to town." Queenie slapped Emma's hand and blushed. "I'm going to be with you turkeys up until my man does his drive through. Then I'm gone."

"I heard that. Do you know for sure if Terrance is coming? You mentioned it once."

"Emma, not to worry. I'm sure Terrance is going to be riding shotgun with my boo." Queenie winked at her. "So, you're thinking about giving Terrance another chance?"

Emma smiled. "Girl, I'm weighing my options. I've come to the realization that I don't want to be by myself."

"Well, listen to you. Maybe we'll become sisters-in-law."

"I didn't say anything about getting married, Q. I just need a little lovin' on."

"There's nothing wrong with that. Let me go and speak to Connie and YoYo before I get started."

"They're in charge of selling baked goods. Connie baked red velvet and carrot cakes. I've already got my pieces set aside."

"I've got to get me some, too." Queenie was about to move on and turned around. "Why don't we double date tonight? We can go out to dinner."

"I'll think about it. I may want to be alone with Terrance."

"Suit yourself. Don't think for one minute that I was planning to be tied up with you and yours the entire night." Queenie and Emma laughed.

"Alright, Q. Let's see what goes down first."

Queenie stuck out her thumb in approval and walked away. She enjoyed seeing everyone get together for a good cause. The choir needed new robes, and hopefully they would sell enough stuff to make that happen.

She hugged Connie and Yolanda when she came to their station. "Hey, divas, what ya been cooking? I hear that red velvet and carrot cake is on the menu."

"You got that right," Connie said, with a glow on her face.

"I've already had a piece of carrot cake," Yolanda said. "I didn't trust that there would be any left."

"But it's so early in the morning," Queenie added.

Yolanda sighed. "That piece of cake contained all of the four basic food groups."

Queenie and Connie laughed.

"That's a stupid excuse for eating all of those sugar calories this early in the morning. What do you think your Italian stallion would say if you pack all of those calories on that caboose of yours?"

"He'd love it. I'll be flying to New York next weekend to see him and possibly meet his mother."

"Oh," Queenie retorted, while twisting her neck like a bobble head doll. "So your relationship has advanced to meeting your future mother-in-law."

"No one said anything about getting married, Q. We're excited about where our relationship is going. I'm having fun as a Silver Bullet."

Queenie and Yolanda slapped each other's hand. "Ain't mad at you, girl. You do you, and I'll do me. My baby should be arriving anytime."

"Well, you better get in and help," Connie said, with her hands on her hips. "After all, the proceeds will benefit your behind too, although you'll need extra yardage for your robe."

Queenie shook her hand in Connie's face. "I'm going to beat you down to the white meat, if you throw shade at me again."

"Well, get to work."

"I forgot to tell you, Q, that I heard through the grapevine that Linden and Drema D are getting divorced." Yolanda watched Queenie's discomfort.

Queenie arched her shoulders and leaned back. "So why in the hell are you telling me? Linden Robinson is ancient history. There's no way on God's green earth that I'll ever touch or speak to that no-good, can't-get-it-up Negro. He got what he wanted, and so did I."

Yolanda hugged Queenie. "That's my girl. You don't deserve a loser like Linden."

"Enough talk; let me go and make myself useful. I don't want anyone talking bad about me behind my back when Donald shows up and take me away from here."

"People are going to talk about you anyway, Q," Connie said, stifling a laugh. "These church folks already say that you're pushy and vocal and need to be tuned down a bit."

"Who said that, Connie? Next time tell them to come and say it to my face, if they have something they want to say about me. Christians aren't any better than sinners. Anyone who has to ask for forgiveness every day of the week ought to wait to come to Jesus until they're ready to be a real Christian."

Connie couldn't control her laughter. "I don't know what you're talking about, Q, and you're not making much sense, but you sure are funny to watch. I made that up, although I'm sure somebody has said something about you. Anyway, God wants your heart now." She waved her finger in front of Queenie. "Waiting until you're ready may be too late."

"Give it a rest and give me two slices of red velvet cake. How much is it?"

"Six dollars."

"Dang, that's highway robbery."

"It's an expensive cake to make. If it wasn't for the church's yard sale, I'd be selling these slices for five dollars a slice." Connie handed Queenie her cake in a box. "Six dollars please."

Queenie handed Connie the six dollars while Yolanda was distracted with her cell phone. "I'll see y'all. Better leave that young bird alone, YoYo."

"You got your boo; I've got mine. Run along."

CHAPTER FORTY

MY BOO IS COMING

*N*o sooner than Queenie walked away from Connie and Yolanda, First Lady Jackie stepped up to her.

"Q, you're supposed to be working at the book booth. But I understand, Connie's cake is to die for."

"I'm not trying to die. I wanted to make sure I had mine before, as you put it, all those other heathens ate it up. Only the church folks will be buying it at three dollars a pop."

"Stop being so cheap. You spend all of your money on those designer clothes and shoes; the church would be happy if you paid your tithes the way you should."

Queenie stepped back on her heels. "Take it back, Jackie. I don't want to fool up with you today and get upset. My boo is coming, and I'm not going to let any of you heifers steal my joy today."

"Well, stop prancing around and get to work."

"By the way, where are the reality show cameras? The yard sale would surely put you not only on the map but in a good light with the other first ladies."

"I don't need spotlight..." Jackie put her finger to her mouth and seemed to ponder what Queenie said. She cocked her head. "You know, that's a brilliant idea, Q. You do use that thing on top of your head for something other than a coat rack. Let me call somebody now."

Before Queenie moved a hundred yards, a horn began to blow. She snapped her head around so hard, she almost caught a crook in it. Her mouth went wide as she saw the gold-colored Escalade move to the curb. Her arms went up, almost causing her to drop her cake.

As fast as she could go, she ran to the sidewalk. Donald and Terrance exited the car and Queenie flew into Donald's arms.

"I thought you would be getting here later. I haven't done anything yet except for show up."

"While I'm not in a hurry, I am in a hurry to be with you," Donald said, winking his eye at her. "But I'm going to stroll through and see what you have and give my regards to the pastor and his wife."

Queenie blushed and was grinning from ear to ear. "Alright. I'll put in at least an hour."

Terrance finally spoke up. "Is Emma here?"

Queenie hit Terrance on the shoulder and pointed in the direction Emma was working. "See, she's looking this way. On the low, she's had a change of heart about you."

"Well, I aim to find out."

"Don't tell her I said that," Queenie warned. "She'd be upset with me from now until next year, if she knew I let that cat out of the bag."

"I'll be discreet," Terrance said, moving in Emma's direction. "I've never given up on her."

Queenie smiled and put her arm through Donald's. "I'm so happy you're here. I've missed you something terrible."

"I've missed you too, Q. I want us to plan our wedding. How does December 31st sound?"

Stopping in her tracks, Queenie lifted her hand and patted her chest. "That sounds good to me. That's only a minute over three months, but I'll be ready."

Donald kissed Queenie on her cheek. "I've been ready to make you mine. If I could take you away today, I would. Here comes your First Lady. Will talk about our plans later."

CHAPTER FORTY-ONE

CAMERAS! ACTION!

The yard sale was officially open. Stragglers who were passing the church on foot stopped ever so often to browse. In the next half hour, more people from the community stopped and supported the cause.

Emma and Terrance were deep in conversation. Queenie could see her face punctuated into a smile. She hoped that Emma would stop pining over Billy and let some sunshine into her heart. Terrance was a good man, and they were hard to come by, but this would be an opportunity for Emma to bounce back, since she seemed to be so lonely.

"Hey, baby," Donald said, looking into Queenie's eyes, "you about ready to go?"

"I've been ready, in fact, I'm not sure why I showed up today. My mind certainly wasn't on the yard sale, although Emma and First Lady would've had my head if I hadn't shown up. Let me tell First Lady I'm leaving. Getting Emma to leave won't be so easy. This event is to support the choir in getting new robes, and with her being the director, there's no way she's going to tear herself away from here."

"We can always come back and get her."

Just as Queenie and Donald headed in Emma and Terrance's direction, there seemed to be a lot of commotion. A van with antennas arrived on the scene.

"I wonder what that's all about," Donald said to Queenie.

"Oh my goodness. We can't leave now, Donald." They watched several men with large professional video cameras exit the van. "It's the T.V. network that's shooting the reality show that the pastor and Jackie are doing. They're going to get some footage of the yard sale. I must go back to my station."

"Queenie, you're a trip."

"I'd do anything for one minute of screen time on the tube so I can brag about it to my co-workers. My appearance alone will boost ratings."

Donald laughed. "Girl, you are too funny, but I love you. The other thing I like about you is that you are honest and don't hide your feelings, although sometimes I feel you need a filter for some of the things you say."

Queenie stopped, put a hand on her hip and gave Donald a nasty glare. "You met me the way I am, and I'm too old to change my ways now. If you're going to be trying to control this sister, think again buster. I can make December thirty-first go away."

"It's not that serious and you know I love you."

"I'm only saying. Oh, I've got to go. The camera crew already has their cameras ready to shoot." Queenie stopped and turned toward Donald. "I'll be walking down the aisle on New Year's Eve." Donald smiled.

The production team gave Pastor Franklin and First Lady Jackie some instructions. Queenie watched as they took direction and got into place. She was amazed at Jackie; she was a natural for the T.V. camera. She and pastor strolled through the length of the yard sale and stopped where Emma and Terrance were. They engaged in conversation, and Queenie was miffed.

People began to pull their cars over to the curb, some stopping in the middle of the street, no doubt to see what was going on. Before long, people were coming from everywhere, buying up stuff like they were made of money. Queenie saw Connie in the distance throwing her hands up in the air.

"Sold out," Connie shouted to the delight of First Lady.

Queenie assisted customers who'd stopped buy and purchased books—books that were donated by the members that consisted of Christian commentary, Christian fiction novels, and some biographies. And then she looked up, and First Lady was walking her way.

"This is Sister Queenie Jackson, our angelic soloist. This one is a song bird, if I've ever seen one." First Lady winked at Queenie. "So how are we doing with the book sales, sister?"

Queenie was all smiles. "Doing good, First Lady. Oops, I've got to help another customer." And the First Lady moved on.

When Donald made his way over, Queenie couldn't hide her delight. "I'm going to be a star. Jackie made it a point to come to my table and highlight me."

"That's my baby. They'll probably put a star on the Hollywood Walk of Fame for you after you blow up."

"You're damn right."

"Q, were at church."

Surely, her man didn't read her in public. He meant well, but she was going to have to school him on Queenie etiquette. She was a grown woman and didn't need a man to tell her what to do, at least not this late in her life. "Sorry, Donald, the excitement is too much for me. This day is already perfect and it isn't half over."

"Why don't I help you for the next few hours? We don't want First Lady to think you've taken advantage of her ability to put you in bright lights by leaving now."

"You're always the voice of reason. Get on over here. It doesn't look like Terrance was about to leave Emma behind."

"You got that right. My brother can be very persuasive, and I don't think he intends to leave Raleigh without some kind of commitment from your girl."

"She's a hard nut to crack, but I'm sure Terrance can handle it."

Donald kissed Queenie again on her forehead. "I can't wait for you to be Mrs. Donald Griffin."

CHAPTER FORTY-TWO

DÉJÀ VU

The yard sale was going better than anyone had predicted. Of course, they wouldn't make the amount they needed to purchase the new robes, but they were on their way. The church was going to subsidize a portion of the costs, but the choir members were pleased that they, at first count, had made almost two-thousand dollars.

Queenie watched Emma and Terrance hold hands, as they walked in her direction. Even Donald seemed pleased that things seemed to be moving along.

"Hey, ladies," Yolanda called out, as she and Connie approached. "What do you all have planned for tonight? It's not something I wouldn't do is it?" Yolanda laughed.

"That wasn't nice," Connie interjected. "My sister doesn't know how to keep her mouth shut."

"It's alright," Donald said, giving each of the ladies a peck on the cheek. "It was all in fun, and YoYo is good with me."

"Me, too," Terrance added.

"Well?"

"We're going on a double date," Queenie said with a smile. "I'm sure you don't have time for us anyway, YoYo, since you have a heavy long-distance courtship going."

Yolanda smiled. "Indeed I do. I'll be flying to New York next weekend. Oops, I forgot; I've already told you."

"It's the first time I'm hearing it," Emma chimed in. "So you're serious about entertaining a relationship with that young man."

Queenie pushed her hand to her mouth to hide her smirk.

"Emma, Stefan is more than a young man, if you know what I mean. Yes, yes, yes, and he's only a few years younger than me. Age is just a number. You've got to live, Emma. I'm glad to see that you and Terrance have rekindled an old flame."

"Well, yes," Emma said with a sarcastic tone to her voice. "We better get going. I'll see you at church tomorrow."

As the group began to disperse, an unexpected visitor sauntered to where they were. Everyone stopped in their tracks, the ladies shocked by the very appearance.

"Hey, Q, how are; how have you been?" a very lean and soft spoken Linden Robinson said, ignoring everyone else standing around to include Donald, who had his arm around Queenie's shoulder.

She examined him like the cashmere coat she wanted for Christmas, except that her face was a little contorted. He'd seen better days, but he still seemed to be in good physical shape, at least on the surface. Those brown eyes of his burned through hers, catching her slightly off guard. And that bald head that she used to hold on to when they were in the throes of passionate love making was like an aphrodisiac calling her name. But she looked away and then back.

"Hi, Linden. How are you and your wife, Drema D?"

Linden paused and rubbed his hands together. "We're getting a divorce. It didn't work out."

Looks were passed between the four ladies, but Queenie didn't flinch.

"Sorry about you and Drema D. You seemed to be a match made in heaven." Queenie moved closer to Donald and put her arm around his back. "I'd like you to meet my fiancé, Mr. Donald Griffin." Queenie was all smiles.

Linden reached out and shook Donald's hands, but not before piercing Queenie's eyes again with his own.

"And this is Terrance Griffin, Donald's brother," Queenie continued, pointing in Terrance's direction.

"Well, I see that you all are busy." Linden looked around, pretending to be interested in what was going on. "Having a yard sale, I see. And what's with the cameras?"

"The pastor and his wife are on a reality T.V. show called *Preachers of Raleigh*."

"Shut up. My man Franklin is on the big screen. I think I may start coming here again."

Queenie was quiet. She could see that Donald was getting testy and had about all he was going to tolerate.

"Well, we were leaving. It's good to see you again."

"And you, too. I see that you're still hanging around with your angry black girlfriends." Connie, Yolanda, and Emma sneered at him, while each had their arms wrapped around their middle.

"That wasn't called for, Linden," Queenie said, coming to the defense of her friends.

"Sorry 'bout that ladies. So, Q, be sure to invite me to the wedding. When is it? I'd like an invitation just to see if it will happen." A sarcastic smile rolled across Linden's face.

"There will be a wedding," Donald said in a gruff voice, finally speaking up. "The date is December thirty-first. You can come if you like, but Q will become Mrs. Donald Griffin."

"Straight-up," Linden said, extending his hand again.

Donald ignored it, turned away, and led Queenie to the car. Queenie was in seventh heaven. Her man had stood up for her and it was a proud moment in her life.

Linden watched as the crew left him standing on the sidewalk by himself.

CHAPTER FORTY-THREE

ANOTHER CHANCE FOR LOVE

The camera crew rolled off as Queenie, Emma, Donald, and Terrance were about to leave. Off in the distance, Queenie could see First Lady Jackie advancing on them.

"Hurry, let's get in the car and get out of here. If Jackie gets a whiff of Emma, Emma can kiss leaving at this moment goodbye."

"True, but I need to let Jackie know that I've got her back and will handle the rest of the business. As the appointed choir director, I owe her that much."

"Whatever."

Jackie seemed out of breath as she closed in on the car. She rapidly waved her hand, and Emma got out of the car.

"Whew," First Lady said as she tried to catch her breath. "Whew, I haven't moved that fast in ages. Where are you going, Emma?" First Lady bent her neck down to view the occupants in the car. "You were going to leave with Queenie without telling me?"

"I got caught up, girl," Emma said, looking back at Terrance.

"Ohh, the man has got your nose wide open."

"No, Jackie, but we're going to talk and see if we can salvage our relationship. Don't worry about anything. If you close up the sale, I'll be at church tomorrow to tally everything up and close out the event. From what I've already seen, we've done a good job."

"We sure have and with the T.V. spot, I may be able to pull in some donors."

"That's real good."

"Well, go on and have a good time, Emma. I've got my good man; go and get yours. I liked him when we first met him in Hawaii last year. I prayed that you wouldn't let him get away." First Lady put her hand on Emma's heart. "Billy will always reside in there. Terrance will never take his place."

Emma smiled and hugged Jackie. "Thanks, First Lady. I appreciate your words."

"Said from the mouth of a true friend. Remember that always."

"I will never forget."

The ladies hugged again and Emma got in the car. First Lady waved at the others as she walked away.

"What was Jackie saying to you?" Queenie wanted to know.

"You're so nosey. It was personal."

"Okay, be that way. We could've left your boney ass...ah, ah, boney behind at the church."

Emma began to crack up. Terrance and Donald joined her.

"You weren't leaving me anywhere, right Terrance?"

"Amen, Miss E."

Emma and Queenie slapped hands. "That's what I'm talking about," Queenie said. "I'm ready to have a good time."

The two couples headed off to lunch. Their spirits meshed, and they had a wonderful time. Queenie and Donald talked about the wedding, while Emma and Terrance reminisced about the few months they spent together.

Terrance cleared his throat. "Ummm, Emma and I are going to opt out of the movie."

"So what are you going to do?" Donald asked.

"We're going to Emma's house so that we can talk in private.

Nothing wrong with your company, bro, but I came to Raleigh with a purpose."

Emma couldn't contain her smile.

"Are you in agreement with that, Emma?" Donald asked.

"Very much so. I'm sure you and Q would prefer to have time to yourself."

"We would, but we can tolerate a few more hours with you. The day is still young." Queenie laughed out loud. "Naw, you all have fun."

"I guess it's settled," Donald said, trying to control a great big grin that emerged on his face. "I'll drop you two lovebirds off, while the Queen and I indulge in some matters of the heart."

"I like that," Queenie said, throwing her hands up in the air.

"Well let's go," Terrance interjected.

Donald drove to Emma's with the help of Queenie's guidance. When they pulled up into the driveway, Emma and Terrance glanced at each other with smiles on their faces.

"Ready?" Terrance asked.

"Ready." Emma replied. And they got out of the car, and in the next minute Donald and Queenie had disappeared out of sight.

CHAPTER FORTY-FOUR

YES, I'M READY

"$\mathcal{I}$t smells nice in here," Terrance said, as he and Emma entered her house. "It feels so warm and inviting."

Emma laughed to herself and put a great big smile on her face as she sat her purse down on the couch in the living room. Even the few months that she and Terrance were semi-dating, she had never allowed him to come to her home. The memories of her now departed husband were too fresh then, and in her mind, to allow another man into the sanctity of her home would've been an abomination.

Terrance crossed the room and began to sit down in the recliner. Emma rushed over and blocked him from doing so. "What's up?" Terrance asked perplexed.

"That's... that's Billy's chair. That's the chair he was sitting in the day he died. I haven't got the heart to give it away yet. There's so much sentimental value in it."

"Look, no problem. I prefer to sit closer to you anyway."

"I feel so stupid for always babbling on and on about my dead husband. Forgive me; I'm working on it."

Terrance stood in front of Emma and put his arms around her

waist. "There's nothing to forgive. Your husband was part of your life for forever. I get it. You were best friends. Now, I'd like to be your friend, if you let me."

"I'd like that a lot."

Terrance kissed the top of her nose and then dropped to her lips. His kiss was tender and sweet. Emma could hear his heartbeats and no doubt he heard hers. The time they'd shared together shortly after Billy's death was magical—it was good for the soul. And what she liked most was that Terrance was a Godly man, sincere, honest, and everything a woman could ask for in a man. That aspect alone is what probably made her pull back—too afraid of what might happen next, too afraid of the truth, the truth being that she really liked Terrance more than she was ready to admit to her own friends while being unable to detach herself from the husband who lived and died for her.

Emma pulled back. "Would you like a glass of wine?"

"No wine, but how about a glass of water? I want to be able to think clearly when we're talking."

Emma smiled. "Okay. I'll be right back."

Terrance looked around the room while Emma left to get the water. He got up from his seat and strolled around the room, scanning the pictures on her mantel. He stopped and picked up one with Emma and a gentleman, whom she was hugged up with. He jumped when Emma returned to the room with a tray in her hand.

"That's me and Billy. We were vacationing in the Caymans many years ago. In fact, we'd talked about going on a cruise right before he had the heart attack. Never put off what you can do today until tomorrow." Emma handed the glass of water to Terrance. "And the cake is compliments of Connie. She made red velvet cake and sold it at the yard sale today."

"Yum, it's my favorite."

"I was going to be selfish and keep it and eat it all by myself, but I realized that this piece of cake was something that I wanted to share with someone special. You're special to me, Terrance." She sat the tray on the coffee table with two pieces of cake on it.

It was Terrance's turn to smile. He sat down and patted the couch.

"Come and sit next to me. I want to be able to look you straight in the eyes." He took a sip of water.

For more than a few moments, they sat sipping water and eating cake. Emma glanced in Terrance's direction and saw that he was staring at her, while stuffing his mouth with Connie's cake. She dropped her eyes, put her fork down, and sighed.

"I don't know why this feels awkward," Emma finally said, although she wasn't sure what she was saying.

"You need to relax."

"I'm a bit nervous."

"It's not like you met me yesterday. I realize it's been a while, but it's not like we haven't been out on a date before. I will say that you seemed to have digressed some from the woman I met in Hawaii and had a brief relationship with."

"Really? I don't feel as if I've digressed, but if you say so, maybe it's true. Truth is, I've been having a lot of dreams about Billy. I believe he's visited me in the night… even made love to me."

Terrance looked at Emma with reverent eyes. "I'm not here to judge you. I haven't been through the type of loss you've experienced, so I can't begin to know what you're going through. I hope I can help you work through it."

Emma listened and let Terrance's words marinate. Respectable was the word that came to mind. "I've thought about you often."

"We can take it as slow as you like, Emma. I'm here for you."

"Thanks, Terrance. You're too kind. You know, I was a feisty thing all of my life. I was the life of the party. I strutted my stuff and looked good doing it. Billy always told his friends that he had the prettiest and smartest wife of all his friends. And I wasn't a trophy wife either; I had my own identity and Billy knew which boundaries he couldn't cross." Emma stopped and a tiny tear trickled down her left cheek. "I loved that man, but I realize he's not coming back. Everyone keeps telling me to move on…get over it, and it only makes me mad. But I do want to move on, Terrance, and hopefully you can help me."

"I aim to do my best, and I'll start by being a good listener."

Before Terrance had an opportunity to say anything else, Emma clamped her arms around his neck and kissed him full on the lips. He put his arms around her in a warm embrace and kissed her back. There were three minutes of silence as the two renewed their feelings for one another. And then Emma came up for air.

"We better stop. The immoral side of me is trying to fight the logical and practical side of myself that keeps saying, stop and don't let your heart rule your head."

Terrance ran a hand over her cheek and kissed her lightly on the mouth. "I've been thinking about this for some time."

"Thinking about what?"

"Let me finish so I can get through this."

"Okay," Emma said, somewhat puzzled.

"I've committed myself, my body and soul to the Lord. When I met you in Hawaii, I was on this spiritual quest to be the best man that I could be. I had a spiritual thirst for righteousness and God has blessed me in so many ways that I can't even count them all."

"A God-fearing man," Emma said. "That's what I like about you. You keep it one hundred in your commitment to the Lord, something I haven't been able to do. He forgives seventy times seventy, and I know the Lord is tired of forgiving me when He knows that I'm going to come to Him in a matter of a few days and ask for repentance for something else."

Terrance was quiet, deep in thought. He clasped and rubbed his hands together. Emma was sure that he was digesting her words.

"Emma, I don't want you to take this wrong."

Emma bucked her eyes and sat up on her seat.

"I want to make love to you."

Emma gasped. She reached for her water and spilled half of it on herself. Jumping up to get something to wipe up the water, she turned around when she was no longer able to move. Terrance had his arm around her wrists.

He pulled a handkerchief out of his pocket. "Here, wipe up the water with this. Don't leave."

"But I… but I need something more absorbent…"

"Emma, don't run away. I was serious in my statement to you."

175

Emma relaxed a little, dabbed the handkerchief against her pants, and sat back down. "You caught me off guard. But, what about the vows you made to the Lord?"

"I'll have to ask God for forgiveness."

"It doesn't work like that. God isn't going to forgive you when you so blatantly tell Him to his face that you're going to commit a sin and then have the nerve to turn around and ask for favor ten minutes later."

"I'm going to be longer than ten minutes."

"Oh my goodness!" Emma covered her mouth with her hand.

"Emma, you're not a prude. We both know this. I listened to you only moments ago tell me how you ask God for forgiveness—let alone that you're about to be on your third strike. And then you said, to sum it up, you know he'll forgive you anyway if you ask, even if you don't deserve it."

"Yes, I said that, but that's not you, Terrance. I'll have to be accountable for my actions." Emma pulled away and turned back toward Terrance. "You're a God fearing man..."

"What are you afraid of? I've been thinking about this for a long time. I want you...not only your body, the whole person. Yes, my flesh is weak, but my soul hasn't been able to rest. When you broke off our relationship, my heart almost stopped beating. The woman I had fallen in love with deserved more from me."

Alarm registered on Emma's face. "Terrance, I honor your vow... your commitment to the Lord. I can't let my selfishness...my desire for more from our relationship be the reason you want to backslide on your promise to God. I'll admit, in the beginning I was coming on strong, but now I'm at peace with letting God direct my steps."

"Shhhhhh... listen to me. It may be my hormones, and for sure it's the intense heat I'm feeling from your body being next to mine, but I want you. I want all of you, Emma. I want to kiss you... not just on the lips..."

"Hold it, hold it one damn minute. My husband didn't put his lips on anything but my lips."

"If you think I believe that lie, you're deceiving yourself. You're a sensuous woman who desires more. Maybe you've forgotten all of the sexy and sometimes erotic things you used to say to me. Yeah, girl, I had to fight the spirit that wanted me to make love to you whenever we were together."

Emma began to laugh. "Wow, I had no idea those kinds of thoughts were running through your head. We would've been in serious trouble."

Terrance scooted closer to Emma. "I'm ready, are you?"

A smile crossed Emma's face. "Yes, I'm ready."

CHAPTER FORTY-FIVE

NOTHING STAYS HIDDEN FOREVER

*T*he search was on. With the vast amount of technological devices and entities to choose from, there was no doubt in Illya Newsome's mind that he wouldn't be able to find something on Marjorie Porter, since she used that name as her stage name. The World Wide Web was alive and well, and he hoped it would render the results he was looking for.

Illya went to the White Pages online and typed in Marjorie Porter's name. There was one Marjorie Porter who lived in New Jersey, and he was going to call her. He wrote the number down, picked up his cell phone, and logged the numbers in. This was the moment of truth.

Illya was taken aback by the voice that came on the line. The voice was female and the voice of a woman who was much younger than Marjorie.

"Hello, may I speak with Marjorie Porter?"

"May I ask who is calling?" The voice was prim and proper.

Illya cleared his throat. "Ah, yes. My name is Illya Newsome. I went to college with Ms. Porter."

"Okay. Wait a minute."

Listening intently, Illya could make out conversation in the background. The conversation was muffled—the voices going from soft to scratchy. After a few moments, a more mature voice came on the line.

"Well, how many years has it been? Too many to count I'm sure."

"Hi, Marjorie, I'm sure you're surprised at the sound of my voice."

"Well, yes, I am. Last I remember, you left me in the wilderness and ran off and married some skinny girl with a model's figure and faded into the sunset. So how's family life? In fact, what is the purpose of this call after all these years?"

"First, I'm happily divorced."

Marjorie grumbled.

Illya dismissed her dig and continued. "I have two girls, who've made it through college and are now on their own."

"That must be nice," Marjorie said matter of fact.

"Anyway, you came across my mine—out of the clear blue sky. I couldn't get you off my mind, so I Googled your name and was surprised to find you on the list."

"I should've taken it out a long time ago, however, no one ever looked me up; and for twenty-something odd years I've been safe. Now that you've called and spoke to me has your curiosity been satisfied?"

"I'm sorry if I upset you. I didn't mean to. I guess I wanted to hear your voice and see how you were doing."

"I'm doing fine. Living life as free as a bird."

"Are you and your sister still singing?"

"Oh, you remembered. That's a plus on your side. To answer your question, though, my sister, Tracey, sings, I don't perform any longer. I had a bout with lung cancer and I gave up the hole in the walls for clean-filtered air. Every now and then, I will go to the club to hear Tracey sing. Also, she has a son, who's a talented artist. He plays in a band and is a producer. My sister married an Italian man with money and I'd say she's doing pretty well for herself. She sings with Stefan from time to time. Stefan is her son, but mostly singing is her first love and she can't give it up."

179

"What about you? Are you married? Was that your daughter who answered the phone?"

"You sound like a detective."

"I kinda... sorta am."

"That was a wild-and-out answer. However, for your information, I was married once and have two daughters, also. The voice you heard belonged to my granddaughter, Gina, who stays with me most of the time. Her mother is also a musician, and she sings background with some singer; I can't remember her name right now. She's on tour at the moment. The lead singer is on Stefan's label."

"That all sounds interesting. You seem to have a colorful life."

"It's been more than that, Illya. Look, maybe you'd like to come to New York...hang out and reminisce about old times."

"Sure, I'd like that," Illya said, jumping at the request that he hoped would fit right in with his plans. The timing had to be right, but that wouldn't be a problem. "I'll let you know when I'd be able to come."

"Okay, great. Well, it's been real talking with you. I hope this won't be your last call."

"I guarantee you that it won't," Illya said. "You may see me in the very near future."

"Well, call me if you do decide. Take care." The line was dead.

A broad smile came over Illya's face. Ms. Yolanda Maxwell Morris could play her games, but he had one up his sleeve.

CHAPTER FORTY-SIX

MAKING PLANS

olanda felt mighty good this morning. She was going to wear her classic blue-and-white St. John suit to church. She flitted to her closet and pulled out a hat box that contained a large blue and white hat with a large satin ribbon that was cocked to one side. When Yolanda's daughter, CiCi, first saw her hat that she called her pride and joy, CiCi told her mother that she looked like the Cat in the Hat. It was tall, and surely the church members who sat behind her wouldn't be able to see a thing. Yolanda reminded her that they had several screens in the sanctuary on which the sermon was projected. If the folks didn't want to watch the screen, the other alternative was to get up and move.

Still reeling from seeing Stefan earlier in the week, Yolanda hummed to herself as she got ready. She and Stefan hadn't missed a day of talking to each other. She felt like a young girl in love and was enjoying the new-found excitement that she now experienced.

Sitting on the edge of her bed, she applied her favorite lotion over her skin, smoothing it under her chin, down both arms, and to the rest of her body. Next she put her favorite Victoria's Secret underwear on and paraded in front of the mirror. Putting on a body shaper, she went back to the bed and picked up the skirt to put it on. Just as she was about to step into it, her cell phone rang.

Yolanda didn't move. The ringtone was recognizable, one that she'd given to Illya. Annoyed, she let it ring until it stopped. Yolanda proceeded to get dress, when her cell phone rang again. This time she went to her nightstand, looked at the caller-ID, and picked it up."

"Hello," she said flatly.

"Hello, YoYo. I bet you're getting ready for church."

"If you knew that, why did you choose now to call? I'm running behind schedule, so whatever it is you have to say, please do it in the next minute or so."

"I didn't think we were at this place. You're treating me like I've done something to you...like I'm the trash you couldn't wait to get rid of."

"No, I'm sorry if I seem harsh. I'm in a hurry and don't want to be late for church."

"Alright, I'll make this short. I understand that you've moved on, but I don't understand what happened."

"Not right now, Illya. I'm trying to fix my mind on Jesus and you want to talk about us."

"Jesus is fine, but I'd like to get together with you...let's say this coming weekend and talk, bring some closure to the way I'm feeling."

"That wouldn't be a problem, however, I'll be flying to New York on Friday. So this weekend is out of the question; maybe another time."

"This weekend, huh? Umm, the new man in your life must be awfully special."

"It's not up for discussion. Look, I've got to go; I'll call you when I return home from New York."

"Okay, I guess I can wait until then. Say a prayer for me and have a good day."

"I will." Yolanda clicked the off button and pondered the call. Illya seemed different. Maybe that's how men acted when they're given the boot. He'd been absent a lot due to his job, but now that she'd moved on, he seemed to be all of sudden readily available.

Yolanda looked at herself in the mirror. Pleased, she splashed herself with her favorite perfume, picked up her purse, and headed for church.

SITTING ALONE in his hotel room, Illya smiled. The television was blaring, reporting the latest news out of Raleigh. He had no idea that he'd be calling Marjorie so soon. Who knew that Yolanda would be going to New York this weekend?

He'd make contact with Marjorie, and if everything was a go, he'd catch a Red Eye to LaGuardia Friday late. Some answers would soon be forthcoming and he was about to get them his way, all while having some fun with an old college mate in the process.

Making plans was next on his agenda. He wasn't sure how it would work out, but he was ready for the challenge and, of course, Yolanda's reaction, if it all played out how he hoped. After all, he was with the FBI, and fact-finding and apprehending was part of his nature.

CHAPTER FORTY-SEVEN

LET THE CHURCH SAY AMEN

Shiloh Baptist Church was full this Sunday morning. It was young people's day, which meant that Queenie, Connie, and Yolanda didn't have to sing. Emma was the adult choir director, so she also had a break from choir duty. First Lady Jackie was still a constant at the piano as she banged away and the children's choir bounced up the aisle and into the choir stand, singing one of Tye Tribbit's songs.

Yolanda rushed down the aisle after the choir came in and sat next to Connie, Preston, and baby, Desiree. There were times that Yolanda would feel sorry for herself, always sitting with her sister's family, with no immediate suitor or friend to call her own. Now, she was content and would probably have a hard time concentrating on the word that Pastor O'Neill was going to give today for thinking about Stefan. She'd ask the Lord for forgiveness, as He was truly first in her life—at least that's what she kept telling everyone.

She watched as Queenie strolled down the aisle holding tight onto Donald's arm, as if she was afraid a mighty wind or the Holy Ghost was going to blow him away. But it was the sight of Emma and Donald's brother Terrance that caused Yolanda to hurt her neck.

Emma had a sway in her walk, and that smile she had on her face. Oh my God!

Yolanda nudged Connie in the arm, leaned over, and whispered in her ear. "Does Emma seem different to you?"

"What are you talking about? Emma doesn't look any different than she did yesterday at the yard sale other than she's walking in church with... with what's his name. Shhh."

"Connie, Emma got her some last night."

"YoYo, we're in church. Get your mind out of the gutter. How's Desi going to feel knowing that her auntie is thinking lewd things in the house of the Lord?"

"That's why I'm whispering, fool."

Connie looked in Emma's direction. "You may be right, but let's talk about it after church. All you have is sex on the brain. That young boy turned you out, and now everybody's getting some. It isn't a competition."

Yolanda hit Connie in the arm again. "You're such a hater since you and Preston got married. I'll be quiet, but I can't wait until after church."

"Help her Lord." Connie put her finger to her mouth and shushed Yolanda.

Reverend Franklin O'Neill raised the roof. The sermon touched hearts and souls and the service was high.

"The Lord gave him a good word...and a long one too," Yolanda complained to Connie under her breath.

"Isn't that why we come to service every Sunday... to get a good word, sister? Jesus, you should've stayed home if you didn't want to be here. Anyway, Franklin is finished. The doors to the church are open."

Yolanda and the rest of the congregation sang a hymn while they waited for people who wanted to join the church to come down front.

It was Connie's turn to hit Yolanda's arm. "Sis, did you see that?"

"Did I? Was that Linden I saw walking to the front of the church?"

"In the flesh."

"Q is probably peeing on herself. Linden is trying every trick in his sorry book to get Q back into his good graces."

"Do you think she'll fall for him again?"

"Connie, please. If Queenie Jackson is stupid enough to give dead-beat Linden Robinson any of her time, then she doesn't deserve Donald. But my girl is no fool; you've got to get permission to get next to the Queen. That arm is going to stay wrapped tight around Donald Griffin's arm. He treats her like a lady."

"And that rock she has on her finger is a true testament of his love for her."

"Church, our prodigal son has returned home," Reverend O'Neill said, holding Linden's hand up and interrupting Yolanda and Connie's train of thought. "Let's welcome Brother Linden Robinson by saying amen."

A thunderous crescendo of amens flooded the sanctuary.

"Q and Donald are slipping out the side door, YoYo. I wonder what that means."

"It means she doesn't want to face Linden and that she and her man were getting the hell out of here so there won't be any commotion. And I don't blame them."

"They had toxic relationship. I would've been stabbed Linden in the heart while kicking his ass out on the street."

"Listen to you, Connie. You're worse than I am. Remember, sis, we're in God's house."

The sisters were quiet, and baby Desi cooed. In the next fifteen minutes, they were dismissed.

CHAPTER FORTY-EIGHT

NOTHIN' BUT THE DEVIL

*Y*olanda rushed out of the church, leaving Connie and Preston behind. She had to find Queenie before they got away. She'd hoped they could all get together and have lunch before the brothers left.

She searched the yard, turning this way and that, but to her dismay, there was no sign of Queenie or Donald. Yolanda turned yet again and spotted Emma and Terrance out of the corner of her eyes and rushed to meet them.

Waving her hand, Yolanda caught Emma's attention. Out of breath, she settled down when she got near. "Hey, y'all, glad to see you."

"Good to see you, too, Yolanda," Terrance said, reaching over and giving her a kiss on the cheek.

"Hey, girl," Emma said.

"Are you all going out to eat?" Yolanda asked.

Emma looked up at Terrance and back at Yolanda. "I'm not sure what we're going to do. Have you seen Queenie and Donald?"

"I was looking for them, too. Look, if you have plans, I'll understand. You've got a nice smile... no glow on your face today, Emma."

"Thank you, YoYo. I'm sure my smile isn't any different from how it always is, although I'm happy that Terrance is here. We're an item again."

Yolanda hollered. "Emma, that's great. Terrance this is good news."

"Dang, YoYo, I didn't intend for the whole church world to know. Not that I'm keeping it on the low, but I don't want to be part of a three-ring circus either." Emma got closer to Yolanda. "Did you see Linden Robinson take his sorry-ass self to the altar? The embers are still burning bright on that hell-bound dog. He's only coming here to be a thorn in Queenie's side."

"Girl, I was about to die when I saw him walk to the front. I thought hell might open up and swallow him whole. If there's an ounce of remorse in his body about how he's treated Q in the past, I'm sure she's never heard the apology."

"Donald isn't going to stand on the sidelines and let some creep mess with his woman," Terrance said, jumping into the conversation. "And I'm his back-up."

Emma smiled. "Look, I'm sure we'll be eating something. We may have to ride with you since Q and Donald are nowhere to be found. Oh, my cell phone is ringing; it's Q."

Emma answered the phone, shook her head a few times, and listened some more before finally saying yes. "YoYo is here and we'll catch a ride with her." Pause. "Okay." Emma hung up the phone. "Q said to meet them at McCormick & Schmick's Seafood & Steaks. They wanted to avoid a potential confrontation with you know who."

"Got it. Let's go."

"Hey," the familiar voice boomed. As if by magic, Linden Robinson appeared from out of the shadows. "Where are you all running off to? Have you seen Q?"

"Look, buddy," Terrance said, moving in front of Emma and getting all up in Linden's face. "We don't want any trouble, and its best that you move along."

Linden's eyes traveled the length of Terrance's body. "Boo. Whoever you are, I'm not scared. And I wasn't talking to you anyway."

Linden punched Terrance in the chest with his finger. "My question was simple."

Terrance tried to remain calm. "Buster, I don't want to have to tell you again…"

"Hey, everybody," First Lady Jackie said, as she and Pastor O'Neill approached the group. "Isn't it a blessing that our brother, Linden, here has returned to the flock?"

"Praise God," Pastor O'Neill said.

Linden managed a fake smile. He gave Pastor O'Neill a fist bump and pecked First Lady on the cheek. "It's good to be back."

First Lady Jackie looked at her watch. "So where are you all going for lunch? I saw Q step out early." She tapped Emma on the shoulder. "She's probably trying to get in a few extra minutes of alone time with her fiancé."

"Could be," was all that Emma would say, looking between Yolanda and Terrance.

"Well, look, I'll be seeing y'all around," Linden said, giving Emma and Yolanda the V sign with his fingers, first pointing them at his eyes and then back at the two ladies.

"See you later, Linden. Glad to have you back among the worshippers." Pastor O'Neill shook Linden's hand, and Linden moved on.

"Whew," Yolanda said. "I'm glad he's gone."

First Lady Jackie put her hand on her hip. "Don't you all see that he's trying to get his life back on track?"

"Don't you see that he's trying to weasel his way back to Q?" Emma said sarcastically. "Drema D divorced his rusty butt, and now he thinks Q is going to drop everything and come back to him. He's still a heathen using the church as the tool to activate his plan."

"Emma, you're exaggerating. The Lord can change anyone, and that's what he's doing for Linden."

"Jackie, you're so naïve. Believe what you want, but I'm telling you, that fool isn't here to get closer to God."

"Okay, Sister Emma," Pastor O'Neill said, cutting into the conversation. "God knows Linden's heart best, and I trust that Linden's coming to the altar in front of all these worshippers today had nothing to do with Queenie. I'm surprised at you all, and God isn't pleased either."

"Let's go, Terrance…Yolanda."

"So, you all are going to lunch without us?" First Lady asked.

"Looks that way." Emma rolled her eyes and grabbed Terrance's arm and walked away with Yolanda tagging behind.

CHAPTER FORTY-NINE

THE TRUTH WILL SET YOU FREE

*D*ays and then weeks passed faster than Harrison could count. He had yet to tell Jefferey that he was leaving her. No time was the right time, but in less than a week and a half, he would be heading back overseas, and he wanted everything to be in order when that day came.

He'd already filed the papers with his attorney and had put off having them served for a few days. Opting out of doing it without witnesses, he invited Jefferey's parents over for Sunday dinner. He hadn't seen the elderly Jacksons in years, and he hated that he had to choose this route to make his plans known.

A good cook in his own rite, Harrison put the brisket that he had slow cooked on the grill for the past eleven hours on a carving board. He sliced it with the electric knife, placed it on a china platter and drizzled au jus over it. The meat was so tender that it fell onto the plate like velvet falling on top of velvet. Harrison was pleased. The meal was rounded off by garlic mashed potatoes, a sweet-potato souf-flé, grilled asparagus, tossed salad, and dinner rolls. Harrison purchased a deep-dish apple pie and vanilla-bean ice cream from the grocery store for dessert.

He didn't see her come into the room nor did he feel her upon him until her arms were wrapped around his waist from behind. She blew warm air on the back of his neck.

"Thank you for doing this, Harrison. It's been a long time since I've seen Momma and Daddy, and this dinner will hopefully be the thing that will get our family back on track."

Harrison didn't move or say anything. He hoped that she would remove her arms from around his waist without having to manually do it himself. He closed his eyes, prayed and asked God to give him the strength to make it through dinner. He prayed that Jefferey would accept what he was going to say. She needed help but after being away so long, he didn't have the wherewithal to stay around and subject himself to a woman with violent tendencies—a woman who nearly killed him fourteen years prior.

"It'll be good to see Marshall and Bertha. It's been…it's been…"

"Fourteen years." Jefferey removed her arms from around Harrison and stood beside him.

Harrison continued with what he was doing, without any eye contact Jefferey's way. "Yes, it's been fourteen years since I've seen them. I've always loved them, especially your dad. That man loved to fish."

"Well, I hope they've forgiven me for some things that I said and acted upon when I had one of my spells. I'm sure they were aware of what I was going through."

For the first time since Jefferey entered the kitchen, Harrison turned toward her. "Did you ever sit down and talk to them about it?"

"Not really. I hemmed and hawed about my illness, but I could never come out and say; I was in denial myself. There was no way to express to them what I didn't understand myself."

"H. J. told them some things. He was very upset with you at the time."

"You're bluffing. What could H. J. have said about his own mother?"

"You kept H. J. prisoner in his own home. You didn't allow him to have any friends. When you got angry, you beat up on him."

"It was all in the name of discipline, Harrison. I would never hurt H. J."

"He didn't quite see it that way." Harrison raised his hands. "Let's not talk about it; it's in the past. I don't want you to get upset before your parents come."

Little beads of sweat began to coat Jefferey's face. She threw her fists out and began to shake them. "I will not get upset. I will not get upset," she repeated over and over.

Harrison put his arm around her shoulder, hoping to calm her spirit. Her erratic breathing began to slow. She exhaled, picked up a napkin, and wiped her face.

"It's going to be alright." They both turned at the sound of the doorbell. "I'll get it, you relax.

The noise was inviting when it neared the living room. Mr. and Mrs. Jackson made their way through the foyer after giving Harrison their coats and hat. Jefferey watched as her parents moved through the hallway to where she was waiting.

They were old and moved slowly—her mother, Bertha, even more so under the weight of her body that had grown well out of proportion. Dad was feeble, almost to the point that he seemed to be holding on to her mother for dear life with one hand while tightly gripping a cane in the other. Dad wore a pair of overalls over a red-and-black plaid shirt. Momma wore a large colorful shift to accommodate her body size. Jefferey was saddened by the thought that she hadn't done anything in a long time to help her parents, even as minute as going to the grocery store, fixing them a nice meal, or nurturing them with a little TLC.

"Hi, Momma and Daddy," Jefferey said in a school girl's voice.

Her parents smiled back. "Hello, Jaybird," Marshall said, kissing his daughter on the cheek. "You're a sight for sore eyes. Wished it hadn't been so long since the last time we saw you, especially for your momma."

Jefferey managed a smile. "Me too. Momma, how are you doing?"

"It's been real tough. Your daddy's health is declining although he swears out that he's still tough as nails. As you can see, I need to lose some weight...well, maybe a whole lot of weight. It's been a struggle taking care of your daddy all by myself, but we're making it."

Jefferey could feel her inner turmoil begin to churn. They hadn't been in the house two good minutes before they started to complain. Sure, she asked them how they were doing, but damn, talk about cutting to the chase in under a minute. They definitely deserved a prize.

"Harrison and I will be here to assist you from here on out," Jefferey volunteered.

Harrison didn't say a word. His face was devoid of expression.

Bertha seemed pleased. "Well, that's good to hear. What is it that smells so good? Harrison did you cook your famous brisket?"

"You remembered after all these years."

"A stomach doesn't forget where the real chefs live. You were always a better cook than Jefferey." Jefferey frowned.

"Jefferey is a good cook, too, Mother Bertha," Harrison rushed to say. Jefferey smiled. "Why don't we all go to the dining room so we can eat? The food is hot, and I've got to say that I'm a little hungry too." Everyone laughed.

They sat at the table like a happy family and partook of the wonderful meal that Harrison had prepared. "May I have another glass of wine?" Bertha asked.

"Anything for you, Mother Bertha," Harrison said, pouring Pinot Grigio into her wine glass.

"I can't get over it," Marshall said shaking his head. "There's nothing like a change of heart—you and Jaybird working it out. That's great."

"Why can't you believe it, Daddy?" Jefferey wanted to know. "Harrison is my husband. Even after a fourteen year separation, we're still married."

"Because I spoke with H. J. only two days ago and he said that his daddy was going to divorce his mother."

Deathly silence pierced the room. Marshall took a sip of his wine and burped. When no one replied, he got another piece of brisket and a roll and began to eat.

CHAPTER FIFTY

HELP IS ON THE WAY

*S*ilence ensued. Bertha wiped her mouth with a napkin after consuming the last bit of her Pinot Grigio. Marshall was still nursing his pie and ice cream when all of a sudden Jefferey stood up from her seat.

"Is it true, Harrison? Is it true that you're planning to divorce me?"

Harrison exhaled and continued to sit in his seat, deliberately not looking at Jefferey.

Blam. Everyone jumped when both of Jefferey's fists hit the table. The china levitated and fell back down, and the silverware made a musical sound as it danced across empty plates. "Damn it, I want an answer now. Did you plan this charade to benefit me or yourself? Answer me, damn it."

"Sit down, Jefferey," Harrison said, still sitting in his seat. "This dinner wasn't for the purpose of exploiting what you've been through. I was hoping it would bring the family together."

Jefferey sat down. "So, are you saying that H. J. told Daddy a lie… that there's no truth to it at all?"

Harrison dropped his head. "H. J. wasn't lying. I do plan to file for divorce…in fact, I've already filed. I'll be leaving for Afghanistan in a week and a half."

Jumping up from her seat again, Jefferey lashed out. "You sorry bastard! You come riding up to Queenie's in your golden chariot like you were coming to rescue me, when all along you were rescuing that evil witch, Queenie, from me. How did she know you were in town? The both of you were probably in cahoots with each other all this time." Jefferey ran into the kitchen and came back with a butcher knife.

"Okay, Jaybird, we've had enough. Let's talk like civilized adults."

"Shut up, Daddy. You've always sided with Harrison. I'm your damn daughter; he's only the man I married. Maybe you haven't noticed, but we aren't civilized adults. Husband's don't treat their wives the way Harrison has done me."

"Baby," Bertha said, cutting in. "Maybe there's a reason Harrison is acting the way he does. You need some help."

"You, too, Momma? I can't believe y'all. Nobody has tried to understand what I'm going through. All I do is give, give, give, and you take, take, take and take some more." Jefferey placed the knife under her chin, and everyone gasped. "I'm through with all of you. I've had it up to here."

Harrison got up from his seat and moved toward Jefferey.

"Step back, motherf'er," Jefferey shouted, waving the knife.

"Jaybird, what's wrong with you?"

"Do you want some of this too, Daddy?" Jefferey moved in Marshall's direction.

Bertha screamed. "Get her away from Marshall. She's crazy."

"I'll show you crazy," Jefferey screamed out as she moved toward her mother.

In the next instant, Harrison grabbed both wrists. "Jesus," he hollered, as Jefferey stabbed him in the arm. He loosened his grip on her to nurse his wound. "Bitch, you won't get a chance to do it again."

"This time, I'm going to kill your ass."

Blood oozed down Harrison's arm and onto the carpet. With all the strength he had in his arm, he pushed Jefferey back and then slapped her across her face. Jefferey stumbled back, almost losing her footing. Harrison got a linen napkin from the table and wrapped it around his arm.

Like a raging bull, she was back, steady on her feet and ready to do damage. Welding the knife over her head, she dared anyone to step to her. Terrified, Marshall and Bertha squeezed into a corner of the room, their faces twisted in fright.

Jefferey's face was red with rage. Blue veins stuck out of her neck like schematics on a circuit board. She looked like a samurai warrior ready for battle. Harrison pleaded with Jefferey to put the knife down, but the only thing coming down was the water that seemed to pour out of her pores. And then she charged at Harrison, and he stepped out of the way. Jefferey and the knife landed in the wall.

"Help," Bertha called out. "Help, something is wrong with Marshall. He's slumped to the floor."

Harrison ran to Bertha's side and fell down on his knees to help Marshall. He felt for a pulse, but it was faint. "Call nine-one-one."

"I think it's his heart," Bertha called out. "He has a bad heart, Harrison."

"We're going to get him some help. My phone is right there on the table. Hand it to me."

Bertha rushed to the table, dialed nine-one-one and handed the phone to Harrison. He talked with the nine-one-one dispatcher and gave them the address. Momentarily, Jefferey was forgotten until she was back on her feet, still holding the now bent up knife in her hand.

It was time for Bertha to take control of the situation. She stood tall and still. Her girth guarded the area where Marshall lay. "Come on over here so I can knock some sense into your crazy ass. Yes, I said it. I'm sure it wouldn't matter to you if you beat up your momma, but we've had enough of your foolishness, and if you want to step to me, I can dance with you. Ali wasn't the only one who could dance in a ring."

Jefferey stared at the woman in front of her, the woman who bore her, the woman who set her free from her womb. With a crazed look on her face, Jefferey took a step forward while still holding on to the butcher knife, and Bertha took a step back. "Momma, are you for real? You'd treat your own daughter like this?"

Bertha began to cry. "I love you, Jefferey. I've always loved you, in spite of all the hurtful things you've done to us, Harrison, and H. J. over the years. You're the one who's refused help when we tried to get it for you. We're old now and barely able to help ourselves." Bertha's hand went up and began to point. "Your daddy is lying over there unconscious, but it's still all about you."

"It's never about me. No one cares what happens to me. You all discarded me when I was no longer useful to you."

"You're a lie and the truth ain't in you, child. Shut up that foolish talking."

"His pulse is still there, Mother Bertha," Harrison said, ignoring Jefferey. "I hear the ambulance now." Harrison continued to hold Marshall in his arms. "Help is on the way."

CHAPTER FIFTY-ONE

DON'T MAKE ME HAVE TO BEG

One of the paramedics placed a tourniquet around Harrison's arm to stop the profuse bleeding. The other two were already on their way to the ambulance with Marshall in tow.

With his back turned to Jefferey, Harrison whispered to the paramedic. "I need a psychiatric physician with a straightjacket." His eyes rolled back into his head.

The paramedic noticed Jefferey for the first time. Jefferey was still holding the knife in her hand, watching the action taking place in front of her.

"Do you want to ride to the hospital in the ambulance?" the paramedic finally said, taking his eyes off of Jefferey and meeting Harrison's head on. There was a frown on the paramedics face—a frown that had worry written in it.

"I'll be okay. If you take care of that little thing for me, I'd appreciate it. I'll come to the hospital once that business is taken care of."

"You sure?" the paramedic asked again, taking a parting glance at Jefferey.

"I'm sure. Since my mother-in-law is riding in the ambulance with her husband, I'll be alright staying here."

"Okay. I've got to go."

The paramedic exited the house and ran to the ambulance that zoomed off to its destination, once he was in it.

"So," Jefferey began, "look what you caused. Because of your selfish desire to be rid of me, you caused my daddy to have a heart attack."

Harrison ignored Jefferey. He went into the dining room and began to stack the dirty dishes on the table. Jefferey followed him, the knife still in her hand.

"We're alone. Please make love to me. I'll forgive all that happened today, if you would make love to me like we did when we first met." Jefferey placed the knife on the table. "I need your love, Harrison. I love you from the depths of my soul; I need you to love me."

Jefferey sat in one of the chairs and broke down in tears. She covered her face with her hands and cried. "I need love. I need someone to love me. Harrison, please make love to me."

Harrison stopped what he was doing and looked at Jefferey. She was a pitiful sight, but the love he once had was no longer housed in his heart.

"It pains me to say this, Jefferey, but I don't need your kind of love. I've loved you for most of my life, but I can't do it anymore. You're the mother of my child, the one gift that I'll never regret, but this—you and I—are over."

Harrison waited for Jefferey to retaliate, but she kept sitting and balling. Clinching his lips together, Harrison went and stood behind Jefferey. He rubbed her shoulders while keeping a watchful eye on the knife that sat close to her hand. He prayed that the psychiatric team would arrive soon, but until that time he had to make do.

"I need love. I need you to love me, Harrison." Jefferey pushed back in her seat and stood. She turned around and put her arms around her husband. "Please don't make me have to beg. I want you to make love to me. Right here, right now."

Harrison sighed, pulling on the tourniquet that was still wrapped around his arm. He looked into her waiting eyes and brought his lips to hers and kissed her for the first time in years.

Jefferey was greedy, taking advantage of the moment. Harrison tried to hold back, but Jefferey was all over him. So he kissed her, rough and tough liked she liked. Her hands traveled over his chest, causing her to make audible, sexy innuendos that only Harrison could hear. Grabbing Harrison's buttocks, Jefferey pushed her body up against his, sucking up all of the air that was between them.

As much as Harrison hated being nestled up against his wife, his growing member wouldn't obey. It responded wholesomely to the warm body that rubbed up against it. There was no way on God's green earth that he was going to step out of his clothes for some sexual R&R, even though the heat between his legs had become so intense that it might have been cause to reconsider. "Resist, resist," he muttered to himself.

"Harrison, baby, I know you want me. I feel your hardness against my leg. Oh, baby, make love to me now."

Jefferey released his buttocks and began to undress herself. Just as she was pulling the straps down on her bra, there was a knock at the door.

"What was that?" Jefferey asked in a panic.

"It's the door. Let me get it. The neighbors probably saw the ambulance and are curious."

"Let them knock. They've interrupted a beautiful thing."

"There it is again. Let me get it and send them on their way."

"If you have to, but hurry back."

Harrison hurried to the door and opened it. Two guys in white medical uniforms stood on the front porch with a gurney in between them. A patrol car was also pulling into the driveway. Harrison smiled within; he'd been saved.

"Are you Mr. Quick?"

"Yes."

"We're here from Carolinas Medical Center to pick up a patient for psychiatric evaluation."

Without flinching, Harrison stretched out his hand. "This way; follow me."

The medics followed Harrison into the foyer.

"Who was that?" Jefferey asked from the dining room, her breasts now free and dangling as she entered the foyer. She stopped in her tracks when she spotted the medics, covered her breasts with her arms, and screamed. "Noooooo. Noooooo. I'm not going anywhere with them."

"I'm sorry, Jefferey…"

Before another syllable dropped from Harrison's mouth, she turned and ran. Following Harrison, the medics ran after Jefferey. One carried a straightjacket in his hand. They cornered her, and she looked like she was portraying a scene from *The Rocky Horror Picture Show*.

"Don't touch me." Jefferey's hands were up in the air, covering her face. Her hair was wild about her head, and her breasts were still free to roam the universe.

A male medic reached out and grabbed one arm, but was unable to keep her from hitting him. The other attendant caught Jefferey's arm, and by some miracle, the straightjacket was on in under two minutes. Two police officers, who'd just entered the house, were there to assist.

Jefferey growled at Harrison. "You will pay. You will pay. You've betrayed me. You betrayed us. You will pay."

Harrison looked at her without saying a word. The medics strapped her to the gurney and got ready to leave.

"Is that it Mr. Quick?" the older of the medics asked.

"Yes. Now I have to get to the hospital pronto. Not only have I got to see about my father-in-law, I have a wound to be looked at."

"Good luck with that."

With pad and pen in hand the black police officer watched as Jefferey was wheeled away and turned back to Harrison. He noticed for the first time the blood-soaked tourniquet around Harrison's arm. "I need to ask you a few questions; I'll make it quick."

"You saw for yourself, officer. The woman, my soon-to-be ex-wife, is crazy. She has mental problems and I hope she stays locked up this time. She lost it again today; I'm through."

"I hear you dawg." The officer gave Harrison a fist bump. He took Harrison's information and then he and his partner were on their way.

CHAPTER FIFTY-TWO

NINE, ONE, ONE, WHAT'S YOUR EMERGENCY

*L*unch was enjoyable. The two couples—Queenie and Donald; Emma and Terrance—plus Yolanda swapped stories and laughed the afternoon away. Queenie was in seventh heaven. She was going to be married in three months, and the man she was to marry was a supreme gift from God.

Queenie was happy for Emma, also. It had been hard on her after Billy's death, and now that she and Terrance had rekindled their friendship, Queenie was hopeful that something would come of it. While Emma would never admit it, she was needy and had always depended upon Billy to make her whole.

"Linden thought he was slick today. Everybody knows what his MO is," Yolanda said.

"Phsssh. If he has any thought of ever being with me again, his head is permanently twisted. Linden is evil and I guess Drema D finally realized that she was the one left holding the lemon."

"I hear you on that, Q," Emma interjected. "I mean… to come into God's house and perpetrate a fraud. It's an abomination. He was asking for God to slap his ass down."

The girls laughed. "And did you hear Jackie trying to defend him?"

"I was some kinda of pissed about that, YoYo. You should've heard her, Q. She acted as if she didn't remember all the trifling things he'd done to you. Nothing about him coming to the altar today displayed that his heart was in the right place."

"Emma, I'm glad Donald was sitting next to me. It was all I could do to keep from getting up and going to where he stood and shake the devil out of him."

"Q, you ought to quit," Yolanda said. "That would've been a sight."

"As long as he doesn't step to my fiancé," Donald added, "I'm good. The brother no longer has jurisdiction here."

"You go, Donald," Emma said, laughing along with the others.

"I won't see you all next weekend," Yolanda volunteered. "I'm flying out to New York on Friday evening."

"YoYo met this younger man," Queenie explained to Donald. "She's one of our fast sisters—praise the Lord one minute and chase a nigga down the next."

"Dang, Q, that depiction wasn't representative of me at all. You make me sound like a…"

"Like a hoochie mama," Emma exclaimed, laughing at her own analogy. "She's really a love them and leave them kind of girl."

"Alright now. I've had a pleasant afternoon, a good meal, and I'm not about to play raunchy with y'all. Gentleman, how your women have portrayed me isn't realistic or should I say characteristic of the woman I am. It's hard to find a good man, as both Q and Emma know, and I'm weighing my options and throwing the bad catches back into the sea."

Donald and Terrance laughed. "You're funny, YoYo," Donald said. "I've been around you long enough to know who you are, and I agree, you're not the portrait they painted."

"Don't let her fool you, baby," Queenie said. "That's my girl, though. And if she wants to be a cougar, more power to her. As long as the man treats her with respect and dignity, I'm down with it."

"Thanks, Q. I appreciate that vote of confidence. I've got a young constitution; there ain't nothin' dead about this sister."

Everyone roared with laughter and slapped high-fives.

"My cell is ringing," Queenie said, reaching into her bag. "I wonder who it could be."

"All I'm saying is that it better not be that old playa, ex-boyfriend of yours."

Queenie smiled at Donald. "Since I changed my cell number a while ago, Mr. Linden Robinson has no way to contact me. And, he's been snatched from the database. Let me get this call; it's a Charlotte number." Queenie hit the TALK button. "Hello?"

"Queenie, this is Bertha."

"Bertha Jackson?"

"Yes," she said somberly.

"Is something wrong with Jefferey?" Queenie could hear sorrow in her voice and could tell she'd been crying. "What is it?"

"It's Marshall…your dad. He's had a massive heart attack today and they don't expect him to live. The doctors are doing everything they can. He's asking for you."

Queenie grabbed her heart and started rocking back and forth. "Oh my God. Jesus, don't let nothing happen to my daddy."

"What's wrong?" Donald asked concerned.

Queenie began to take in big gulps of air. "Uhh, Bertha, I'll be there right away. Where are Jefferey and Harrison?"

"Harrison is here. Jefferey…"

"What's wrong with Jefferey?"

"I'll tell you the whole sordid story when you get here. Queenie, I'd be lost without Marshall. Please come as fast as you can."

"I'm on my way."

The stoic group watched as Queenie threw her cell phone in her purse. "I've got to go guys. My dad had a massive heart attack and isn't expected to live."

"I'm going with you," Emma said, snatching up her purse. "You don't need to be there by yourself."

"Terrance and I are both going," Donald interjected. Not wasting another moment, he was on his feet. "We'll take you ladies home so you can grab a suitcase and we're going to the hotel and get our things."

"I can drive Q and Emma home," Yolanda volunteered. "That way you and Terrance can go straight to the hotel and get your things and meet over at Queenie's. I won't be going, but my prayers are going up right now."

"Let's move," Queenie said. "This is an emergency."

CHAPTER FIFTY-THREE

TIME IS OF THE ESSENCE

*T*he silence was deafening. No one spoke and the radio was silent. Cars whizzed by going to their various destinations, and Queenie stared out of the window with a worried look on her face.

"Lord, there must be an accident up ahead," Donald said. "I can't believe that we're almost in Charlotte and now the freeway is backed up."

"Let's get off," Queenie said, her voice slightly above a whisper. "I've got to get to my dad. He's calling for me."

"We're going to get there. Look for an alternate route on your phone's navigator, Terrance."

"I was in the process of doing that, bro. Here we go."

"We need to go to Carolinas Medical Center on Blythe Boulevard."

"Got it, Queenie," Terrance said. "We don't have far to go."

Queenie sat back without responding. Emma held Queenie's hand while the guys kept their eyes on the road. The silence in the car darkened the mood until Donald let it be known that they had arrived at their destination.

Before the car had come to a complete stop, Queenie's hand was on the door and the next second she was out. Emma exited on the other side and chased behind Queenie until she caught up with her. Donald and Terrance were close behind.

Queenie dialed Bertha's number and within fifteen minutes, Bertha was standing in the lobby. As if they were long-lost sisters, Queenie ran into Bertha's arms that she wrapped tightly around her. The two were sobbing, sobbing for a man they both loved, although Queenie hadn't said so in years.

Finally parting, Queenie introduced Bertha to the group and followed her to and into the elevator. The group was quiet—Emma, Donald, and Terrance observing Queenie with a watchful eye. Queenie's fingers were intertwined with Bertha's and the soft purring of words of prayer under their breaths was the only audible thing anyone heard.

The elevator chimed and Bertha pushed her body forward and exited it. The group followed without a word. As big as Bertha was, she moved at lightning speed, as if she was going to miss a train that was getting ready to take off. When they reached the waiting room, Queenie saw Harrison, who stood when the group approached.

He sighed and shook his head. Hugging Queenie, he looked her in the eye and turned to Bertha. "No word yet. I've been sitting here and praying that Dad will be okay. Right now, no news is good news."

Bertha threw up her hands to heaven. "Lord, look after my husband in there. Guide the doctor's hand. Restore my Marshall to good health. In your name, Jesus, I ask right now. Amen." Tears rolled down Bertha's face and she took a seat.

The agonizing hours stretched on. Donald soothed Queenie as best he could. While Queenie hadn't cried openly, the tears continued to fall from her face. Donald's arm hadn't left Queenie's shoulders and Emma held her hand like there was no tomorrow. Bertha cried herself to sleep while leaning on Harrison's shoulders.

It was well into the night when the doctor made an appearance. He seemed drained and his blue scrubs were well worn. He made a beeline to Bertha, who jumped up from her seat when she saw him approach.

"Dr. Sutton, how's my husband? Is he alright?" Bertha's eyes were pleading for good news. "Oh, and this is Marshall's daughter, Queenie Jackson." The doctor nodded his head.

The others stood and waited for the verdict, holding on to each other for support.

Dr. Sutton stretched his arms in a downward motion. His head dropped a little and he squeezed his lips together. That was not a good sign.

"He didn't make it."

Before the last syllable was out of Dr. Sutton's mouth, wailing sounds spread throughout the floor. Bertha collapsed to the floor and Queenie cried and screamed while holding her face up with her hands.

"I'm so sorry," Dr. Sutton offered. But no one was listening. He stood by and waited for the cries to subside.

Harrison picked Bertha up from the floor and fanned. Dr. Sutton called for a nurse to bring some smelling salt. Clasping his hands behind him, Dr. Sutton backed up a few feet to give the family their moment to grieve.

Tear stained, Queenie uncovered her face and looked at the doctor. "I'd like to see my daddy." She turned to Bertha. "If you don't mind, Bertha, I'd like to see him by myself."

"Follow me," Dr. Sutton said.

Queenie followed Dr. Sutton, her heart pounding hard in her chest. The past forty-something of her years passed by—the years she spent hating her father when all he wanted to do was love her, even though he and her mother weren't together.

She thought about all the times she'd promised that she was going to let bygones be bygones and reach out to him, call him and ask for forgiveness. She thought about all the times he'd call and left messages but she was too stubborn and ornery to call back. She remembered the times that he'd sent birthday and Christmas wishes, money for school and other things, but she hadn't once said thank you. The few times they were in each other's presence, she was a bitch with a capital B. And now the father that she loved in secret would never know how she really felt...how much she loved him.

The doors to the operating room were ahead. She balked when they were on top of it. Marshall had been moved to another room just off the emergency room. Queenie followed the doctor when she felt she was ready.

"Daddy, I love you," Queenie cried. She went to where his body lay and kissed his face. She reached down to try and hug him, but the attending nurse pulled her back. "I love you, Daddy. I wish you could hear the sound of my voice. I hope you knew that the love was there."

Queenie sobbed and finally fled the room, unable to stay another minute. She found a wall, leaned up against it, and cried until there were no more tears.

When she decided to walk back to the waiting room, Bertha passed her as she walked in to see her husband. At that moment, Queenie hated herself...hated herself for being a bitter old woman. She wanted to blame it on her mother, but she was an adult and had no one to blame but herself.

Donald wrapped his arms around Queenie when she returned to the waiting room. Nothing was said. Queenie sunk into the chair next to Donald and cried some more.

CHAPTER FIFTY-FOUR

SHE DID WHAT?

*U*pon Bertha's return, the group gathered their things to leave.

"You can all stay at the house," Harrison said, eager to accommodate.

Queenie stopped in her tracks and turned to look at Harrison. "Where in the world is Jefferey? No one has mentioned her name since we arrived."

A somber look crossed Harrison's face. He looked in the direction of his mother-in-law and then back at Queenie. "She's here in the hospital."

"Here... for what?"

"She's being evaluated." Harrison sighed.

"Did she have a breakdown because of what happened to Daddy?"

"She is the reason your daddy is here in the first place," Bertha said, taking control of the conversation. "Let's not talk about Jefferey right now. If we do, it might cause me to roll right up to the Psychiatric Ward and choke her mean ass to death."

"What are you talking about, Bertha?"

"Queenie, let it rest until we get to the house. Harrison and I will explain everything."

Queenie sighed, not liking one word of what Bertha was saying. She looked back and forth between Harrison and Bertha but couldn't figure out what all the secrecy was about Jefferey's hospitalization.

"Alright, but as soon as we get to Jefferey's house, I want an explanation."

"You'll get it," Harrison said, bluntly.

The somber group left the hospital quietly. Besides Queenie giving Donald the address to put in his GPS, no one uttered a word. Although they followed behind Harrison, there was something soothing about letting the white lady from the navigator tell them which way to turn. And when the silence had become too much, Queenie asked the first question.

"What do you all think is the big secret they're keeping about Jefferey?"

"Will find out soon enough," Donald said. "There's no need to speculate when the answer will be forthcoming as soon as we reach our destination, which, according to GPS is under ten minutes."

Looking out into the dark night, Queenie sighed. "If Jefferey had anything to do with my daddy's death, I will kill her myself."

"Come on, Q," Emma said. "That's anger talking; you aren't going to kill anyone."

"Emma, you've done a good job keeping your mouth shut. Don't get on my last nerve."

"You aren't going to kill anyone either. Jefferey is sick, and if she had anything to do with your father's death, she'll have to pay for it."

Queenie sucked in hard and bit her tongue. She knew Emma was right and the last thing she wanted to do was take the bitterness and anger that squeezed her heart out on her friend. "I'm sorry, E. Seeing my daddy today...lying dead on that table got the best of me. The person I should blame is myself." Queenie huffed. "I wasn't a good daughter..."

"Come on, Q. You handled your relationship with your father the best you knew how."

"Did I, E? I'm a grown-ass woman who knows right from wrong. Regardless of how angry my mother was for my father leaving us, he never disowned me. I keep playing it over and over in my head the many times Daddy tried to reach out to me, but my stubborn ass refused. I killed him as much as Jefferey may have, if that's what their little secret is. Why else would she be at the hospital for an evaluation?"

"We're almost there," Donald said. "Let's not jump to conclusions until they tell us what happened. There's a logical explanation; hopefully it's not one you'll regret to hear."

"Why do you always try to be the voice of reason?"

"Q, that's who I am and that won't change."

"Change is good, but I'll take you the way you are, Mr. Griffin. I do have one regret, though. I regret the fact that I didn't make it in time to tell Daddy how much I loved him."

There wasn't much to see in the dead of night. The motion sensor that came on when they crossed it offered some light in which to see by. Jefferey and Harrison's house was a large two-story brick home. Although the home was twenty years old, it seemed to still be in good shape.

Everyone piled inside and Queenie took the liberty to look around and gawk. It was the first time that she'd been in Jefferey's house. While it was an older house, it appeared to have had some upgrades, as the kitchen was furnished with stainless steel appliances that looked fairly new, which wasn't the fad at the time the house was built. And the furniture was modern, almost as if the plastic had been torn off months ago. The thing that made Queenie raise her eyebrows was how clean the house was. Jefferey hadn't lifted a finger to help her in the couple of months she'd been with her, but in her house, Queenie could smell the oil that had been rubbed into the rich wood and the carpet fresh that gave off a nice, flowery smell.

"Would anyone like something to drink?" Harrison asked the group. "I have Coke, Sprite, water, sweet tea…and the hard stuff if you like. I sure could use a stiff drink."

"Water for me," both Donald and Terrance said.

As bad as Queenie wanted a Long Island Ice Tea, she settled for a Coke.

"I'll have coffee, although I could swallow a whole bottle of that good wine you had earlier," Bertha said, not caring what the others thought.

Harrison left, returned with a few glasses of liquid that he passed out, and headed back into the kitchen. "Coffee coming up for Mother Bertha and Emma."

It had been years since Queenie had even spoken to Bertha. The short communication today about Queenie's dad being ill was the most the two had said to each other in years. It was obvious that Bertha loved her father and that her heart was hurting and yearning for him, but she wasn't sure what to say to her.

Bertha opened her mouth, seemingly sensing Queenie's dilemma. "Your dad loved you, Queenie." Bertha turned her head away and wiped a tear. "He talked about you all the time." *Sniff.* "He was so proud when you went to work for the paper as an editor; in fact he thought for sure that you'd be writing your own novel soon."

The revelation caught Queenie off guard. If she had a relationship with her father, she would've known this. "I never knew."

"Don't beat yourself up about it. He told me on a few occasions that he also loved your mother, but whatever it was that tore them apart, he couldn't deal with it. He hated that your mother didn't allow him to come near you."

Bertha's words tore at Queenie's heart. Guilt had clouded any remote chance for her and her father to reconcile, although she had wanted to in the worst way. She pretended in front of everyone that she didn't care about her father. The hurt was deep, but in her heart of hearts, she loved him. Normally, she would've chewed Bertha out for talking about her mother in that condescending way, but in truth, Queenie's mother was selfish, and if she couldn't have her father, her father wasn't going to get the opportunity to see his firstborn grow up. And he didn't.

"What happened today, Bertha? What caused Daddy to have a heart attack? I had no idea that his heart was that fragile."

"He's had heart problems for some time. The old ticker was getting weak, but that didn't stop him. He had a zest for life and whatever he could muster up enough strength to do, he did it. Sometimes he got along better than I did."

"So what happened, Bertha? What happened today?"

Queenie watched Bertha as she turned and looked at Harrison. It was apparent that something had gone awfully wrong and Queenie wanted the truth.

Harrison put his drink down on the coffee table and went and sat on the edge of the sofa where Queenie and Donald were sitting. "As you are aware, Jefferey is a very sick woman. I invited Mother Bertha and Dad over for lunch today to bridge the gap between them. Jefferey hasn't always been the model daughter as she has let on, and we've come to realize that a lot of the discord is due to the sickness. But today didn't go well."

"But I thought she was making progress."

"She seemed to be, Q. After that fiasco coming from Raleigh where Jefferey ended up being held for observation, she seemed to be herself. But today we saw another side of her." Harrison sighed. "Dad shared something with her that made her go off. He'd talked to H. J. a few days ago, and H. J. told him that I was getting a divorce."

Queenie looked puzzled. She looked at her friend, Emma, who was curled up in the corner of the loveseat being the supportive person she always was. Emma had a weird look on her face also. In the few conversations Queenie had with Harrison, he never once mentioned that he was planning to divorce Jefferey, although she thought they were already. Maybe it was a decision he'd made in the past few days, but for sure, Queenie didn't see it coming. "So what did that have to do with Daddy?"

Sadness was etched in Harrison's face. Everyone watched as he fought back tears. He tried to speak but couldn't get anything to come out of his mouth. Queenie squeezed his hand.

"Jefferey lost it. She got a kitchen knife and stabbed me in the arm."

"She did what?"

217

Harrison held up his arm to show them the bandage that was wrapped around it. "She shouted and screamed at all of us, and we were somewhat afraid for our lives."

Seeming to feel more confident about what she had to say, Bertha took over the conversation. "Your dad asked her to stop and she tried to get close to him, wielding that dangerous weapon in the air and shouting for him to shut up. Harrison tried to stop her and then I noticed that your father had fallen to the floor gasping for breath. I shouted for help and Harrison tried to assist. He called the ambulance. The next thing I knew, I was riding in the ambulance hospital at your father's side."

"I called the mental health division at the hospital," Harrison interjected, "and had them to pick her up. They're going to render their decision more than likely tomorrow."

No one had noticed that Queenie was numb. It was as if she was there but again she wasn't. All of a sudden she got up from her seat and began to walk back and forth in front of the group without saying a word. Halfway during her next revolution, she abruptly turned and faced the group with tears rolling down her face. Pointing her finger in the air, Queenie became unglued and now more defiant. "She robbed me of my father. I gave her a home, a safe haven from whatever was ailing her from the time she landed on my doorstep, although I hadn't seen her in years. She blamed me for our torn relationship when all the time it was that bitch who's been the selfish one." This time, Queenie threw her fists in the air. "I hate her, and I don't want to ever see that bitch again."

Donald rushed to Queenie's side, held her, and let her cry until she had cried her last tear.

CHAPTER FIFTY-FIVE

NEW YORK CITY, HERE I COME

*D*ressed in a red, lightweight-wool, two-piece pantsuit and beige calf-skin boots, Yolanda sat patiently at the terminal gate, as she waited to board the plane. The week hadn't gone by fast enough, but the time had finally arrived.

There was an explanation as to why Yolanda was in seventh heaven and anxious to get to New York as fast as the jet could fly. She could play it off and say that she'd met a really nice man, whose company she rather enjoyed. However, the truth was in the pudding. Yolanda had fallen in love with a man in a matter of weeks—a man she barely knew and was seven years her junior. Don't mention her heart that kept tripping over itself, as the desire to be with her friend and lover was so strong.

Yolanda was a little down in the dumps upon arrival at Raleigh/Durham Airport, but once the ticket agent announced that boarding would begin in a few minutes, she was okay. Earlier that evening, she and Queenie had serious words. There was nothing Yolanda could do to rearrange her trip in order to attend Queenie's father's funeral. In her hand was a non-refundable ticket, and she was going to use it. Preston and Connie would represent their family.

"We're now boarding First Class and all passengers who need assistance at this time," the ticket agent announced.

Yolanda was up and out of her seat. Stefan had purchased a first-class ticket for her; she was loving and living every moment of her new-found status.

Comfortable in her first-class seat, she took her cell phone out of her purse to change it to airplane mode. Before she was able to do so, it rang. Not wasting a moment's time, she clicked the ON key and smiled. "Hey, baby, I'm on the plane."

"I'm as anxious for you to get here. We're going to have a fabulous time, and you'll get to meet my parents. My mother will be performing a few sets tomorrow night, and I can't wait for you to hear her."

"I'm ready, Stefan. I've been ready since you said you wanted me to come. Queenie is a little upset with me though. Her father had a heart attack last weekend, and he'll be funeralized tomorrow. My heart goes out to her and her family."

"We'll have to send flowers."

"I've already taken care of that."

"That's why I fell in love with you. You're smart, beautiful, and definitely on top of things."

"I will be on top of you in the next hour or so."

Stefan laughed. "And I'll let you. Have a safe flight. See you in a few."

"Smooches." Yolanda ended the call, set the phone on airplane mode, threw it in her purse and smiled. She didn't care what anyone thought of her relationship with Stefan, he was the man she wanted to be with.

She sat back in her seat and waited for the other passengers to be seated. And then they were off into the wild blue yonder.

CHAPTER FIFTY-SIX

HOMEGOING

*P*ain, stress, and anger lined the stoic faces of the grieving family, as they marched into the church. Mourners came from all over Charlotte to bid their farewells to a small man but a well-loved and respected one in the community. The church that Marshall Jackson had answered the call to the Lord in and served as a deacon for many, many years was much too small for his services. One of the larger churches in the community opened their doors for his Homegoing.

Queenie couldn't believe that so many people had shown up for her father's funeral. The men and women were dressed in their finery, almost as if they were from aristocratic families, such as the Queen City suggested. It was a proud moment but one that Queenie couldn't fully relish in. Her lost years getting to know her father were gone forever, and she felt like a fool...no, a hypocrite, sitting on the front row next to her stepmother and Donald, as if she had adored her father all her life like it was nobody's business.

Flowers were placed all along the front with their condolences expressing sweet sorrow. Queenie smiled and admired the beautiful spray of white and red roses—the red in the shape of a heart that was draped on her daddy's coffin. She had picked it out herself with no protest from Bertha. The brief time that she and Bertha shared since Marshall's death, Queenie wished she'd gotten to know her sooner. Bertha was a decent and beautiful woman inside, although she'd spawned a demon child.

Queenie was adamant about Jefferey not coming to the funeral, but at Harrison's insistence and after he spoke with the doctor, she agreed to let Jefferey come. Who was Queenie anyway to not allow her sister to see their father one more time? She hadn't been a model daughter either. But it would take only one misstep and Queenie would be all over Jefferey's ass—funeral or no funeral, public or private.

Co-workers from the Raleigh News and Observer and many of Harrison and Jefferey's friends were there. Emma and Terrance, Connie and Preston, Pastor and First Lady O'Neill were also there to lend support. But Queenie was some kind of pissed when Yolanda refused to postpone her trip to New York and support her during this time of grief.

Shaking her conversation with Yolanda from her mind, Queenie drew her head back when she saw H. J. come in. He hadn't come to Charlotte until now, stating that he couldn't handle his grandfather's death.

H. J. was as tall as his daddy and had all of Harrison's features. He was handsome, and if he hadn't been her nephew, as well as too young to touch, Queenie would've had to do a Yolanda—be a cougar. There wasn't a trace of Jefferey embedded in her son, as far as Queenie could see, although there were faint, microscopic similarities, if she was fair in her assessment. H. J. was quiet, but he had a beautiful, dark-skinned girl wrapped around his arms, her silky mane twisting and turning about her head with enough body in it to give to four other people.

The Homegoing service was beautiful. The eulogy was insightful and touched almost every soul in the building. Every now and then, Queenie wiped tears from her eyes. She'd never get the opportunity to say what was really in heart to her father. It hurt even more when all the people who came up to speak said nothing but good and kind things about him.

It was time to view the body one more time. Marshall Jackson looked peaceful...like he was taking a nap. As the eldest child, Queenie was first to view him with Donald by her side. She touched him and threw him a kiss. "Goodbye, Daddy. I love you."

It was equally hard on Bertha, who couldn't stop touching him. She wept openly and almost collapsed on top of Marshall. Several nurses ran to assist with a box of tissue in one of the nurse's hand. They helped Bertha back to her seat where she continued to weep.

All was silent when Jefferey got up from her seat. Henderson stood next to her, holding her up like the foundation to her frame. Jefferey inched her way to the casket, her once silent voice becoming large moans.

"Daddy, Daddy," she screamed to the top of her lungs.

A hushed whisper fell over the church and a nurse rushed to Jefferey and began to fan.

"Daddy, I'm so sorry. I'm so sorry for all the heartache I caused you. Daddy, I love you, don't go."

Jefferey held on to the side of the casket, while Harrison tried to ease her back to her seat. She shrugged his hands from her shoulders and began screaming and crying at the same time. Even bubbles formed outside of her nose.

"Daddy, I want to go with you. Don't leave me. I love you." And then Jefferey tried to climb into the casket.

Harrison grabbed her around the waist and tried to pry her hands from the top of the casket. The funeral director ran to the front to assist Harrison. Bertha was on her feet, begging and pleading for Jefferey to stop. And Queenie watched, her mouth turned up into a frown.

Appalled mourners stood up, some to try and get a better vantage point in which to witness the fiasco. Ooohs and ahhs could be heard throughout the sanctuary, while several bands of conversation were heating up in the congregation. Others with their cell phones took pictures. And in a matter of minutes, Jefferey's outburst had hit social media—*Facebook, Twitter, and Instagram* and became viral before the service was over.

Harrison saw Queenie stand up, but he put out his hand. He remembered Queenie's threat, but they had had enough theatrics for the day. Queenie sat down, but her face was turned up, and she was mad as hell. The viewing ended when they were able to pin Jefferey to her seat. And the preacher, who had already eulogized Marshall, quickly said the benediction and put the service back into the hands of the undertaker.

Instead of going to the gravesite, Harrison pushed Jefferey in H. J.'s car and told him to drive straight to Broughton Hospital, whose mission was to deal with psychopathic maniacs. Today was the last straw for Harrison. All of Jefferey's promises of maintaining a calm decorum at her father's services fell on deaf ears. Maybe, he should stay and help her through this ordeal, but he was tired of this woman who'd nearly destroyed his life and that of their son's. And the doctor said that Jefferey might get well, but he was hard pressed for a good outcome.

H. J. kept his eyes straight ahead, not once acknowledging his mother's presence.

CHAPTER FIFTY-SEVEN

UPSIDE DOWN

*D*aylight filtered through the room, arousing the lovers from their sleep. Only a thin, Egyptian cotton sheet covered their bodies. Yolanda stretched her arms over her head and sighed, not wanting to move the rest of her body. She'd done a lot of that in the wee hours of the morning. Stefan gradually opened his eyes, his body not willing to give into the command of his brain that whispered, *get up... get up.*

Turning over to face Yolanda's back, Stefan lovingly placed his arm around her waist and nuzzled up against her naked body. Her petite frame fit his like a missing piece to a puzzle. He rubbed his nose on her neck. She was warm and smelled like the wonderful fragrance she showered with after they'd conquered the jungle of their lust for each other.

"Hey, are you awake?" Stefan whispered in Yolanda's ear?"

He heard her faint whisper. "No."

Stefan tickled her side and Yolanda threw back her head, laughing as he continued to taut her. She turned over so that she was now facing him and smiled.

He was in love with not only the woman but also her body. It was obvious she cared about it—her muscles taunt and firm in all the right places. Moving the sheet away, Stefan took a liberty and closed his mouth around one of her extended, ripe nipples, sucking it with painful pleasure, while carefully taking the free nipple in his hand and squeezing it to Yolanda's delight. She pushed him away gently, although his hard erection wasn't happy.

Rubbing his chin with her finger, Yolanda playfully moved closer and seductively kissed Stefan on the lips. So in tune to this woman, Stefan kissed her back, laying small kisses about her lips, but this only made his desire to enter her and soak in her passion much more urgent. And then he became ferocious, gobbling up her lips in one fell swoop, kissing and sucking them like he was going for the center of a Tootsie Roll Pop. Then he tenderly examined her mouth with his tongue and her body shuddered next to him.

She held his face and kissed him back with the same force. With no reservations, Yolanda eased on top of her man, stopping the foreplay in mid-air. He entered her with reckless abandon, and she rode him like a cowboy in a hurry to get to the next town. Stefan held onto her juicy tenderloin—her buttocks flapping in the air until they hit Dodge City and screamed for release.

"My, my, my, my, YoYo; you are so damn good. I don't want to get up; I could make love to you day and night." He pulled her head down to his and kissed her on the forehead and then on the lips, panting and sweating from their torrid lovemaking.

"I wish you could be in me all the time. You make…you make me feel so wonderful, Stefan. I'm alive when I'm with you, and then there's your other side, out from under the sheets that I love too. You're so transparent in the way you feel about me, and I believe you do love me."

"I do love you, baby, and I want to take it to the next level. I want to announce to the world that I've found my friend…my soulmate and that I want to live the rest of my life with her. I want to give you whatever it is your heart desires, shower you with adoration and show you off at family picnics and other social gatherings."

"Do you really love me, Stefan? People say a lot of things when they're in the throes of passion. While they may feel good shouting out their feelings at the moment, it was never their intention to say it in the first place."

Stefan bucked his eyes and then put his finger to Yolanda's lips. "Shhhh. You say crazy things. If I say I love you, I'm one-hundred with it. I mean every word I say. I don't know how you were treated before I found you, but my truth is what I say. Trust me; I'm the real deal."

"Where did you come from? I've never met a man like you before —so sure of his ideals and where he's going. I do believe you, though, and I want to trust you with my whole being. That's a hard thing for me to do, but you've given me no choice but to do so."

Stefan rolled Yolanda off of him and turned to look at her. "I'm going to marry you, Yolanda Morris. I'm going to make you my wife and live a happily ever after."

"That's what they say in fairy tales."

"But this isn't a fairy tale. It's real."

"What if your family doesn't like me? What if your mother says that I'm too old?"

Stefan gazed into Yolanda's eyes and stared. "Do you not want to be with me—this Italian, African-American stallion?" He held out his hands for her to get a good look at him.

Yolanda hollered. "You're the one that's crazy. Of course, I want to be with you." Yolanda kissed him, sat up, and gazed out of the window.

"What's wrong now?"

"Nothing's wrong. I'm happy, the happiest I've been in a long time. Stefan, you've turned me upside down. Sometimes I can't think clearly. For so long, I didn't think I could ever love again."

"I'm glad. You've turned me upside down and round and round."

"Diana Ross."

"You started it. Would you like to meet her? She and my mother are friends and lives right here in Manhattan."

"Do I want to meet Diana Ross? Hell yeah." Yolanda bent over and kissed Stefan for more than a minute and then came up for air. "That was for the lover in you who always gets it right."

"Anything for you, babe. Now let's get up, bathe, and I'll take you to lunch. We've got a long and exciting day ahead. I can't wait for you to meet my family."

"Ciao Bella."

Stefan looked at Yolanda and began to laugh. "Do you have any idea what Ciao Bella is?"

"It sounds good. Does it mean ok...goodbye?"

"No crazy woman that I love. It is an American Italian company that specializes in gelatos and sorbets."

"That sounds good too." Yolanda got up and tried to rush to the shower.

"It is good, but not as good as you." Stefan gently slapped her on the butt. "Get ready."

CHAPTER FIFTY-EIGHT

IN PURSUIT

*U*nable to get a Red Eye, Illya took an eight-thirty flight on U.S. Airways from Raleigh/Durham to New York. He arrived at LaGuardia Airport a couple of hours later. Without fanfare, he checked into a hotel in Queens.

Settling into his room, he took out his wallet that contained the piece of paper with Marjorie's name and phone number on it. He fingered the paper and looked at the digits written on it. *I should call her,* he thought. But as soon as his mind accepted the idea, the other voice in his head said stay on course—you're in pursuit.

Quickly, Illya folded up the piece of paper and put it back in his wallet. Tomorrow would be soon enough for him to see Marjorie. The hurt part of his pride wanted to see her, but he was afraid that if he saw Marjorie tonight, memories from the past would envelope him and he wouldn't be able to resist the lure of the beautiful woman he once loved. His purpose was to make Yolanda jealous so that she would run back to his arms. And for that reason, he was going to stay on task.

His head clear, Illya got up, left the room, and went downstairs to the bar. He'd have a drink and toast prematurely to a successful trip. It was going to be worth the wait and definitely a pleasure to watch Yolanda stumble all over herself when he walked into the family gathering.

CHAPTER FIFTY-NINE

I'M IN LOVE

$\mathcal{I}$t was a New York gray day. Thick clouds threatened rain. True New Yorkers were used to the weather and went about their business as usual.

Dressed in all white, Yolanda looked like a goddess. At least that's how Stefan described her to his mother. Yolanda smiled at him... smiled that the man she'd fallen in love with and who was still on the phone with his mother would give her such a compliment. Hopefully, they would get along, Yolanda mused to herself. She was too old for games, although if she did decide to let Stefan make her his wife, she'd be with him, not his family.

After ending the call, Stefan smiled at Yolanda. "I want you. I want you in my life for forever."

Yolanda went to him and held his head in her hand. She closed her eyes and kissed him seductively, tasting only the tip of his tongue. Drawing back and letting her hands slide down to his chest, Yolanda looked at him straight on. "I love you and I want to be with you for forever."

"We'll have to do something about it. The course of our lives is about to change, YoYo. I'm serious about how I feel; I've never felt this way before."

"What is it about me that made you say that, Stefan? You are an extremely handsome man who could have any woman you want. There are so many prettier, younger women out there who could be your ideal."

A frown formed on Stefan's face. "As I've tried to tell you before, it's your intellect, your maturity, and of course your raving beauty that sold me. I've tried pretty and young, and what I've found is these women only want status and what I can give them. Their conversations drip with designer names and when am I'm going to update their wardrobe. Where will we eat today and what venue full of A-list celebrities will I take them to? Hearing that crap twenty-four hours a day bores me to death. With you I can talk about life—politics, community awareness, world issues and what we need to do to solve them. I love that we can express to each other our desires, struggles, and what's important to us as individuals. You are a global person with global ideas and your conversations are of the same mindset as mine. I trust you with my life. Now the icing on the cake is having that someone whose lovemaking is what I call A-List. You're the total package, YoYo."

Yolanda clasped her hands together. Her eyes became tight slits as she tried to keep from crying. And then she opened her mouth and measured her words. "That's the kindest thing anyone has ever said to me, Stefan. It's not so much what you said, but how you said it…with compassion and love. Your honesty is what drew me all the way in, and I appreciate you for it. I love you, and I won't question your love for me again."

Stefan pulled Yolanda close to him, held her around the waist and kissed her passionately. "I love you so much. You're my queen and my future wife. Now let's get something to eat."

Grabbing a cab, they went to one of Stefan's favorite eateries. The couple ordered a light breakfast and in between bites, held each other's hand.

Yolanda was ready to conquer the world with Stefan by her side, and she wasn't going to allow any negativity, to include her sister and girlfriends, get in the way of being with him.

CHAPTER SIXTY

MY HEART IS SURE

*a*rm in arm, Yolanda and Stefan headed to SoHo. Instead of getting a cab, Stefan drove his silver Bentley. Yolanda loved this car; it felt as if she was riding on air.

Light jazz flowed through the speakers. It was so calming that it almost put Yolanda to sleep. But her nerves were on edge, as this would be the night she'd meet Stefan's family.

They arrived at the club around six-thirty. Upon their arrival, a jazz band was doing a mike check. The place was dimly lit, and a few tables were filled with patrons who seemed to be in deep conversation while nursing spirits of their liking.

With one hand on her back and the other pointing the way, Stefan directed Yolanda to a side door that opened up into a short, well-lit hallway. "We're going to my mother's dressing room."

Yolanda felt her nerves taking over her body. Would this woman be judgmental? Would she look at her with disdain? Yolanda wanted to turn around and go and sit incognito in one of the empty seats inside the club.

"You seem tense," Stefan said, rubbing the small of her back.

How in the hell did he know? It was scary that Stefan could read her feelings so easily, as if they were joined at the hip or were encased in the same body. "I'm fine," she lied.

Stefan abruptly stopped in front of a door and smiled. A sign was stuck to it with the name Tracey Porter emblazoned across it. For a moment, Yolanda was confused but remembered that Stefan's mother used her stage name when she performed.

Stefan rapped on the door. *Knock, knock.* He listened.

"Come in," said a sweet voice.

Stefan took Yolanda by the hand and ushered her into the room. Yolanda was astounded and transfixed by how gorgeous Stefan's mother was. She was an ageless beauty. Her skin was a roasted-honey color, which gave Stefan that smooth buttery look against his other dark features. She wore dreads that were neatly swept up into some kind of ball and held in place by long, brownish-yellow wooden sticks that had Chinese symbols at the end of each. On her body, she wore a black, form-fitting dress that stopped above her knees and hugged her body like a thin coat of paint. On her feet were three-and-a-half inch black, ankle boots, and when she turned around the boots boasted a gold strip that zipped straight up the back. Bling, bling. What caught Yolanda's attention was the beautiful tattoo that ran the length of Tracey's arm that bared a musical note and a rippled set of black and white piano keys, entwined by the stem of a red rose whose petals lay partially on the keyboard and the musical note. The artist's rendition was breathtaking.

Yolanda reached out her hand, but Tracey smiled and hugged Yolanda to her chest. She pushed back. "I see why my son has been so enthralled with you. When he told me you were older than him, I was unsure of your intentions/his intentions. Not that I'm any wiser now, but I do understand his initial attraction to you. But I'm quite pleased with your other fundamental qualities that my son says has drawn you to him. We're going to be friends; you'll see."

Stefan smiled at Yolanda. "Mother this is Yolanda Morris and YoYo, this is my mother, Tracey Porter Morsilli. Isn't she gorgeous mother?"

"I have to agree with you, Stefan. She's beautiful. She reminds me of myself."

"I'm pleased to meet you…"

"Just Tracey, girl. I'm old enough to be your older sister."

This time Yolanda laughed. "I'd like to give you a real, big-sister hug this time."

"Girl, come on and hug your big-sister, and from what I hear, possibly mother-in-law."

Yolanda tapped Stefan on the shoulder. "You told your mother?"

"Stefan and I are very close, but for your edification, I'm not the meddling kind. In fact, you're two grown individuals, who despite your age differences love each other."

"I do love him," Yolanda said. "My girlfriends are calling me a cougar, but he's taught me a lot."

Tracey began to laugh. "That's my son. I look forward to chatting with you further at dinner afterwards. We're going to the restaurant where you met, Stefan. A few of my husband's relatives are in town and it would be a great time to make an announcement." Tracey winked at Stefan. "Oh, and you'll also get a chance to meet my sister, Marjorie. She'll love you."

"Whew," Yolanda said, blowing air from her mouth. "My nerves were all bunched up in my chest when I got here, but you've made me so at ease. I look forward to your performance tonight."

"Nothing to worry about…what did you call her, Stefan?"

"YoYo. It's short for Yolanda."

"I got it, baby." Turning to Yolanda, Tracey looked at her and smiled. "There's nothing to worry about, YoYo. Do you, sistergirl. I'm from the old school, but if it's love, why deny it. Okay, I've got to finish my rituals." Tracey picked up a glass of water with lemon in it and sipped. "I've got to warm and loosen up the pipes. I'll see you both when I come out on stage."

"Thank you for making me feel comfortable, Tracey."

"You made it easy, YoYo. You were an easy read, but I'm pleased for my son's sake."

Stefan rolled his eyes at his mother, gave her a peck on the cheek, and ushered Yolanda from the room.

When they were outside in the hallway, Yolanda turned to Stefan. "I love your mother, and if you should ask me to marry you today, tonight, or whenever, my answer will be yes."

"Damn, I should've brought you here sooner."

"This was the moment; this was the time. My heart is sure."

CHAPTER SIXTY-ONE

ALL IN THE FAMILY

racey Porter was off the chain. Her soulful, bluesy and jazzy numbers set the roof on fire. The packed out room, with its eclectic group of patrons that were unique to SoHo, were feeling the melody, the beat, and the sultry lyrics that exploded from Tracey's mouth. To Yolanda, she sounded a lot like Jill Scott with a twist of Ella Fitzgerald.

Yolanda raised her hands and rocked her head from side to side, feeling what everyone else in the room was feeling. At the end of Tracey's last set, the applause was loud and intense, the audience begging for an encore.

Smoke swirled about the place, while ice cubes clinked in glasses. The band continued to play and engage the crowd. And when Tracey reappeared with her hands raised in the air, the crowd burst into a thunderous applause.

"Sing, Tracey!" someone shouted. "Sing "My Funny Valentine.""

"Wow, you all are special to me," Tracey said, grabbing the microphone from the stand. "I'm going to do one more number for you and then I've got to run. I heard "My Funny Valentine," and since it is one of my favorites, although it's not one that I wrote, I'm going to sing it for you."

"Yes!" someone screamed.

Wiping sweat from her face, Tracey closed her eyes and caressed the microphone. "My Funny Valentine…"

The audience went wild. Couples got up and slow danced on the small dance floor, hugging their partners with all their might. Other than Tracey and the few couples dancing, the room was still, the patrons ingesting every word she sang.

Stefan took Yolanda's hand and ushered her to the dance floor. They melded together in a lover's embrace. With her head on his shoulder, Stefan began to sing the words along with his mother. "You make me smile…"

And when Tracey finished singing, she gently replaced the microphone back on the stand. "I love you. Goodnight." She kissed her fingers and threw it to the crowd. And then she was gone.

Sitting across from Stefan, Yolanda smiled. "Tonight was special. Your mother was awesome. I don't understand why she didn't emerge as a big superstar like Aretha or Gladys."

"She could've if she pushed hard enough. However, she was all about the family. And my father didn't want her gallivanting all across the country singing to drunks and pimps, as he used to say; it's an Italian thing. My mother loves my father, so she gave up the big life for him with a caveat that she be able to sing from time to time in some of the local clubs, to which my father agreed."

"Kudos to your mother. That woman sang from the heart, and I was glad I had an opportunity to hear her."

"I'm glad too. Ready to go and meet the rest of the family?"

"I think so."

"Let me collect Mom, and then we'll be on our way."

It was a short drive from SoHo to the restaurant. Yolanda raved over Tracey, although Tracey contended that her voice was a gift from God that she wanted to share with others from time to time.

So modest, Yolanda thought. She prayed that the rest of the family was half as nice. But she didn't care how they felt about her. She'd already told Stefan that she was his.

There seemed to be a lot of merrymaking when they arrived at the restaurant. A private room had been reserved for the family. Vincent Morsilli, a burly man who was all of six feet with cold black, wavy hair at the back of his bald head, was entertaining some of the relatives when the group entered the room.

"To my lovely wife, Tracey," Vincent said, raising his glass of vino in the air and then taking a sip. "And a toast to my handsome son, Stefan, and his beautiful lady friend." Vincent raised his glass again and then downed the rest of the liquid.

Vincent met Tracey at the end of the table and kissed her on the lips. "You look fabulous, sweetheart."

"I love you, too, Vinnie."

After his mother and father finished kissing, Stefan stepped to his father and patted him on the back. "Pops, this is Yolanda Morris."

Vinnie moved back so that he could take in all of Yolanda. Yolanda blushed but was a little nervous at how forward Stefan's father was, especially since Tracey was also in the room. "You're a beautiful woman and it's so nice to meet you." Vinnie kissed her hand. "You have a thing for my son?"

Yolanda was caught off guard and then she saw Tracey's smile. The confidence she had when she first arrived, then left, had somewhat returned. "Yes, I'm in love with him."

"Shut the chicken up. You're in love with my Stefan? How old are you?"

It was time for Tracey to intervene. "Vinnie, please stop antagonizing Yolanda. I'm already enthralled with her."

"And so am I," Stefan said in agreement with his mother.

"I am, too," Vinnie added, nodding his head. "Sweetheart, don't take any offense. You're beautiful and if I know my son, you've got an amazing head on your shoulders. I...I just thought he would be bringing a much younger woman to the celebration."

Yolanda managed a smile. She wanted to run as far away from

Vinnie as she possibly could, but then Stefan stepped up to the plate. That man always knew the right thing to say.

"This is the woman for me, and I'm going to marry her. She's only a few years older than me, but she has brains and intellect, which most of the women I've dated in the past lacked. YoYo isn't with me for what I have or what I can give her, except for my heart. We're true soulmates and we're in love with each other."

Tracey stood up and clapped her hands. Other family members followed suit. And before Yolanda knew what was happening, she was lifted up into the air by Vinnie, who after placing her feet back on the floor, kissed her on the cheek.

"Welcome to the family! Let's get this party started." Vinnie pointed toward the back wall and turned to Stefan. "Stefan, introduce YoYo to your Uncle Frank and Aunt Sylvia; Uncle Michael and Aunt Rita and your cousins. We truly have something to celebrate. My boy is getting married. Drink up."

Within seconds, Yolanda was engulfed in the arms of Stefan's relatives. She received more kisses in that one moment than she'd received all year from all of her friends collectively. It was a good feeling to be embraced by these people who didn't judge her on the color of her skin or ethnicity, although it was already obvious that they were colorblind.

The merrymaking continued, while calamari and platters of spaghetti, ravioli, lasagna, Veal Parmigiana, and endless bowls of Carmine salad littered the table. Plenty of wine was at their disposal. Bouts of laughter filled the room, as each of Stefan's uncles told stories about growing up in the old country and then coming to the United States. Yolanda joined in the laughter.

And then there was a momentary silence as a new couple entered the room. The woman was dressed in a sleek, nut-brown pantsuit and her straight black hair fell past her shoulders. She looked much like Stefan's mother, Tracey, except that she might have been a few years younger. But the man...the man who escorted her into the room was all too familiar to Yolanda. She gasped and quickly covered her mouth, as the woman holding onto Illya Newsome's arm approached.

CHAPTER SIXTY-TWO

THE SPY THAT CAME IN FROM THE COLD

a million thoughts ran through Yolanda's mind. Tiny beads of sweat began to form on her forehead. What in the hell was Illya Newsome doing in the same room with her?

Tracey got up from her seat and embraced the woman. "Marjorie, I'm glad you made it." And then she looked into the face of Marjorie's guest and grabbed her chest. "My goodness, Illya Newsome is that really you? How long has it been?"

"Yes, it's me. It's been a long time."

"The last I recall, you left Marjorie for another woman…the woman you married. So, I'm puzzled by your being here."

"We reconnected, sis," Marjorie said, holding up her hand in surrender.

Vinnie offered Marjorie and Illya a glass of wine. "Sit, take a seat. We were wondering when you were going to get here. Grab a plate and dig in. For everyone who doesn't know Marjorie, she's my sister-in-law, Tracey's sister. We're celebrating."

Marjorie looked at Tracey with a puzzled look on her face. "What are you guys celebrating? I thought this was supposed to be a family get-together."

"Oh, it is," Vinnie said, with a proud look on his face. "But we also got some good news.

Tell her what we're celebrating, sweetie."

"Stefan is getting married."

Illya Newsome's eyes rolled in his head, and the brief smile of vindication that had once crossed his lips while he watched Yolanda's discomfort was long gone.

"Married?" Marjorie stared at Stefan and noticed Yolanda for the first time. "When did this happen, Stefan? I can't believe you didn't tell your Auntie. I thought we were close like that." Marjorie tapped her heart with two fingers that formed a V.

"Aunt Margie, this is Yolanda Morris, the love of my life. We haven't known each other long, but we were made to be together. And I'm not going to live my life without her."

"Well, alright then. You do have something to celebrate. It's nice to meet you, Yolanda."

Yolanda's knees were knocking together. She couldn't believe that Illya was in the same room with her. He hadn't once acknowledged her presence, and she was afraid to look in his direction. The few times she'd spoken to him in the last couple of weeks, he never once said that he was going to New York.

Something in the back of her mind caused her to stop...think. She remembered that Illya had been inquiring in a subtle way about what she was doing on the weekend. Actually, when she told him that she couldn't meet with him this weekend, he hadn't put up a fuss, although she'd been cocky enough to tell him that she was going to New York. But how in the world did he know who she was seeing? How had he hooked up with Stefan's aunt? Had he been following her? Whatever sick game Illya was playing, he was messing with the wrong woman.

Coming back to the present, Yolanda reached out to shake Marjorie's hand. And just like her sister, she wasn't having it.

"No, we're a family of huggers. A friend of my nephew is a friend of mine. Where are you from, Yolanda?"

"North Carolina."

"It's a small world." Marjorie stood next to Illya and wrapped her arm in his. "Illya has been working in North Carolina and flew here to meet up and get reacquainted. We were an item in college. I thought we were going to be married, but it didn't quite work out that way."

Illya smiled but said nothing.

"Did you fly from Raleigh?" Yolanda asked, now regaining some of her nerve.

Illya looked Yolanda square in the eyes without any emotions. "Yes I did."

Flabbergasted, Marjorie drew her neck back. "Wow, you both may have been on the same plane. When did you fly in, Yolanda?"

"Yesterday."

"So, did I," Illya rushed to say. "I would've remembered if we were on the same plane."

Yolanda turned away, noticing for the first time that Stefan was watching the exchange. She hated Illya's smugness. But not owning up to the fact that he knew her was even more puzzling. There was something she wasn't seeing...that she was missing. Illya had a purpose and she had to find it. Surely, his work with the FBI had nothing to do with his being here. It couldn't or could it?

"Coincidences," Marjorie said, already on her second glass of red wine.

As Marjorie and Illya found their seats and began to eat, Stefan stood up. "I'm so happy to be surrounded by my family. You all are important to me. Mother and Pops, you're the best."

"I'll drink to that," Vinnie said, while pouring another glass of wine for himself. Tracey smiled broadly at her son.

"As you all have heard, I've been blessed to meet a special woman. Yolanda is the ying to my yang. She's my true beginning and end. I'd like to seal that love by asking her to marry me before all of you drunken people."

Everyone laughed.

Stefan kneeled down on the floor, turned to Yolanda, and produced a Tiffany's box from the inside of his jacket. He took her hand and looked into her eyes. "Will you marry me?"

Yolanda was elated and temporarily forgot the elephant in the room. She covered her mouth with her hand, unable to control her emotions in seeing the beautiful platinum diamond ring. And then she looked up at him. "Yes."

The room lit up, and everyone sang their congratulations and toasted the couple. Stefan fixed his fiancé with a passionate kiss and the cheering crowd continued to roar—all except Illya Newsome, whose fixation with Yolanda hadn't gone unnoticed. Tears flowed from Tracey's face as she watched her son in the moment. When the room quieted down, Stefan lifted Yolanda's hand.

"The center diamond is 3.83 carats, and the diamonds circling it are another carat. But you're worth more than gold or the weight of these diamonds."

Yolanda looked at the ring on her finger and cried. "I love you, Stefan. Now, I feel like a giddy school girl with everyone gawking at me."

"Another round of drinks," Vinnie called out. "My son is getting married to a beautiful woman. You did good, Stefan. It's about damn time." Everyone laughed.

Yolanda smiled. And then she thought about her girlfriends at home. How would they take the news? How would her sister feel about her moving to New York? Damn, she hadn't given that much thought. Oh, and Queenie; she had to call her. The pain of losing her father after not being in touch with him in all these years must be taking a toll on her. Yolanda smiled, but when she looked up, Illya Newsome was staring at her and for a fleeting moment she was frightened. The look of contempt on his face said that she'd done something awful to him and he was going to pay her back. And then it came to her; Illya wanted her for himself.

With the amount of drinking Yolanda had done, it was a wonder she could stand up straight. She had an urgent need to go the restroom, and she'd better do it soon. She kissed Stefan and off she went. Just as she was about to open the door to the restroom, a hand grabbed her arm.

"I not sure what game you're playing, YoYo, but so that you're aware, you're playing with my affections."

"Take your hand off of me, Illya, before I sound the alarm and have my fiancé kick your ass out of here. You came in here with another woman, who happens to be Stefan's aunt. That's suspect. Don't you agree?"

"You're not marrying that guy. I'm your man."

"Illya, the steam has run out of our relationship. You've been spending a lot of time with your ex, which leaves me to believe that you're rekindling your marriage."

"Had you asked, I would've told you that my ex-wife is having severe medical problems and my daughters asked for my help."

"If you had been more forthcoming, I would've known that. But now, I'm in a different place and a different space. I love Stefan and that's the end of this discussion."

"He's not your equal. He's a young kid with a lot of money. Please don't tell me you're settling to be a kept woman."

"I've had enough of you. I've worked my whole life, and YoYo has never needed a man to take care of her. I can't believe I really did care for you, but let it be known, the fire is out. Let me suggest that you go back to your lady friend, save face, and get out of Dodge. It would be awful for you if she knew you were using her to get to me."

"This conversation may be over for the moment, but nothing is over. I'll see you when you return to Raleigh."

"Don't hold your breath." Yolanda watched as Illya walked away. Her hands were shaking and her mind frazzled. She had given all she had to her relationship with him, but the return on her investment wasn't worth the risk. She had to move on. Her stock portfolio looked pretty good, but her reality was that she'd fallen deeply in love with Stefan and Illya Newsome was out.

CHAPTER SIXTY-THREE

FRIENDS

*N*ow that the funeral was over, Queenie had lots of time to think. Her life flashed before her—some of it good, some of it bad. There was a long string of men that she'd opened her door to. She thought about all the time she'd wasted on her relationship with Linden Robinson. There was nothing good about it, but it opened her eyes to her own insecurities. She needed validation—that she was worth something to someone, but she failed to see her own self-worth.

All the time and energy she spent on worthless relationships could have been spent forming a better union with her father. All the good things she heard people say about him, she couldn't vouch for; she had shut him out of her life and never would get the chance to know the beautiful human being that was her father.

She was happy to have the love of her friends and fiancé. Donald, Terrance, Emma, Connie, and Jackie were troopers, giving her all the love and support she needed. It was Yolanda who had surprised her the most. She hadn't heard from her all weekend until a few hours ago when she expressed an interest in stopping by.

Wiping a lone tear from her eye, Queenie got up from her bed, showered and put some clothes on. She'd taken a couple of weeks off from work to heal and help Bertha with some of her father's paperwork. Jefferey had been admitted to Broughton Hospital where she hopefully would get the help she needed. Queenie was drained.

The doorbell rang. Masking her feelings, Queenie went to the door and there stood Yolanda. She looked radiant in a crisp pair of jeans, an off-white, cashmere twin sweater set, and off-white boots. She had the look of one who'd returned from a luxurious vacation where she'd been pampered and doted on. Her hair was freshly done.

"Hey, Q." Yolanda reached up and kissed Queenie on the forehead.

Hesitant at first, Queenie mellowed out and embraced her friend. "Get in here. I was pissed at you, but as always, you're always there for me."

Yolanda followed Queenie to her living room. Queenie sat on the Queen Ann couch while Yolanda plopped onto the loveseat.

"How are you feeling?"

"YoYo, it's been a three-ring circus. I still can't get over the fact that my daddy is gone. He looked good and the service was wonderful. His wife, Bertha, my step-mother, is the nicest person you ever want to meet. I'm going to Charlotte this weekend to help her with a few things."

"If you want, I'll go with you."

"Feeling guilty about not being there this past weekend?"

"Maybe a little bit, but this is coming from the goodness of my heart."

"Thanks, YoYo."

"So, did Jefferey show up?"

"Did the bitch show up? She showed up and showed her ass off. That heifer tried to climb into the casket with Daddy. I thought Harrison was going to haul off and strike her, but being the gentleman he is, he pulled her back and tried to calm her down. If he didn't, I was. He was a mad brother, though. He took her straight to the psych hospital."

"Wow, y'all had a made for TV movie going on."

"YoYo, it was ridiculous, but the rest of Charlotte paid humble tribute to my dad." Queenie reached over and took Yolanda's hand. "So glad you're here."

"I love you, girl. And if you take that moo-moo off, I'm going to take you to lunch and a spa treatment."

"Say what? You don't have to tell me twice. This is what I need."

"I neglected my friend, but not on purpose, and that's why I took off work today to spend time with you."

"I'm up and changing my clothes now. You've got to tell me all about New York. I want all the juicy details."

"Hurry up. I've got lots to tell you."

CHAPTER SIXTY-FOUR

DOGGIE BAG

Queenie slipped into a pair of jeans, a white blouse, and a red blazer. She picked out her natural hair, put on some lipstick and was ready to go.

"Ready. Let's go somewhere we can get some good drinks."

"You mean like Coke or Sprite?"

"You've got jokes, YoYo. I'm talking about something that's going to give me a little buzz."

"Oh, I see. Let's go to TGI Friday. Their alcohol is good, although I believe I consumed enough this weekend to last me through to the end of the year."

Queenie began to laugh. "You and your younger man had a good time."

"A real good time. I met his parents."

"Shut the front door. Stefan introduced you to his parents? This must be more serious than you're telling me."

"It's serious." Yolanda removed her left hand from the steering wheel and flashed it in Queenie's face.

Queenie gasped. Her mouth was wide open. "Damn, YoYo. What

did you have to do to get this massive rock? Didn't he give you a ring not long ago?"

"It's my engagement ring. Stefan asked me to marry him. Let's wait until we get to the restaurant so I can tell you everything. You're going to throw up."

"Throw up? Why will I want to throw up?" Queenie's face went from surprise to a big smile. "You and Stefan were doing all that freaky stuff. Did you take any of your toys with you?"

"Hush, Q. You're going to make me wreck my car from laughing at you."

"I know better than that. You aren't going to let anyone including yourself inflict any harm to this Lexus. Been with you too long. Now, hurry up so I can throw up." The ladies laughed.

In twenty minutes, Yolanda pulled up to the entrance of TGI Friday. The lunch crowd had just about dissipated, with the exception of the few who lagged behind talking about politics or having a late luncheon meeting.

"I can eat a whole slab of ribs," Queenie said, getting out of the car in a hurry. "I've eaten everybody else's food since Daddy passed. I'm ready to eat some stuff I love."

"I hear you, Q."

The ladies walked into the restaurant and were seated without waiting. After giving their orders to the waitress, the two friends sat back and relaxed.

"So is everything in order for your wedding?"

"Yeah. Donald is leaving everything up to me. Men don't want to be bothered with all that wedding stuff. All they want is the goodies after the reception is over, that's if they haven't already hit it."

"Q, I don't know what I'm going to do with you. Your mind is always in the gutter."

"So, are you saying yours isn't? Seems to me, you've been hitting the sheets hard and heavy with your steamy romance."

"It's like this. I'm truly in love with Stefan. The ring is only the icing on the cake. The love that we share isn't only between the sheets. Our hearts are in tune with one another."

"Umm, you're getting all soft on me. Where's the YoYo I know?"

"She's still inside of my body, but I don't want to discuss my love life with Stefan like it's something nasty or dirty. It is a beautiful thing, and the fact that my man can throw down makes a much more powerful statement."

"Shut the hell up. YoYo, I never pegged you for a girl with these kinds of feelings. I'm used to rough and ready. Remember doggy bag?"

"Speaking of doggy bag, it's the part of the story…my weekend that I have yet to share with you."

Queenie sat up straight and looked at Yolanda quizzically. "What are you talking about? Don't leave a girl hanging. Wait, here comes our drinks. Let me sip on some of this Long Island Ice Tea before you begin."

Yolanda waited, and when Queenie gave her the nod, she took off. She told Queenie about meeting Stefan's mother and hearing her sing. "That woman is gorgeous and has a fabulous voice. His father is cool, too. He's a true Italian man. They are so loving and embraced me with open arms."

"But this is the point where you go…dum de dum-dum."

"You're right. The night was going so well. We were eating and drinking, drinking and eating, and then this couple walks in."

"Don't tell me…"

Yolanda held her hand up. "Let me tell my story. The couple stepped into the room like they were a power couple. The woman was tall and gorgeous and looked a lot like Stefan's mother. The only difference, Stefan's mother wears her hair in dreads and the woman, who happens to be Stefan's aunt, has beautiful, straight hair and she is a little darker. But that's not the kicker. Guess who was rolling on her arms?"

"Denzel Washington? I knew he was a player."

"No, silly, it was Illya Newsome. You remember him—my long, lost FBI agent boyfriend."

"Shut the freak up!" Queenie said it so loud, other patrons turned in her direction. Queenie waved her hands. "I'm sorry."

"Yes, but he would never acknowledge me. He was funky and acted as if he never met me before. It was the strangest mess I've ever witnessed. Q, my legs were shaking so bad, I thought I was going to wet my panties. Illya was acting some kind of weird. But it got worse after Stefan got down on his knees, proposed to me, and gave me the ring."

"What did he do?"

"He accosted me when I went to the bathroom and told me that I wasn't going to marry Stefan…that he was my man."

"Girl, you're going to need a restraining order. How in the world did he know that you were going to see Stefan and how did he end up with his aunt?"

"Those are the same questions I asked myself. This is some scary stuff. I told him that our relationship was over and that this was the end of the road."

Queenie took a couple of swallows of her drink. "So what did he say to that?"

"Oh, he had something to say alright. He said he'd see me in Raleigh. I may have to hide out at your place."

"Look, I just got rid of a nut. That crazy man isn't going to tear up my house coming after you."

"I'm only talking, Q. I'm not sure what I'm going to do. I don't want to go to Connie's now that their lives are on track."

"I can understand that. I never figured Illya for a stalker…at least not outside of his job."

"You and me both. He seemed so gentle…couldn't hurt a fly, except when he had to take somebody down."

"Truth be told, if he could do that as part of his job, he probably wouldn't find it hard to revert to that tactic in his real life."

"Look, this afternoon is about you, not me. I can hardly eat my food, though."

"You downed that drink mighty fast." The ladies laughed. "Anyway, YoYo, I'm glad to be talking about something else other than my dysfunctional family. Your situation gave me a few laughs, but this thing with Illya is serious. You're going to have to talk to someone about it. So when are you getting married?"

"We haven't set a date. It's too soon."

I'm happy for you, but don't try to upstage a sister by getting married first. This is my year. Oh, and Emma seems to be back on track with Terrance, although she probably won't marry again."

"That's good. Emma needs someone in her life. Oh, oh, my cell phone is ringing."

"Is it Illya?"

Yolanda smiled. "No, it's my baby checking in. Excuse me."

Queenie picked up her Long Island Ice Tea and sipped. As soon as she spotted the waitress, she called her to the table and ordered another. She was happy for YoYo.

CHAPTER SIXTY-FIVE

SOMETHING'S UP

*A*fter lunch, Yolanda drove to the spa in Cameron Village. She loved the quaintness of the old shops mixed with the new. Cameron Village reminded her of the days when department stores were separate buildings downtown and you had to walk outside to get from one to the other. Malls were a good idea, especially when the weather was bad and she understood the economics of having stores under one roof, but it made her miss the good ole days.

She was happy that Queenie was enjoying their outing. It was therapeutic for her also, considering she hadn't had any resolve with her Illya situation.

As they prepared to get out of the car, Yolanda spotted him out of the corner of her eye. She grabbed the back of Queenie's coat and pulled her back into the car.

"What's wrong with you? You almost made me fall."

"I saw him, Q."

"You saw who?"

"Illya." Yolanda pointed.

Queenie looked in the direction that Yolanda was pointing. "I don't see anyone. YoYo, I'm serious. Your encounter with Illya is going to drive you batty and have you looking over your shoulders twenty-four seven."

"Q, I'm telling you. He was standing by that building, watching me as I was getting out of the car. I swear I'm not making this up."

"Okay, okay, I believe you. He may have hopped inside when you took your eyes off of him."

"I'm afraid. That man is with the FBI, and they use all kinds of tactics to draw out their victims."

"I thought he wanted to be with you?"

"That's what he said, but I'm not so sure. Anyway, if there was ever a chance of us really being together, that opportunity is long gone. I've been debating, though."

"Debating about what?"

"If I should tell Stefan about Illya. I don't want to cause a stink, especially since his aunt is involved."

"His aunt needs to know that she's being used, and they'll blame you later for not telling them. How do you think that will sit with Stefan and his loving family?"

"You've got a point, Q. I may have to meet with Illya to try and bring closure to this mess."

"Be careful, whatever you do. But if you did see him, YoYo, how is it that he was here before we arrived?"

"Beats me? Not…not unless he has my telephone tapped, but I never said anything to you about going to the spa until I was at your house."

"Maybe your car is bugged."

Yolanda sat there a moment and digested what Queenie said. If Illya had indeed bugged her car, he was more of a threat than she realized. "I'll take my car to the police station and have it tested for bugs. But I'm going to call Illya and have a face-to-face with him. This is going to stop."

"Sounds like a good idea. Now, can we go in and get our massages?"

Yolanda hit Queenie on the arm. "You are too much. You don't care what happens to me; all you care about is getting that massage."

"You did say that today was about me. I'm a friend in need and I thank you for my blessing. Look, YoYo, everything will work out; you'll see. Right now, tell Illya to kiss your ass, if he's listening to us on some device, and let's get our massages." The girls laughed and went inside.

Out of nowhere, Illya materialized. Making sure the ladies were inside the spa, he walked cautiously toward Yolanda's car. He hadn't anticipated how smart she would be, and he needed to get the tracking device and transmitter from under and inside of the car as soon as possible. He couldn't risk Marjorie finding out that she was a ploy in a scheme to take her nephew's fiancé away from him.

He tiptoed and then went into a fast sprint. He dropped beside Yolanda's car that was parked next to another, felt for the tracking device and extracted it. Using a tool for breaking into a Lexus that was fully armed, he opened the door and took out the listening device. This was a trick of the trade, and he thanked the FBI for that small wonder.

Maybe Yolanda was coming to her senses. And he wasn't about to squander an opportunity to meet with her without trying to convince her once and for all that he was in love and that she was the woman for him.

CHAPTER SIXTY-SIX

YOU'RE MINE

Dropping her keys on the coffee table, Yolanda plopped down on the sofa. She must be losing her mind; she was sure she saw Illya this afternoon. However, the trip to the police station helped to ease her mind, finding out that there were no bugs or other electronic devices attached to her car.

She snatched her purse off the couch and retrieved her cell phone. The last thing she wanted to do was have a conversation with Illya. However, it was necessary in order to get an understanding about a few things and bring closure to a decaying relationship.

Fingering the phone, she sighed and decided to make the call. It hadn't been a good second after she dialed before Illya answered.

"I've been waiting for your phone call."

"How presumptuous of you."

"Well, it has been a few days since I saw you in New York. I figured that our meeting was imminent."

Yolanda blew air from her mouth. His arrogance was getting on her last nerve. She felt backed into a corner—a position she didn't relish. "First, I need to ask you something."

"Ask away."

Yolanda paused, trying to keep from cursing him out. "Have you been following me? I'm sure I saw you at Cameron Village today."

"It wasn't me; I've been out in the field all day."

Silence ensued. She knew he was lying his ass off. Beyond a shadow of a doubt, it was Illya she saw, hiding like a coward on the side of a building instead of being man enough to approach her and say what was on his mind. She sighed and huffed.

"Look, if you want me to begin the conversation, I will," Illya said.

"Suite yourself."

"YoYo, let's be civil."

"If I can. What do you want me to say, Illya? You show up in New York at the same private party I'm attending and act as if you've never met me before. The only reason I didn't give you away was that I didn't want to embarrass Stefan's aunt. You're playing her to get to me; that much is obvious. My question is how did you know with whom I'd be with and where I was going to be?"

Illya snickered. "I do work for the FBI, and it didn't take a lot of research to get the four-one-one on you. How I did it is irrelevant."

"But why? The way you're acting scares the hell out of me."

"YoYo, I thought you and I had something special. When we met, I was skeptical. I'd gone through so much with the divorce from my ex. You were a breath of fresh air and I felt that I could be open to love again."

Tears welled up in Yolanda's eyes. Why hadn't he said these things to her when she needed to hear them? There were months when it seemed that they were so detached from each other. She knew he had a job that required him to be undercover and away from her for periods at a time. But he'd never once expressed a deep affection for her. They loved each other's company, the sex was good, but there was never any indication that it would go to the next level.

"Why are you telling me this now, Illya? For the year that I've known you, I waited for you to express your true feelings for me. I shared mine with you, but other than your obvious interest in me, you've not once said that you wanted a long-term relationship."

"You slay me. I don't wear my feelings on my sleeves. I thought we were in a good place, that we understood each other and were taking our time to get to know one another. I put my trust in you. Marriage, however, wasn't in my immediate future due to all the hurt, humiliation, and financial trouble I was in. And I thought you understood that. I even went the extra mile for your brother-in-law because I cared about you. What do you know about this Stefan dude that you can accept a marriage proposal and a ring after being acquainted with him for only a few weeks? Sounds strange and desperate to me."

"I appreciate you being honest with your feelings. Unfortunately, it's a little too late. I'm in love with Stefan and how it all evolved and how long we've known each other is no one's business but ours."

There was a long silence at the other end of the phone. She heard him grunt and let out a long sigh.

"You can't marry him."

"Why? Is he a rapist or a murderer?"

"Is he? Have you done a background check on him? You go to New York and fall all over yourself because some guy makes a pass at you. And the next thing I know, I'm getting walking papers."

"You're truly a piece of work. We talk, Illya, but that's it. When was the last time we've been on a real date? I understand your job requires that you have to make certain sacrifices where our relationship was concerned, but you've been so consumed with whatever it is you're doing, that you took me for granted…that I would always be waiting on you whether it was a week, month, or two months. I was tired of it, and when this new opportunity presented itself, I went for it. I may not have handled it well, but it is what it is."

There was another long pause and then a sigh. "I'm trying to be civil, YoYo. But let me put it this way; you belong to me."

"I don't belong to anyone. It hurts me that I've hurt you, but it wasn't intentional. Maybe all of this happened so that you and Marjorie could reconnect."

"I'm doing my best to remain calm." Pause. "You're in my system, and I'm not giving you up for another man…rather a boy who has expensive toys and for now enjoys what you can give him between the sheets. When he tires of you, what will you do then?"

"Damn, Illya, you sound like a jealous man. There was no need to hit below the belt. What I have with Stefan is more than a sexual liaison. Our love is bigger than the stratosphere. We are in tune and reading from the same sheet of music."

"Oh, I get the picture, but it doesn't sound realistic at all. I'm not sure if you're quoting some song or pulling something out of your fairytale mind, but listen to me and listen well. You're mine, and I'm going to have you. We were meant to be together."

"I'm beginning to see why your ex may have walked away from your marriage. I hadn't seen this possessive side of you before, but I'm getting the picture. It's funny how now that there's someone else in my life, you've suddenly become more attentive. It's best that we go our separate ways. I did care for you, Illya, but I've closed that chapter of my life."

"You will never marry him. I'll see to it that you don't."

"Is that a threat? Is a federal agent threatening me?"

"You'll see the results of my threat if you continue to see lover boy."

Silence, and then Yolanda clicked the phone off. Her life was in jeopardy and she needed to tell Stefan what was going on. But before she talked with him, she needed to talk with her sister. They had their disagreements, but it was time to move beyond it. She needed Connie and Preston.

CHAPTER SIXTY-SEVEN

CONNIE MAXWELL-ALEXANDER

*U*nhooking Desi from the car seat, Connie picked her up and strolled into the house. She was surprised to see that her loving husband had already arrived home and had dinner sitting on the table, although with compliments of the Chinese cooks at The Wok House.

"Hey, baby, how was your day?" Preston took Desiree from Connie, kissed her, and sat down at the table.

"Babes, it was tiring. If I didn't enjoy the lifestyle that I've become accustomed to, I'd give the university my resignation papers."

"You can call it quits at any time. God has blessed us, Connie, and things have never been better on my job."

"As much as I'd love to quit, I'm going to work until I get my state retirement check. I've put in too many years with the State to start acting like I'm bourgeoisie."

"It's your call, baby. Wash your hands so we can eat before the food gets cold."

"Okay." Connie took Desi, who'd already fallen asleep, and placed her in the playpen. She quickly washed her hands and rejoined Preston at the dinner table.

"I got all of your favorites."

"I see. Looks good and I'm going to eat all of it."

Preston laughed.

As Connie placed food on her plate, her cell phone began to ring. Preston gave her a look, and Connie ignored the call.

"That was YoYo's ring."

"When was the last time you all spoke? She knows better to interrupt our dinner time."

"I'm not sure what's up with my sister, Preston. She's gone coo-coo for Coca Puffs over this Stefan guy. Every time I look up she's flying to New York like she's acquired a ton of frequent flyer miles. If you ask me, she's acting like a first-class whore."

"Come on, Connie. That wasn't a nice thing to say."

"But Preston, I can't talk to her. She won't listen to reason. YoYo didn't even go to Queenie's dad's funeral and they've been friends for years. She's known Stefan for how long?"

"I feel sorry for Illya. He really likes her a lot; at least that's what he told me."

"Hopefully, it's a faze, but she needs to snap out of it soon."

"Well, finish your food and call her back. You guys need to mend your broken fence."

Connie smiled at Preston. "That's why I love you. You make so much sense. Thanks for the meal."

"You're welcome, baby."

Thirty minutes later, Connie retrieved her cell phone and called Yolanda. Preston sat close by, reading the paper.

"Hey, sis, I'm returning your phone call. You caught me in the middle of dinner."

"I'm sorry. Didn't mean to interrupt. How's Preston and Desi?"

With Preston watching her, Connie rolled her eyes and bunched up her shoulders. "Everyone's doing fine. Are you alright? You seem far away."

"Can I come over? I need to talk with you and Preston."

"You want to come over now? Is it something we can discuss on the phone?" Connie made eyes at Preston. She couldn't believe that Yolanda wanted to come over in the middle of the evening to talk.

"I'd rather talk with you in person; it's important."

Connie shrugged her shoulders and looked at Preston who had a quizzical look on his face. "Sure, come on over."

"Great, I'll be there in twenty minutes."

Connie ended the call and looked at Preston, who had put the newspaper down. "I wonder what that was all about. She wants to talk with both of us."

"It has to be tonight? My new favorite show is coming on television, and I don't want to be interrupted when "Black-*ish*" comes on. That Anthony Anderson makes me laugh."

"You might have to DVR it tonight. My sister sounded like whatever is on her chest is serious."

"Maybe she finally realized that she bit off more than she could chew with Stefan. I hope that girl has come to her senses."

"Well, we'll have to wait and see."

CHAPTER SIXTY-EIGHT

STALKED

$\mathcal{I}$n less than twenty minutes, Yolanda was on Connie and Preston's doorstep. She took a deep breath and inhaled. Illya Newsome had her on pins and needles and hopefully her family could give her some good advice.

Composed, Yolanda rang the doorbell. She kept looking over her shoulders and down the street to make sure she hadn't been followed. There was no telling what lengths Illya would go to get his point across. She gave a sigh of relief when her favorite brother-in-law answered the door.

"Hey, YoYo." Preston hugged Yolanda as she entered. "Connie is in the family room."

"Okay."

"Are you alright?"

Yolanda sighed. "Not really. That's why I'm here."

"We're your family and you can talk to us anytime."

Yolanda followed Preston to the family room without saying anymore. Connie got up from the couch and hugged Yolanda when she entered.

"How are you doing, sis?" Connie asked. "You've got me and the hubby worried. I haven't heard from you since you went to New York. How did that go?"

Yolanda let Connie get all of her questions out in the open. She was well aware that Connie wasn't feeling her association with Stefan, but she planned to squash that tonight. "New York was fine. I met Stefan's parents; they are wonderful."

Connie glanced in Preston's direction. It didn't get past Yolanda.

"So, are you still seeing him?" Preston asked.

Yolanda sat for a moment without saying anything. Finally, she sat all the way back in her chair and threw her hands up. "I'm going to cut to the chase. I'm in love with Stefan. We're getting married." Yolanda threw her ring hand out so everyone could see the large diamond ring that sat on her finger.

Both Connie and Preston gawked but said nothing, while they continued to look at the ring.

"So, what's so urgent that you had to talk with us tonight?" Connie finally asked, not taking her eyes away from the rock on Yolanda's finger.

"Someone followed me to New York."

Connie's eyes sounded an alarm. "Who?"

"I was having a great time in New York. I got to hear Stefan's mother sing. She has a wonderful voice. After that, we went to Carmine's for a family get together. You'll never guess who shows up there with Stefan's aunt?" There was a long period of silence. "I almost fell to the floor when Illya walked through the door."

"What was Illya doing there?" Connie asked, concern written on her face.

"He acted as if he didn't know me. However, when I went to the restroom later, he grabbed me by the arm and threatened me."

"Hold it one damn minute," Preston said, sitting on the edge of his seat. "He did what?"

"You heard me. The son-of-a-bitch grabbed me by the arm and told me that I wasn't marrying Stefan, and that he was the man for me."

"But how did he know that you were with Stefan and that you'd be at the restaurant?"

"How was it that Illya was with Stefan's aunt? The answer? He's been stalking me, Preston. Today, Queenie and I went to the spa. I swear Illya was hiding beside one of the buildings watching me. I called and confronted him about it, and although he denied it, I'm positive it was him. He said that if I didn't stop seeing Stefan, I would regret it."

"I can't believe you're talking about Illya. He's crazy about you."

"Yes, he's crazy alright, and I'm scared as hell. I don't want to stay in my house alone."

"You're more than welcome to stay here, sis. Preston and I have your back. If Illya thinks he's going to mess with my sister, he'll have to come through the both of us."

"Guys, we don't know what he's capable of. But to see him in New York at the same place that I was, a place that I told no one that I'd be, scared the living daylights out of me. I told him we were through."

"Wow, YoYo. I can see about arranging protection for you."

"I don't want to go there, yet, Preston, but it may be an option if he continues to harass me."

"Stay the night, sis. We've got leftover Chinese food if you're hungry."

"Thanks, I'm going to take you up on that offer."

"As a thought, you may need to tell Stefan what's going on, especially if you plan on making a life with him."

"Thanks, Connie. It's already on my "to do" list."

CHAPTER SIXTY-NINE

AN INTELLIGENT WOMAN

The hours ticked away. His time was getting short for remaining in the United States. As much as he was ready to get away from Jefferey and return overseas, he was conflicted. He needed to make sure that she would continue to get the best care possible, and hopefully one day get well.

He walked into the dark room...the bedroom they once shared. He stood a moment in the dark, remembering a time when their life together was great. Flipping up the light switch, Harrison glanced around the room. He picked up what-nots that sat on the dresser and then rummaged through her drawers looking for what, he wasn't sure.

His finger hit a hard object. When he removed the nightgown, he was surprised to see a journal underneath.

Harrison pulled the journal out of the drawer, took it to the bed, and sat at the end of it. He patted the cover, not sure that he wanted to open it.

Visions of Jeffery right before she was taken to the hospital loomed in his head. She was all out of sorts, wild and crazy, begging him to make love to her. Maybe she jotted down some of her thoughts when there were moments of clarity. He'd have to open the journal to find out.

He felt like he was invading her privacy. It was Jefferey's thoughts and dreams on the paper. Harrison smiled as he stared at her scribbling; Jefferey's penmanship was beautiful. The words flowed across the page like that of an established writer. These were words of an intelligent woman.

Harrison's mouth flew open as he continued to read. Jefferey had penned something in the journal less than two weeks ago. She spoke of her love for him and H. J. and how she wanted her family to be one again.

Tears blurred the words on the page. Where had the woman who'd written these words gone? Abandoning his wife at this time would seem cruel, but he'd given up so much already in hopes that she'd find her way back to his heart.

Not able to read any more, Harrison shut the journal and replaced it in the drawer. He sat on the bed for more than an hour, thinking and going over in his mind what he needed to do. In the end, his head said stay on course, while his heart begged to differ. He got up, looked around, and shut the door.

"My work here is done. I've got to move on while I still can."

CHAPTER SEVENTY

FIX IT JESUS

Octber was around the corner. The fast falling leaves and cool weather was an indication that Queenie's New Year's Eve wedding was on fast approach and she hadn't ordered invitations or made any real preparations for the wedding. She wanted it to be a small affair—not a lot of fanfare. In truth, she wondered if marriage was what she really wanted.

Tossing her daydream, she pulled her car in front of Connie and Preston's house. Yolanda had shacked up at her sister's place since her supposed sighting of Illya. Queenie honked the horn, anxious to get on the road to Charlotte to help Bertha with her father's estate.

Yolanda flew out of the house in a pair of jeans, camel-colored knit top, and a blue-tweed blazer. Queenie smiled at her friend, as she got in the car. She was fortunate to have good girlfriends who had her back and she could confide in.

"What's up, Q, looking all fabulous in your gold and white. I can't believe you're sporting a white jean pantsuit after Labor Day."

"Fashion trends have changed. You're up in the fashion capital all the time; white is acceptable whenever you feel like wearing it. All those southern taboos are for the birds, but you won't catch my behind in a pair of white shoes, though."

Yolanda laughed. "Whatever the new fashion trend is, you're rocking that outfit. Looks like you've lost a few pounds."

"Where? If anything, I've added a few pounds on my feet. I've been having problems with them swelling."

"Haven't you been taking your high-blood pressure pills?"

"Yeah, but I'm sure it's has to do with the stress of Daddy dying. I have so many regrets and I can't do anything about it." Queenie pulled away from the curb and headed toward Capital Boulevard. "How are things going with the Illya saga?"

Yolanda sighed. "I'm really in a dilemma as to what I should do; however, I have made one decision after talking it over with Connie and Preston."

"What's that?"

"I'm going to tell Stefan. Our short time together has been based on honesty, and he needs to know that his Aunt Marjorie's friend who showed up with her at the dinner was perpetrating a fraud...that Illya was well aware of who I was, as I was well aware of who he was, and that he threatened me. The only thing that scares me is that Illya is FBI and he might retaliate. In my wildest dreams, Q, I would've never thought Illya was this kind of man. I really cared about him, but damn, I am afraid of that man."

"It's a wise decision to tell Stefan now. Nip the questions in the bud now. Don't make Stefan have to wonder about you."

"Stefan's family has money and I'm sure plenty of connections. They seem to like me, and I need them on my side."

"Fix it, Jesus."

Yolanda laughed. "Q, quit. You are so crazy."

Hitting the freeway, they drove along in silence. Queenie was deep in thought, wanting to share her feelings about marriage. They had a couple of hours before arriving in Charlotte.

"YoYo..."

Yolanda looked over at her friend who hadn't finished her sentence. "You okay, Q?"

"Yeah, yeah." Queenie kept her eyes on the road and sighed. "Marriage...I'm not sure that I'm ready for it. I love Donald, but I've been so used to my freedom; I'm not sure I want someone sucking up my free time on a permanent basis."

"You've got cold feet. That's what it sounds like to me."

Sighing again, Queenie tapped the steering wheel. "I've been having these gnawing feelings about permanency—someone sharing what I have and the inability to move about like I've been so used to doing. Believe it or not, I haven't ordered invitation the first, let alone made any real plans for a wedding. I've looked at dresses, but I'm indecisive about that."

"You love Donald, and he loves you. Donald is a man of God...a man you can trust with your life. You talked about having a partner who loves you unconditionally. Girl, don't blow this. Weigh the odds —Donald Griffin...Linden Robinson."

"Girl, you're the one that's crazy. Linden Robinson needs to dig a hole and fall in it. I'm sure you're right—pre-wedding jitters. Donald is the one for me."

"Fix it Jesus, fix it," Yolanda sang, making up her on melody while clapping her hands. "Fix it Jesus, fix it."

"He'll do it for you; he'll do it for me," Queenie sang.

Queenie and Yolanda laughed their heads off and then got quiet again until they arrived in Charlotte.

"We're going to my dad's house. I'm nervous; I hadn't been to see him in all those years, and now I'm visiting the house he shared with my stepmother to handle his business. I feel like a hypocrite, YoYo."

"God forgives you; it appears Bertha has forgiven you."

"She's the nicest woman. I hate to say this, YoYo, but she's much nicer than my own momma. I truly believe I understand why Daddy had to get away from her." Queenie frowned. She couldn't believe those words left her mouth.

"It's alright, Q. You're finally growing up."

Queenie exited the freeway. At the stop light, she turned in Yolanda's direction. "I'm so glad you're with me today. Jesus is fixing something on the inside."

CHAPTER SEVENTY-ONE

SAVING MY SISTER

Queenie and Bertha worked well together. Bertha was appreciative of Queenie's time, especially since she didn't understand half of the forms they had to complete. The surprise was that Marshall Jackson left both of his daughters a nice sum of money, and Bertha would be well taken care of.

"We're taking you out to lunch, Mother Bertha," Queenie announced. "I want a good, juicy steak."

"That's nice of you, Queenie, but you and Yolanda don't need to worry about me. You have a long ride back to Raleigh."

"No, you're going to get out of the house and have a nice meal that you didn't cook."

"I'm still eating leftovers that the church folks brought by. I don't eat that much and I had to freeze a lot of it."

"Save it for tomorrow's lunch or dinner. You're going out with us. Right, YoYo?"

"That's right, Mother Bertha."

"Okay, if you insist."

The doorbell rang, startling all of them.

"Are you expecting company?" Queenie asked teasingly. "Daddy is in the ground so you are free to entertain gentleman callers." Yolanda rolled her eyes at Queenie.

"Queenie Jackson, get out of my face and answer that door for me. Marshall Jackson was the only man for me. Anyway, I'm too old to be entertaining, although one of Marshall's old deacon brothers whispered to me at the funeral that he loved healthy women who could cook."

Queenie and Yolanda fell out laughing. "You're kidding, Mother Bertha," Q said.

"If I hadn't been grieving, I would've punched him in his dirty little mouth." The ladies laughed. "Now get that door, Queenie. Whoever it is sure is persistent."

Queenie walked from the living room into the small foyer that was lined with live plants. She opened the door and was pleasantly surprised. Harrison, looking fine and debonair stood on the porch. She greeted him warmly. "Come in." Queenie gave him a big hug.

"This is a surprise. I thought it was your car parked outside. I dropped by to see if Mother Bertha needed anything."

"We've finished transacting some business and are about to go to lunch. Why don't you join us? My girlfriend, Yolanda, is here with me."

"Sure, I don't mind if I do." Harrison walked in the house and greeted everyone. He gave Mother Bertha a big hug and kiss. "I saw Jefferey this afternoon. In fact, that's where I'm coming from."

Queenie took a seat. "How is she?"

Harrison sat down on the vintage couch next to Queenie. Bertha continued standing, while Yolanda also took a seat in a vintage chair adjacent to the couch.

"Now that she's on meds, Jefferey is a totally different person. She was so apologetic, soft-spoken in her words, but she was the gentle woman I married years ago. It was hard not to scoop her up in my arms and hold her, but I didn't want to offer any false hopes.

"I hadn't said anything to anyone, but I found a journal in one of her drawers that she'd been writing in. Her words were like poetry and it touched my heart. Her thoughts were so lucid...so exact. She's an excellent writer. I wished she got the help she needed sooner."

"Since she's doing much better, is the hospital staff planning to release her soon?"

"Mother Bertha, if Jefferey could manage to stay on her meds without supervision that might be a possibility. But there's no way to know...and...and I plan on going through with the divorce; I leave for Afghanistan next week. I'm still doing contract work.

"I'm unhappy; I've been unhappy for a long time. I can't forfeit the rest of my life waiting for Jefferey to get better—if she's going to get better. It sounds selfish, but I've been through a lot, and I deserve a little happiness."

No one said anything. Queenie thought of her own selfishness— how she hadn't been there for her sister or father.

"Daddy left me some insurance money." Everyone stared at Queenie. "I'm going to start a foundation in Jefferey's name...to help underserved families who have mentally ill family members and need assistance."

Yolanda got up from her seat and brought her hands to her chest. "That is wonderful, Q. I'm going to donate. Maybe we can get First Lady Jackie on-board and use that television show she and pastor are on to spread the word for good."

Queenie got up from her seat with tears in her eyes. "That's an awesome idea, YoYo." Queenie turned to Harrison. "I understand how you feel, Harrison, but from this day forward, I'm going to be there for my sister...something I've should've done a long time ago."

"That's great, Queenie. Jefferey will be happy when I tell her."

Bertha sat on the couch with tears running down her face. She was overcome with joy.

"If you all are still interested in having lunch, it's my treat," Harrison said. "I have some other things to take care of, but I don't want to miss the opportunity of having lunch with the three finest sisters in Charlotte."

Bertha looked straight at Harrison. "Thank you, son. Thank you for taking care of my little girl all these years. You were a good husband and father and gave more of yourself than Jefferey probably deserved. I love you for it, and I understand you've got to do what you have to do. I'm not mad. I do have a request, though. If you have time, I'd like for you to take me by the hospital to see my daughter."

"I'd like to go too," Queenie said. "It's past time that I had a talk with my sister and offer her what I can."

Harrison shook his head. "You all are beautiful and I hope Jefferey will understand how lucky she is."

CHAPTER SEVENTY-TWO

COINCIDENCE?

olanda was rejuvenated after spending the day with Queenie and her family in Charlotte. She had a renewed sense of being coming from that experience. Although it was late in the evening, she decided that it was time for her to go home and stop running from the demon called Illya. Tonight, she would tell Stefan all about him and all that occurred during the week since she left New York. Before she did that, she was going to call Pastor and ask him to pray for her.

Retrieving her mail, Yolanda went through her house and made sure everything was in order. It was just as she left it. Feeling much better, she went to the kitchen and put water in the tea kettle to make some tea. She sat at the kitchen table and rummaged through her mail.

There was a letter addressed to her with no return address. It was postmarked in Raleigh only the day before. Yolanda sighed, sliced the envelope open with her finger, and took out the contents.

A paralyzing fear came over her. In letters cut from a magazine, two words appeared on the paper. MARRY ME. There wasn't a signature, telephone number or any identifiable anything that pointed to the sender. But Yolanda knew who'd sent it. It was from Illya.

She jumped when her cell phone interrupted the quiet in the room. Answering on the first ring, she felt solace when she heard his voice.

"Stefan, I'm so glad it's you."

"I told you I'd be calling. You didn't forget, did you?"

"No, I didn't forget."

"Well, I have a surprise for you."

"Stefan, I hope the surprise can wait. I have something important to tell you."

"What is it, baby?"

"Do you remember the man that came to the restaurant with your Aunt Marjorie last Saturday?"

"Yeah, the guy with the dreads. Mom said that the guy used to date Aunt Marjorie when they were in college. However, he dumped her for some other chick that he eventually married. Mom said she was shocked to see him with Aunt Marjorie. She said they hadn't spoken to each other in over twenty years."

"Do you think it was a coincidence?"

"It's what I call six degrees of separation. This is a small world."

"Listen, Stefan. It wasn't a coincidence. I knew the guy the minute he stepped in the restaurant."

"You didn't say anything."

"For one, I was flabbergasted. I couldn't believe my eyes when I saw him walk in with your aunt like they were on a date. And then he acted as if he didn't know me at all, that is until I went to the restroom when everyone was up having fun."

"What happened when you went to the restroom?"

"He appeared out of nowhere and told me that I wasn't going to marry you; that I belonged to him. In fact, he grabbed my arm and said it in a threatening manner."

"Why are just now telling me this? Do you and this guy have something going on?"

"He's an old boyfriend. I broke it off with him, but he saw me in the airport the night you arrived after we'd come back from New York. I believe he's been watching me.

"Earlier in the week, I could've sworn I saw him near the spa where Queenie and I went to have some girl time. I confronted him about his whereabouts, but he denied having been at the place where I thought I saw him. My eyes didn't deceive me. I had not seen this side of Illya before, and being afraid, I've been at my sister's house since Wednesday. I told her about what was going on, and she agreed that it was time to tell you."

"I'm glad you didn't wait any longer. This guy sounds like a psychopath."

"The funny thing is he works for the FBI. He knows how to use all kinds of tactics to get to a person. I've seen him in action."

"We're going to have to do something about it. My surprise is that I'm in town. I flew in only minutes ago. Don't come and pick me up; I'll get a cab and come there. Make sure your doors are locked and windows closed. I'll be right there."

"Hurry, baby. And oh, I received a letter in the mail today; I'm sure it was from him, although it wasn't signed. The letters were cut out of a magazine."

"Damn, baby. What did it say?"

"Marry me."

Yolanda could hear Stefan breathing deeply. "I'm coming."

CHAPTER SEVENTY-THREE

WHAT'S LOVE GOT TO DO WITH IT?

 olanda went from room to room, making sure that all windows were shut and locked, as well as the doors that led outside. She turned every light on in the house and continued to walk from one room to another, not sure of what to do next.

The steam from the tea kettle roared, and Yolanda nearly fell trying to run from the sound. This was no way to live her life; she hadn't been this frightened in years.

She fixed herself a cup of tea and sat down at the kitchen table. The letter was still there staring up at her. She picked it up and analyzed the two words. What was going on in Illya's head? He seemed to shy away from any talk of marriage and she understood.

The doorbell rang. She looked at her watch. Twenty minutes had passed. She ran to the door and pulled it open, glad that Stefan was there, but when she took a second look, there stood Illya with two dozen red roses.

Yolanda stood there, frozen in place. She stared at Illya, her heart sinking to the floor.

"Aren't you going to let me in?" Illya asked, finally pushing past her. "The flowers are for you. Red roses signify love."

Illya moved through her house liked he belonged there. Yolanda followed right behind him. He went to the kitchen and went under the sink where Yolanda kept her empty vases. Pulling a tall slender vase from underneath the sink, he filled it with water, arranged the flowers neatly, and sat them in the middle of her table. Then he took her hand.

"What are you doing here, Illya?"

"I'm claiming what's mine." He finally saw the piece of paper with the words marry me on it and smiled. "I see you received my letter."

"This isn't funny, Illya. Your behavior is bizarre. Never in my wildest dreams did I think you'd be the one to hurt me." Yolanda threw up her hands. "I want you to leave right now."

"If I leave, you're coming with me."

"No, Illya, I'm not going anywhere. This is my house and you're no longer welcome."

Illya knocked the flowers off the table and Yolanda jumped back. She threw both hands up.

"YoYo, I love you. I can't see you with another man. If I can't have you, no one will."

"Why, Illya? Why are you doing this to me? You have not once talked to me about taking our relationship to another level. In fact, whenever I've mentioned the word marriage, you would shy away from the conversation."

"My marriage to my ex was hell. I suffered and stayed with her for more years than I could count, although there wasn't any love in it."

"I'm sorry that you had an unhappy marriage with your ex, but that doesn't change anything between us."

"I want to be with you."

"But I don't love you, Illya."

"What's love got to do with it?"

A confused look came over Yolanda. Who was this man standing in her house ranting and raving about wanting to marry her? "Love has everything to do with it. Illya, if I thought that we had something, we wouldn't be here having this conversation. I'm not trying to hurt you, but I can no longer see us in a relationship...let alone married."

Illya's head snapped around at the knock on the door. "Who's coming to see you this late in the evening? You've got someone else trying to get under your dress?"

"Is that what this is all about? You haven't gotten laid in a while and you need a comfortable spot to put your dick? So you run to the accommodating Yolanda, who will roll over for you anytime, who'll let you have your way with her and allow you to satisfy your thirst until the next time you feel the need to empty your tank? I'm not the one, Jack." Yolanda snapped her fingers. "I'm not the one."

Getting up enough nerve, she pushed past Illya and ran to the door. Illya caught her arm and pulled her back. "The door is unlocked!" Yolanda screamed. "The door is unlocked."

With her neck in a headlock, the door flew open. Stefan tore through the foyer and punched Illya in the face. Illya punched back, releasing Yolanda who fell to the floor. It looked like the WWE, except that no one lifted the other up in the air and let them fall to the floor.

Regaining her composure, Yolanda got up from the floor, ran and got her cell phone and dialed nine-one-one. When she returned, Stefan had blood dripping from his lip.

"Yolanda is mine," Illya retorted.

"I'm not going to argue with you, man. What you need to do is march your ass out of here now before I call the police."

"I am the police, fool." Illya whipped out his badge and pushed it in Stefan's face. "Nobody can touch me."

"Suit yourself, but my fiancé would like for you to leave. I have no issue with you, although my Aunt Marjorie may not say the same. Whoever you are, you've barked up the wrong tree."

Illya stopped and nursed her knuckles. "What do you see in him, YoYo? He's a white punk who thinks he can take our women from us."

"You don't have me, Illya. I'm no longer your convenience tissue you can blow your nose into when the need arises. I'm not sure what went wrong with us, but we've come to the end of the road."

At that moment, there was pounding on the front door. "This is the police department."

Illya rushed to the door and opened it. Four police officers invaded Yolanda's home. "We're here from the Raleigh Police Department," the lead officer said. "We received a call regarding a domestic violence dispute." He looked at the three people standing in front of him.

Illya pulled out his badge again. "I'm with the FBI. I was investigating…"

"Sir, this man," pointing at Illya, "accosted me," Yolanda said. "My fiancé stopped by in the nick of time."

"Is this true?" the officer asked, looking at Illya's badge once more.

Illya conceded. "Yeah, it's true. You'd think that white folks got their run of the country and now they're trying to take our women. It's a damn shame."

Yolanda and Stefan stood back and said nothing.

"Do you want to press charges?" the officer asked.

Yolanda looked at Illya for a long time. She remembered all he had done to help Preston get out of the mess he was in last year. "No, I don't want to press charges; he's had a little too much to drink.

"Come on, Mr. FBI. We're going to take you in anyway. Maybe a night in the slammer will do you some good." The officer handcuffed Illya and dragged him away.

When the cops departed, Yolanda fell into Stefan's arms. She closed her eyes and cried into his shoulders. "I hope it's over."

"Why didn't you want to press charges?"

"Stefan, I'm not sure what was going on in Illya's mind. This was so uncharacteristic of him. The main reason I didn't press charges is that he was instrumental in keeping my brother-in-law out of jail after he got caught up in a drug smuggling situation last year. I owe him for that."

"So, he was the guy before me?"

"Yeah."

"We're you still seeing each other when you came to New York?"

"We were somewhat estranged when I came to New York. I hadn't seen him in a while; mostly we conversed over the phone. We were disconnected as a couple and I had planned to call it off. And that's exactly what I did after I met you."

"So, I'm the rebound kid."

"Not at all. You're someone I fell in love with. I wasn't looking for a relationship when I met you, Stefan. You were all up in my cool-aid, and I'll admit at first that I was flattered. But after we began talking every day and night, I realized there was more to you than what I first thought. You were easy to talk to. You were genuine—a complete gentleman in every way. You weren't pretentious and said all of the right things. I'll agree it was fast, but you were someone I could love. When I told Illya that I didn't love him and he asked me what love had to do with it, I knew right then and there that he was the wrong person for me."

Stefan smiled and kissed Yolanda's nose. "I love you and I appreciate you saying all those wonderful things about me…mainly because they are true. I want you to promise me one thing."

"What is that?"

"First thing on Monday morning, I want you to get a restraining order against your ex. I may not be here to protect you the next time around, not that the piece of paper will either, but it'll be on record should he come around trying the same thing again. If there is a next time, he will be going to jail."

"Okay," Yolanda whispered. "I still can't get over him acting like this."

"He doesn't like to lose." Stefan held Yolanda tight and kissed her with everything he had.

CHAPTER SEVENTY-FOUR

FIX MY LIFE

Yolanda thanked God that her life was spared. She was grateful that Stefan had shown up and was in the right place at the right time. His timing was impeccable.

She lay through the night thinking about her life—her relationship with Illya and her engagement to Stefan. Was she rushing into this marriage with Stefan? Was it heaven sent or was she blinded by what might be false adoration to make her think that Stefan was the one. She wasn't wrong.

As if sensing her mood, Stefan held her and nothing more. "YoYo, you've been in deep thought ever since the police left. What's on your mind?"

She sighed. "I was wondering if you were truly the right person for me and if I said I do, would it be for the wrong reason?"

"I don't believe I'm hearing this. I love you, Yolanda Morris. If I have to wait forever, you're still the woman for me. I've given all the reasons why we are meant to be, and I haven't changed my mind for a second. If you want to wait to get married, I can do that."

"I felt like I a receptacle for him to lay his seed anytime he got ready. Do you feel that way, Stefan? Am I only an old-ass whore who knows how to make you feel good at your beck and call?"

Stefan got up on his knees and stared down at Yolanda. "If you think that's who you are, then I don't want to be with you. You are a real woman, who I'll admit has needs, but you're kind, honest, gentle, educated, and do you want me to go on?"

"Thanks, Stefan. I'd like for you to do something for me."

"Whatever you want, I'm game."

"I'd like for you to go to church with me this morning. I've got to give God praise for who he is to me. If it wasn't for his grace and mercy…"

"I'd be more than happy to accompany you to church. Do they have good singing? That's what I want to hear."

"The preaching is good, too. Jackie's husband is our pastor."

"Jackie is a mess."

"She sure is."

VIDEO CAMERAS and videographers were stationed throughout the church. Yolanda was surprised to see them as she and Stefan walked into the sanctuary. They walked down the aisle and found a seat near the front, not far from where Connie sat holding Desi.

"What's going on?" Stefan wanted to know. "Are they getting ready for a wedding?"

"No," Yolanda whispered. "Pastor and First Lady are part of a television series called *Preachers of Raleigh*. They must be taping a segment today."

"Oh." Stefan sat back in his seat.

The congregation seemed alive today, as they sang along with the choir and patted their feet. Even Sister Minnie had pep in her step as she read the church announcements. After the choir sang, First Lady Jackie O'Neill stood up at the piano. One of the deacons rushed to give her a microphone.

Dressed to the nines in her burgundy, two-piece wool suit,

trimmed with a detachable fox collar, Jackie stood tall and made her way to the front of the church, holding a piece of paper. Her ten-inch tall burgundy hat, whose brim was almost as wide, and had a black three-inch ribbon running around the crown, almost blocked her eyes as she stared out into the audience. The cameramen could be seen searching for the best angle.

"Good morning, church," First Lady Jackie began. "It's so good to see so many of you here. The reason I stand before you is to share something that has been burning on my heart."

Yolanda looked at Connie who stared back. Yolanda had been focusing so much on herself that she had been somewhat out of the loop. She didn't realize Jackie had being going through. She entwined her fingers with Stefan's, squeezed his hand, and waited for Jackie to finish sharing.

A couple of weeks ago, our dear sister, Queenie Jackson, lost her father. He suffered a massive heart attack, and a week ago we buried him. But what you aren't aware of is that her sister's mental illness was an indirect cause of her father's heart attack."

Jackie looked down at the piece of paper she was holding and began to read from it. "What is mental illness? It is a medical condition that disrupts a person's thinking, feeling, mood, and ability to relate to others and daily functioning or the inability to cope with the ordinary demands of life.

"Jefferey Jackson-Quick, Queenie's sister, visited with us here not too long ago. Some of us had the opportunity to dine with her later and judged her harshly, as she was acting out inappropriately. But what none of us knew at the time was that Jefferey was suffering…had been suffering a long time without any help. It grieves my heart that there are men and women, boys and girls, who are out there in the same predicament as Jefferey. We laugh and point our fingers, but hardly do we ever lift a hand to find out the 'what' or the 'why.' There was a reason Jefferey ended up on Queenie's doorstep in July; it was to get help."

Yolanda looked up at Queenie who was sitting in the choir stand. She had a tissue to her eyes as First Lady spoke.

"I've spoken to Pastor O'Neill about Jefferey, and he and I are establishing a foundation in Jefferey's name to help families who need assistance in assisting a family member who needs medical attention due to mental disorders."

The congregation stood up and clapped their hands. And then they sat down.

"Sister Queenie, please come down and stand with me," Jackie said.

Moving slowly, Queenie joined First Lady Jackie down front. Pastor O'Neill also came down and joined them.

"The foundation will be named the Jefferey Shaunice Jackson-Quick Foundation for Mental Illness," Jackie continued. "Pastor and I are donating all the proceeds from our television show, *Preachers of Raleigh*, to the Foundation."

The congregation stood up and roared, clapped their hands and stomped their feet in praise. Queenie laid her head on Jackie's shoulder and cried. Yolanda and Connie got up out of their seats and joined them at the front. Emma came down from the choir stand and locked arms with her girlfriends.

The cameramen were getting close-up shots and zoomed around the sanctuary. It was a glorious morning. And then Stefan moved forward.

Yolanda looked at Stefan, as if he was out-of-order. She was happy that he understood the seriousness of what was going on, but there was no reason for him to be up front. No one knew who he was. And then he whispered something in First Lady Jackie's ear, and she handed him the microphone.

The congregation quieted down and took their seats. Stefan held the microphone to his mouth, cleared his throat and began to speak. Yolanda's eyes bulged from their sockets, wondering what in the world Stefan was going to say.

"Hello, my name is Stefan Morisilli. I'm a friend of Yolanda Morris. Actually, Yolanda is my fiancée; I've asked her to marry me."

A low murmuring could be heard throughout the church. Yolanda looked as if she wanted to die. Emma, Connie and First Lady looked from one to the other.

"The reason I'm up here, however, is to donate ten thousand dollars to the Foundation that First Lady and Pastor O'Neill have set up in Queenie's sister's name. For each of the next five years, I'd like to donate ten thousand dollars, which will make that a fifty-thousand dollar gift. I challenge you to do the same, even if it's ten or twenty dollars a year."

The congregation was back on its feet, cheering louder than before. Queenie hugged Stefan, as did the other four ladies. Yolanda hugged him the longest. Untying himself from their embrace, Stefan said one last thing.

"Mental illness impacts individuals and their families in many ways, but whatever we can do to assist those individuals at the early stages of their wellness would be exceptional. There's no cure, but recognizing the symptoms and getting the help to those individuals early, especially assisting those families when there is a financial need is what this is all about. Thank you for your time. We have to do what we can to fix a life."

People cried and rejoiced—the cameras capturing every minute of it. Pastor O'Neill threw his hands up and said church was dismissed and that the sermon had already gone forth. It was a great day at Shiloh Baptist Church.

CHAPTER SEVENTY-FIVE

LUNCH IS ON ME

They headed for Nantucket Grill. Pastor Franklin joined the ladies, so as not to leave Stefan alone to fend off the wolves who were dressed in women's clothing. Even the camera crew hurried ahead, once they learned their destination, hoping to get some good footage for the show.

As the group took their seat, their faces still had a glow on them—First Lady and Pastor O'Neill, Queenie, Yolanda, Stefan, Emma, Connie and baby Desi. Queenie was rather quiet, not used to being paid the kind of tribute she was paid today, even if it was in honor of her sister. She wished Harrison and Mother Bertha could've been there to hear the announcement; they would've been grateful.

After giving the orders to the waitress, Queenie cleared her throat. "First Lady...Pastor O'Neill, I'm still overcome by your generosity today. It was only last week that I told YoYo, Jefferey's mom, and Harrison that I was going to donate the money Daddy left me to start a Foundation in Jefferey's name for the very same purpose. And Stefan, I can't thank you enough; I'm overwhelmed by it all. As most of you are aware, I wasn't the best sister I could've been to Jefferey, and I hate myself for it. I lost out on many good years with my father because of my self-loathing hatred of my sister and her mother, but I'm glad that it isn't too late to do something for my sister."

"For a long time, Q, I've toiled with how I could be a bigger benefit to others. I'm a preacher's wife and I'm joined at the hip with him in his ministry. But I've always had a desire to do more. And when I learned about Jefferey's illness, I knew this was it. I, too, have a distant family member who suffers from a mental illness." Jackie looked lovingly at her husband, Franklin, and then back at the group. "And while I wasn't close to that family member, Jefferey's illness put it all in perspective."

Everyone nodded and waited for the next person to say something.

"Well, let's change the mood. This is a celebration, and I'm hungry," Pastor O'Neill said. "Down and sad faces have got to go. And I'm not trying to take away from what the celebration is all about. Am I right?"

"Yeah!" the group said in unison.

"So, Stefan...I didn't catch your last name..."

"Morsilli."

"So Brother Morsilli, you announced your intentions of making Sister Yolanda a modern housewife again."

"No, just my wife, Pastor."

"Well, while I'm all up in your business...awww, why did you hit me, Jackie?"

Everyone laughed.

"You said it yourself, Franklin; you're all up in Stefan and Yolanda's business."

Pastor O'Neill threw his hand at Jackie. "This is man talk."

"Um, hum."

"Listen, Stefan, I must ask you. Are you white or black?"

The room erupted in laughter. Jackie rolled her eyes and looked at Franklin.

Stefan chuckled and then looked at the group who broke up in laughter again. "For your edification pastor, I am an Italian/African-

American brother. My black mother married my white, Italian father. They're still together, and it isn't a matter of black or white with us."

"Well, hallelujah," Franklin O'Neill said, slapping the table. "I'm not going to ask any more questions, although I did want to ask how old you were."

This time Yolanda spoke up. "Pastor, please. Leave Stefan alone. He donated ten thousand dollars to your Foundation today. That in and of itself should speak highly of him."

"I'm sorry, Sister Yolanda. Curiosity got the best of me. I haven't any other questions to ask. Lunch is on me."

"Thank you Lord for small blessings," First Lady Jackie said. "And here comes the food now."

Lunch was a pleasant experience. There wasn't any taunting or fighting between the ladies. Everyone was on their best behavior. The ladies seemed to enjoy the company of the two men who'd joined them. When they had finished eating and had pushed their plates to the center, Queenie tapped her water glass with her knife. And when she got everyone's attention, she spoke.

"I can't tell you what today has meant to me. It has brought me a lot of joy. I love you all from the bottom of my heart and I couldn't have a better set of friends." Queenie raised her glass of water. "To Yolanda and Stefan, I wish you all the best. You are the one Stefan, and I'm glad my girl, Yolanda, found you. New York was meant to be."

"I'll drink to that," Connie said. "I'm a woman of few words, but I'm sorry if I judged you harshly, sister. I see what you see in Stefan. And I'm sure the more I'm around him, I'll get to know him even better."

"Yes," said the group in unison.

"My wedding day is coming soon," Queenie began again. "I want to have it at the church and I want it to be simple. Ladies, you all are my bridesmaids, and Emma is my matron-of-honor. I wanted you all to be my matron-of-honor, but I had to choose one."

"I'll play the music for you," First Lady said. "I don't need to be in it."

"That'll work. Pastor, I need you to officiate."

"Ain't nobody else coming up in my church to do it. I'll be there front and center to marry you, my dear Queenie."

"Remember, the day is New Year's Eve. Donald and I would like to bring in the New Year as husband and wife."

"As long as God says so," Pastor interjected.

"YoYo, you and Stefan should join us and make this a double wedding."

"We've already talked about this, Q. You told me I couldn't get married before you, and this is your day—yours and Donald's."

"Pastor can always pronounce you all man and wife second."

"Q, you're a mess." Yolanda looked at Stefan and patted his hand. "We'll wait. In fact, you may have to leave on your honeymoon from New York. I haven't said anything to Stefan yet, but I'd like to get married in New York on New Year's Day."

"But that's so selfish, YoYo," Connie said. "We won't be there."

"How about I fly everyone to New York?" Stefan volunteered. "That way you can meet my family and we can see Queenie and her new husband off on their honeymoon."

Queenie slapped Stefan's hand. "I like this man. New York is where you guys met."

"Right," Yolanda agreed.

"So…, who's going to officiate the wedding?" Pastor O'Neill asked.

"You will, of course, along with the pastor from my mother's church," Stefan replied.

"All right then. This is cause for a celebration!" Pastor waved at the waitress. "Another round of soda, please."

Everyone broke into laugher once again.

CHAPTER SEVENTY-SIX

WITH THIS RING

$\mathcal{T}$he next few months flew by without fanfare. Christmas had come and gone, and New Year's Eve had arrived. Queenie was going to finally marry her king.

Emma, Yolanda, and Connie were gathered at Queenie's house to assist their best friend with final bridal preparations. Yolanda and Connie wore sangria-colored, strapless, cocktail length dresses by Alfred Sung that hit right at the knee. Swarovski crystal pieces were sewn around the bodice to serve as a belt, and they wore earrings of the same crystal that were shaped liked teardrops. Matching four-inch heels adorned their feet. Emma's dress and shoes were the same, but in candy-coral.

Simple and elegant was Queenie's white-satin, strapless dress, with a mermaid sweep train. While white usually magnified one's weight, Queenie's dress settled around her perfectly, not annunciating her full figure to the point that tongues would be wagging.

"You look beautiful," Emma said to Queenie, as she fastened a pearl necklace around her neck. "Donald is going to eat you up."

"I certainly hope so, E. I've been waiting on this day for far too long." The ladies laughed. "I don't believe I'm admitting this, though, but your girl is a little nervous. What if Linden Robinson shows up?"

Emma looked at her friend and smiled. "He's been barred from these festivities. There's nothing for you to worry about. If by chance that sorry jackass tries anything, the girls and I will handle him." The girls all chimed in agreement.

"As for you being nervous, Q, you have every right to be," Yolanda said, looking at herself in the long mirror in Queenie's room. "You're making a big step at your age. Freedom has been your middle name for the last twenty or so years, but you're giving up that freedom for a man who really loves you and treats you like the queen you really are."

Queenie smiled, went to where Yolanda stood, and hugged her. Emma and Connie had their arms outstretched, and Queenie hugged them too.

"Whew, I wasn't sure I was going to look this fabulous in this dress, but one Body Magic and one body shaper works wonders." The ladies flooded the room with laughter. "I guess Donald will get his first glimpse of what it'll be like to take care of a full-figured momma when he has to help me take off the stuff that's holding this stuff in."

"Q, you're wrong for that. I'm trying to keep my make-up on my face, while you keep coming with the jokes that have my eyes tearing. I can't be a beautiful Matron of Honor with mascara running down my face."

Queenie took a tissue and dabbed at Emma's face. "You're perfect now. What you need to do is let Terrance have some to calm you down."

It was Connie's turn to put her two cents in. "Q, you're messy. Emma hasn't said one word about being frazzled or walking down the aisle with Terrance. But as usual, you had to turn this conversation into something about sex."

"Look who's talking. You're getting it on the regular. We all know that Preston is working your pipes. If you weren't taking birth control, I'm sure you'd be an old woman with lots of babies."

Connie laughed at Queenie. "Don't worry about what my man is giving me. I feel so sorry for Donald. He's going to have to take a sabbatical from your horny ass so he can get a breath of fresh air."

"Connie!" Yolanda yelled, jumping into the fray. "What's wrong with you, sis?"

"Q knows I'm messing with her."

"I did? It felt like an attack on my wedding day. You were laying it on, Connie, but you were telling the truth. Honey, honey, honey, I'm going to wear Donald out." The ladies howled.

"A horn is blowing," Emma said, lifting up one of the blinds in Queenie's bedroom and peering out onto the street. "A beautiful, white stretch limo is parked outside. Five o'clock will be here in a minute. It's time to get this party started."

"Amen," both Yolanda and Connie said in unison.

Emma picked up the train on Queenie's dress and the group proceeded down the stairs. Not wanting to wear a veil, a thin circular band with featherlike protrusions that boasted Swarovski Crystal pieces glued on each end, was placed in Queenie's red Afro. She looked like a black-Greek goddess.

Leading the way, Queenie slowly turned around and blew kisses at her girlfriends. "I love you all."

The wedding was beautiful, elegant in every way. Video cameras from the *Preachers of Raleigh* series were there to record the momentous occasion. The church was filled to capacity and was decorated in splashes of burgundy, white, wine, and soft pink. The candelabras stood tall and inviting, waiting to be lit. Mother Bertha, along with several cousins on Queenie's father's side, sat in the front. But as Queenie walked down the aisle by herself, she was surprised to not only see Jefferey sitting next to her mother, but Harrison and H. J. were there too. A tear slipped from Queenie's eye.

A large contingency came from Atlanta to support Donald. The whole Griffin family took up at least three rows.

First Lady Jackie looked as if she was trying to out-do Queenie in her finery—her gold and egg-shell, brocade suit and matching hat that sat seemingly ten feet high on her head, vying for the cover of *Ebony* magazine or *Vogue*. But it was Pastor Franklin O'Neill who took the cake in his gold and egg-shell-colored robe—the gold lame` crosses stitched on both sides and blazing bright. He could've been mistaken for the Pope.

Three turtle doves were released in the sanctuary after *The Lord's Prayer* was sung. You could see people ducking as the birds flew overhead and into a waiting cage. The funniest moment came during the ring ceremony.

Pastor O'Neill asked for the bride's ring. Terrance passed it to Donald who passed it to the pastor. Pastor O'Neill instructed Donald to put the ring on Queenie's finger and repeat after him.

"With this ring," Donald repeated. However, before Donald was able to repeat any more of the vow, Queenie turned the ceremony into a comedy act.

"Yes, oh yes, I promise, I'll always love you." She went on and on before Pastor O'Neill was able to quiet her down.

The audience was in stitches, but with the exception of that moment, everything else was beautiful.

The reception was held in the church social hall that was turned into a lavish room fit for a Queen and her king. From the sit-down dinner to all of the festivities that were part of the reception, Queenie was happy. The only thing missing was the dancing, but Queenie said she'd have a great big party when she returned from her honeymoon.

CHAPTER SEVENTY-SEVEN

A NEW YEAR

$\mathscr{I}$t was time for them to fly to New York. What no one counted on was Stefan arranging a private plane for their flight. The group that consisted of Yolanda; Connie, Preston, and baby Desi; Queenie and Donald; Emma and Terrance; and First Lady Jackie and Pastor O'Neill were elated at their first-class accommodations.

The buttery-colored plush leather seats in the interior of the plane conformed to everyone's body. Even Desi went right to sleep as soon as everyone was situated. One lone flight attendant was onboard to take care of their needs, and the champagne went round and round. By the time they arrived in New York, the group was in a festive mood. It was a quarter to midnight.

The private plane taxied onto the private airfield. The wide-eyed revelers peered out of the plane. On the ground was a black, stretch limo and Stefan stood beside it.

"I'm ready to get off," Yolanda said, unbuckling her seatbelt before the plane had come to a complete stop. "I want to be in my man's arms when the clock strikes twelve." Everyone laughed.

Queenie and Donald were all hugged up, kissing each other every

WHAT'S LOVE GOT TO DO WITH IT

moment they could. They didn't need to wait on the New Year to ring in. They were on cloud nine and the first leg of their honeymoon. Emma and Terrance played patsy with their hands, the mood of the day seeming to encompass them. Connie and Preston were still enjoying the newness of their marriage, so calm and unassuming. First Lady and Pastor were pecking each other's lips in between the sips of bubbly.

The plane now at a full stop, the pilot appeared from the cockpit and wished everyone a Happy New Year. He opened the hatch and let the stairs down. Yolanda was first out, nearly leaping out of the plane and down the steps into Stefan's arms. The chauffeur from the limo began to count down, and when he said Happy New Year, the happy travelers grabbed their mates, held each other tight, said Happy New Year, and kissed each other.

"Happy New Year," Stefan said. "Today, our lives will be changed forever, and only for the better. I love you, YoYo."

Yolanda looked deep into Stefan's eyes. "I love you more than you'll ever know."

Queenie hit Yolanda with her elbow. "Did you see Emma slobbering all over Terrance?"

"Girl, I was lock jawed with my man, but I wish I had seen it. Emma seems to be warming up to him, Q."

"Hmph, I think Emma has already warmed up to Mr. Terrance Griffin; she's just not saying."

Stefan waved his hands. "Let's get in the limo everybody. The night is young and I hope you're ready to hang. My parents are hosting a New Year's Eve party at the Roosevelt Hotel near Central Park, and I was instructed to bring you all straight there."

"Stefan, if you don't mind, First Lady and I would like to go to our hotel. We aren't partyers and we don't want to crimp what you've got going on."

"No problem, Rev, we'll drop you and Jackie off at the Marriott Marquis in Manhattan. I've booked everyone there. I want you well rested for our one o'clock wedding later today."

"Thank you, Stefan. We appreciate it."

"We can't take Desi to the party," Connie said with concern.

"There will be someone there to assist with the children, Connie. You and Preston are coming with us. We'll take good care of your little one."

"Thanks, Stefan."

Connie fell in love with Stefan's mother. She was so gracious. His father was funny, especially with too much to drink in his belly. She was happy for her sister, happy that she found someone who truly loved her for who she was, who adored the ground that she walked on, and was interested in her well-being. While she and Preston danced, she took some time to sit back and watch. Yolanda was in good hands.

The party lasted until four in the morning. Queenie and Donald were anxious to get to their honeymoon bed. Stefan reserved a special suite for them to enjoy before heading out to Australia. They were in wedded bliss.

Emma and Terrance took separate rooms. They had so much fun dancing and getting to know each other again. They were happy that the evening afforded this for them. Terrance escorted Emma to her room, but turned to her.

"You can stay with me the night if you like."

Emma didn't say a word. She wrapped her arms in his and followed him into his room.

Yolanda wanted to be alone to meditate and pray. God had blessed her beyond measure and in less than nine hours, she was going to be someone's wife—a new year with promise.

CHAPTER SEVENTY-EIGHT

YOLANDA MAXWELL MORSILLI

olanda Maxwell Morris looked stunning in a Maggie Sottero gown, with its corded embroidered lace appliqués that sat on top of illusion sleeves and a sweetheart neckline that plunged to her heart. The V-back was as dramatic as the front, and Stefan's heart dropped when he saw his bride walk down the aisle in that beautiful, white gown. It wasn't an understatement as to how gorgeous she looked, as the scores of Stefan's family and friends hung their lips in awe.

The church was an old relic in Harlem. It was an architectural dream—it's stained-glass windows dating back over a century. It had the feel of old-world renaissance where poets, literary artists, jazz and blues musicians, and others came to praise their God but also where they came together to entertain their souls and minds in the arts.

Connie was Yolanda's Matron of Honor, and she looked beautiful in the dress she wore in Queenie's wedding. Likewise, Emma wore her dress, too, and was the only bridesmaid. Queenie sat up front with her new husband, Donald, and his brother, Terrance, she still in a tranquil state after having pledged her love and stating her vows only hours earlier. First Lady Jackie sat on the pew with them, but wore a more subdued suit from the one she wore at Queenie's wedding.

Stefan's mother, Tracey, and her sister, Marjorie, looked gorgeous in their iridescent, sky-blue, sleeveless gowns. Tracey wore a matching short jacket, while Marjorie had a fur stole tossed around her shoulders. Each had a beautiful blue corsage with silver trimming that was pinned on their shoulders. There was a large contingency of Afro-Americans from Tracey's side of the family and an even larger Italian population from Stefan's dad's side. The common thread was that happiness was written on every face that graced the place.

Pastor O'Neill and Pastor Gaston, Tracey's pastor, took turns officiating. It seemed so effortless. In less than an hour, Yolanda became Mrs. Yolanda Maxwell Morsilli. The happy couple couldn't stop gazing at each other, their admiration captured for the world to see. And then they kissed as if it was their first time and that they had just discovered something wonderful about each other.

Clearing his throat, Pastor O'Neill gave the couple a gentle nudge to part lips and prepare for the procession. Everyone in the congregation laughed, the Italians being the loudest.

The reception took place at the Marriott Marquis in Times Square where the bridal party were staying. The room was decorated beautifully, and the guests sat down to a full-course meal that consisted of a choice of Beer Brind Double Cut Pork Chop, Roasted Chicken, and Center Cut Beef Tenderloin that was elegantly noted on the menus that sat at each seat. Ice sculptures were placed throughout and beautiful vases of blue, white, and pink hydrangeas sat in vases that were centered on each table. Soft jazz floated throughout the room.

The real surprise was when Tracey and Marjorie sang a beautiful love song to the newlyweds, accompanied by Stefan on the guitar with his band backing them up. There wasn't a dry eye in the house.

The rest of the evening seemed to sail by—good eating and good dancing. And then it was time to say goodbye.

Yolanda and Stefan rushed to their room, not wanting to waste another moment to be with each other intimately.

"Hi, husband."

"Hi, wife. I want all of you tonight."

"I'm yours for your taking."

Slipping Yolanda's dress from her shoulders, Stefan placed kisses on her lips and along her neck, slowly slipping down to her breasts that sat waiting for him. He tenderly nibbled each one and then proceeded to remove the rest of her clothing. He gazed at the woman he selected to be his wife and then eased her naked body onto the bed. And then he undressed, Yolanda watching him with eagerness in her eyes.

Like an experienced painter, he kissed every part of her body, not missing a corner or a crevice, repeating the ritual as Yolanda's body relaxed and he took full control. He fondled her breasts and took liberties with her extended nipples, sucking them until she cried out for him to stop. So seductive and sensual was the foreplay, that Yolanda wrapped her bare legs around his waist, allowing him to tease her with his manhood before he entered the place of total surrender. It was all good. And the night continued for the next four hours, the heat of passion coursing through their loins and roaring to the ultimate climax not once or twice, but three times until they were spent.

In a couple of hours, they would be up again, getting ready to depart for their honeymoon. But what no one knew, besides the people involved, was that Yolanda and Stefan were going to accompany Queenie and Donald to Australia. Yolanda was amazed that Queenie hadn't let the cat out of the bag. Even her sister, Connie, had no idea.

The newlyweds woke from their stupor at the sound of the telephone. Stefan reached over and answered it, thanking the operator for the wake-up call.

"I'll rush through the shower first, baby," he said, placing a kiss on Yolanda's lips.

"Okay, sweetie, I'm right behind you. All I need is five minutes." She kissed him back.

Stefan got up and went into the bathroom. Turning over, Yolanda yawned and stretched her arms in the air. She heard the water flowing in the shower. Stefan would be finished in no time.

Sitting up in the bed, she looked at the nightstand as her cell phone began to ring. It must be Connie checking to see if she was up. Without looking at the caller-ID, she answered the phone, looking down at her wedding ring, the joy still in her heart as she remembered their day. And then she held the phone out, finally looking at the caller-ID.

"What do you want?" she said in a harsh voice. "Why are you calling me?"

"You've made a grave mistake, YoYo. You married that boy anyway...against my wishes. It was supposed to be me and you forever."

Yolanda's hand shook uncontrollably, and she dropped the phone. She ran into the bathroom. "Stefan, Stefan..."

He stuck his head from behind the shower curtain, shampoo covering his head. "What is it, baby?"

"It's Illya Newsome. He's on the phone, warning me about having married you."

With shampoo still in his hair, Stefan snatched the curtain back, got out of the tub, and raced to where Yolanda had dropped the phone. He picked it, but the line was dead. Without saying anything, he dialed the number that appeared as the last call on Yolanda's cell phone. He touched it with his fingers, and the call went through.

"Listen you sorry son-of-a-bitch, if you call my wife again, I will have you castrated."

"I'm the FBI; remember that boy, if you dare to open your mouth again and threaten me."

"That means nothing to me; I'm not the person you want to tangle with." Stefan clicked off the phone and threw it down on the floor.

"What are we going to do, Stefan?"

Stefan picked up the phone. "I'm calling the FBI. Something is wrong with that dude, and he needs to be dealt with. Go ahead and get your shower; this distraction isn't going to ruin our honeymoon."

Yolanda's stomach was in knots but she trusted Stefan. "Okay. I trust that you'll take care of it." Yolanda went into the bathroom and shut the door.

Stefan called the Raleigh Police Department and notified them of what happened. They said that they would look into the matter and take care of notifying the FBI. They would update him periodically on the status. Stefan had promised to keep Yolanda safe and that's what he intended to do.

CHAPTER SEVENTY-NINE

DOWN UNDER

*C*heers could be heard for blocks as Connie and Preston, Emma and Terrance, and First Lady Jackie and Pastor Franklin O'Neill stood in front of the hotel and waved as the limo pulled away from the curb and whisked Mr. and Mrs. Donald Griffin and Mr. and Mrs. Stefan Morsilli to the airport. Soon, they would be boarding a plane to Australia.

"I guess you and Terrance are next," Connie chided Emma.

"Marriage is a long way off for me, if it's to be. Terrance and I are enjoying each other."

"Well, I'm going to give it my all," Terrance volunteered. "Emma is a special lady. I may have to work hard at winning her heart over, but I'm up to the challenge."

Emma looked at him and squeezed his arm.

Preston and Terrance bumped fists. Pastor O'Neill also bumped Terrance's fist with his. "I'll agree," Preston began, "that our women are special. Ask Pastor how hard I had to work to settle Connie down. And Desi came right after."

"If I recall clearly, my dear husband, it was me who had to put you in check...or should I say motivate you to claim the best woman you've ever had. You were real close to losing me."

Pastor O'Neill and Preston bumped fists, while the ladies laughed. "I'm all right with it fellas," Preston said, giving his wife a squeeze. "She's telling the truth; I can admit I was moving a little too slow for Connie's taste, but that's all water under the bridge."

First Lady Jackie smiled. "I'm praying that those two couples, who just left here and are on their way to a grand honeymoon in Australia, will have a happy marriage. They deserve it."

Connie bumped fists with First Lady. "Yes, I agree."

CHAPTER EIGHTY

JEFFEREY SHANICE JACKSON-QUICK

*J*efferey rummaged through her drawer until she found the object of her search. A smile radiated on her face when her fingers touched the journal. She retrieved it from its hiding place and hugged it to her chest, as if it was a long, lost treasure. She needed to write down the good thoughts that rolled around in her head before they turned ugly. However, she felt so much better now that her moods were being controlled by the drugs she was ordered to take.

Looking around the room, Jefferey spotted an ink pen. Snatching an envelope from on top of the dresser, Jefferey clicked the pen and began to scribble, forming small circles and then stopped. She seemed pleased that the pen was in working order.

New Year's Day,

I can breathe. I'm sitting in my own room, away from the clinical and cynical atmosphere of the hospital. I'm grateful to Harrison, the true love of my life. He was kind enough to ask the doctors to release me to his custody so that I could attend my sister's wedding. It was a surprise to me that he had come home on leave...that he and H. J. had gotten together for Christmas, although I wasn't included. Momma came to see me, though. It hurt because I'm sure, as my mother looked at me, her thoughts were about the day Daddy died. If I could turn back the hand of time, I'd do it in a heartbeat. I loved my daddy.

Speaking of Queenie, she looked beautiful in her wedding gown. She looked radiant and she made me feel special, like she was really happy to see me. Now that I'm a resident of the hospital and have time to think, I often wondered what it would've been like to have had a real relationship with my sister. Momma says that Queenie has helped her out a lot and that she really likes her...like she was one of her daughters.

Hmph, Momma. She's special. I can't fault her for the way she feels about me. I was hoping that some of that forgiveness she talks about all the time would materialize in her heart and that she would love me the way she used to. Bertha Jackson loves me; that I'm sure of. However, I stole the one person she loved more than life itself away from her. But she's Momma and mommas are going to love their children no matter how bad they've been.

I've been waiting for the day that my son would come and see me. H. J. has a heart of stone. He told Momma that I caused nothing but pain and misery in our family. He said I ran his daddy away, a man who truly loved me. I wonder if I'll be invited to H. J.'s wedding; Harrison told me that H. J. was planning a June celebration. I'm going to keep hope alive.

My man, Harrison Quick—the center of my being and my one and only love. He tried to love me; he tried to be there for me, but in the end he said he couldn't wait for me any longer. He's in the next room. I wish I could go to him, make passionate love to him, and tell him all of my thoughts and dreams while he holds me, kiss me, make love to me as only he could. That boy is talented with the tongue. LOL...LOL. Yes, Lord. I'm having a mental orgasm just thinking about how Harrison used to touch all the right parts of me until I was on fire and I'd give it all up to him. I was putty in his hands, but I knew how to love my man, too. Satisfied isn't the word I'd use to describe how I truly made my baby feel...more like satiated to the inth degree. He would have a hard time catching his breath after our episodes of lovemaking. The orgasms were powerful and potent, so intoxicating that it would also take my breath away. But I better stop talking...writing like this. I don't want to get my feelings hurt by getting up enough nerve to go next door and beg Harrison to make love to me and be turned down again. Whew.

Thirty minutes have passed since I wrote that last line. I had to get a hold of myself...take care of myself—you know. Well, if you haven't guessed, I'm not going to explain it.

I hear Harrison out in the hallway. I don't want him to know that I have a journal with my thoughts written in it. But I pray for a good year...that 2015 will be good to me...that I can control my illness so that I can come home permanently. And maybe, Harrison will come home to me.

Jefferey Shanice Jackson-Quick

January 1, 2015

AFTERWORD

Mental illness effects millions of people in the U.S. each year and has many sides to itself which include depression, anxiety disorders, schizophrenia, personality disorders, eating disorders and addictive behaviors. Approximately 1 in 5 adults (43.8 million, or 18.5%) experience mental illness in any given year.

In *What's Love Got to Do With It*, Jefferey Shanice Jackson-Quick, suffers from an undiagnosed onset of bipolar/paranoid schizophrenia disorder. In the story, she displays periods of mania and also depressive symptoms which led to her making poor choices; having extreme mood changes and violence.

Jefferey didn't receive the help or the support she needed, while all the signs were there. In her times of lucidity, Jefferey didn't recognize that she was a sick woman, who needed medical attention, however, she did journal instances of her life—good and bad, that suggested she had problems. Due to several instances of her having to go to the hospital, she was given medicine, and if taken properly would've helped her to cope. Non-support may have been due to a lack of knowledge but Jefferey's own abusive behavior more than likely drove any help she may have had any way.

Should you see a loved one or a friend who's exhibiting this type of behavior, please steer them to a place to get help or in cases of severe behavior, call 911 or a local emergency number immediately. In the case of suicide, call the National Suicide Prevention Lifeline at 1-800-273-TALK or 1-800-273-8255. You may not be able to force someone to get professional care, but you can offer encouragement and support.

16107416R00194

Made in the USA
Middletown, DE
23 November 2018